Tentacles of red, white and blue streaked down from the dark night sky.

"They've started! Come on." Grace pulled Drew by the hand and they ran to the bottom of the staircase.

The fireworks were in full force by the time they'd climbed midway up the stairs to a landing with a long wooden bench. "My dad built this when we were young, so we could have a resting place on our way up from the beach," Grace said as they sat on the bench overlooking the beach and, beyond it, the bay.

Drew pulled her against him as the sky filled with color. When she glanced up at him, her eyes sparkling in the afterglow of fireworks, he felt a burst of emotion that he couldn't quite identify. Something more than pleasure or satisfaction. Was it as big as joy? Or did it even matter whether he could name it or not? He knew only that he wanted to kiss this small woman leaning into him.

Dear Reader,

Lighthouse Cove is a fictional town on the coast of Maine. Despite spending all my life in cities, I'm drawn to the idea of small towns and villages because of the strong sense of community I imagine those places must have.

I also wanted a locale that would feasibly support a lighthouse. In *His Saving Grace*, the neglected lighthouse—its beacon extinguished for years—is a symbol of the sadness and grief that fell over the Cove after a tragedy involving one of the town's teenagers.

Grace Winters was fifteen when the tragedy occurred, and the burden of guilt had a profound effect on her ability to believe in herself and to believe that she could love and be loved.

Enter Drew Spencer, a Coast Guard officer with a traumatic past and guilt of his own, who is driven again and again to prove that he can make things right. This is what he is determined to accomplish when he arrives in Lighthouse Cove to demolish the very lighthouse Grace has vowed to restore. Drew is unaware that his mission is doomed to fail. Why? Because he meets a woman who needs saving and love as much as he does.

Happy reading!

Janice Carter

HEARTWARMING

His Saving Grace

—

Janice Carter

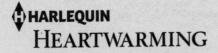

HARLEQUIN
HEARTWARMING

⧫ HARLEQUIN®
HEARTWARMING™

ISBN-13: 978-1-335-88983-6

His Saving Grace

Recycling programs for this product may not exist in your area.

This edition published by arrangement with Harlequin Books S.A.

For questions and comments about the quality of this book, please contact us at CustomerService@Harlequin.com.

Harlequin Enterprises ULC
22 Adelaide St. West, 40th Floor
Toronto, Ontario M5H 4E3, Canada
www.Harlequin.com

Printed in U.S.A.

Janice Carter has been writing romance novels, in particular Harlequin romances, for a very long time. What began as a hobby when she was working full-time and helping to raise two daughters continues in retirement as a wonderfully satisfying hobby! When she isn't writing, she is playing with her granddaughter, enjoying cottage life, traveling and *always* reading.

Books by Janice Carter

Harlequin Heartwarming

For Love of a Dog
Her Kind of Hero

Visit the Author Profile page
at Harlequin.com for more titles.

For my fellow writer and good friend, Dawn Stewardson, who read the early beginnings and who has always encouraged me and inspired me. Thank you!

PROLOGUE

"IT'S ONLY A JOKE. No one's gonna die or anything."

Fifteen-year-old Gracie Winters clutched on to Cassie's reassurance as tightly as the folded paper in her hand. She'd already delivered the first note to her cousin, Brandon. That part had been easy because her mother had asked her to return two eggs she'd borrowed the day before. Gracie made small talk with her aunt in the kitchen but kept an eye on her cousin, playing his new Nintendo game in the den. She made an excuse to go to the bathroom before leaving and on the way, darted into Brandon's bedroom to set the note on his desk next to his iPod so he wouldn't miss it.

Getting the other note to Ella Jacobs was trickier. She and Ella had fallen out halfway through the summer when Gracie began to think Cassie was right and Ella was just being friends with her because she had a crush on

Gracie's older brother, Ben. And it was true that Ella wasn't as much fun anymore. She spent more time reading in the lounge chair on her cottage deck or tanning on the beach across the road. When the three of them were together, Ella was often quiet. Except when she came over to Gracie's house. At first, Gracie had thought the old Ella was back. Then partway through the summer Cassie made a comment that ruined everything for Gracie.

"Haven't you noticed that she only acts like this when Ben is around?"

Other summers Ben never spoke a word to them unless he had to, going in and out of the house without a glance their way. Suddenly he was around more, sticking his head into Gracie's bedroom to ask if they wanted anything from town or if they wanted to use his iPod.

The day Gracie happened to look through the big window of Pete's Grill to see Ben and Ella sitting together in a booth confirmed all that Cassie had been whispering in her ear for weeks. *She's using you to be near your brother.*

The idea for the prank didn't come up until the last week of August, before the end-of-summer beach party. Cassie predicted Ella wouldn't go unless Ben did. Two days before the party Gracie mentioned that Ben wasn't going because he and their father were driving to Augusta early the next morning to take a load of stuff to the college dorm where Ben was registered for his freshman year. Ella's disappointment was painfully obvious and when she phoned later to say she wasn't going to the party Gracie ran to Cassie. They gossiped about Ella and when Gracie blurted that Brandon thought he was in love with Ella, Cassie was silent for a long moment before saying, "I have an idea."

The notes were basically identical, except one was signed "Ella" and the other "B." Cassie wrote them and Gracie's job was the delivery because she could get into Brandon's house, and Ella's cottage was closer to the Winterses' place. Besides, Gracie was the one who was more often alone with Ella than Cassie.

Meet me at the path to the lighthouse about 8 tonight. I want to say goodbye—in private!

Making sure that Ella got her note was more of a challenge. It had to be done in a place where Ben would logically be, so Gracie called Ella to invite her for their annual end-of-summer book exchange. Every year they traded books for the long winter months ahead and returned their favorites each July. Ben would be home packing.

The way Ella's face lit up when she saw Ben ticked Gracie off. After the book exchange, Ben stuck his head in Gracie's bedroom doorway to ask if anyone wanted a cold drink. Ella leaped off the bed to follow him into the kitchen and Gracie tucked the note into Ella's book bag. Then she carried it with her to the kitchen and set it on the table.

Gracie and Cassie arrived early, excited to attend their first end-of-summer beach party. Gracie guessed there were about twenty kids clustered around the bonfire, sitting on blankets and sharing snacks and drinks. Someone brought the fixings to make s'mores and Gracie was toasting her marshmallows on the end of a metal skewer when Ella arrived. Cassie gave Gracie a "what did I tell you?" nudge as they shifted to make room for Ella on their blanket.

"How come you changed your mind about coming?" Cassie asked.

Ella just shrugged, silently scanning the group. Looking for Ben, Gracie figured. Brandon arrived a few minutes later and sat across from them on the other side of the fire. He kept staring at Ella, which made Gracie nervous. A few minutes before eight o'clock, Brandon got up and walked pointedly toward them, veering off at the last second to head for the dark sand dunes behind them. Someone shouted a comment about using the facilities at home first and the gang tittered.

When Ella checked her watch and whispered, "I think I'll go home. This is boring," Cassie caught Gracie's eye and winked. As soon as she disappeared in the same direction Brandon had gone, the two girls scrambled to their feet. Someone called out, "Hey! What's going on?" as the girls dashed down the path leading to the lighthouse and the meeting place.

The line of dunes several yards back from the water formed a natural shelter, protecting the bonfire and the revelers from the coastal winds. Cassie and Gracie hid behind thick scrub edging the junction between the dunes and the grassy trail leading to the long rocky point where the lighthouse perched. The waxing moon and the glow of the bonfire from the other side of the dunes gave Cassie and Gracie enough light, but Ella had thought to bring a pocket flashlight, which she was aiming at Brandon just as the two girls dropped behind the bushes.

"Brandon! What're you doing here?" Ella cried.

Brandon's wide smile, spotlighted by the light's beam, faltered. "You asked me to meet you here."

Ella snorted. "I did not."

Confusion spread across his face. "Yes, you did. I got your note. You asked to meet me to say goodbye."

"Why would I want to say goodbye to you?"

"Then why are *you* here?"

"I'm meeting Ben. I'm here to say goodbye to Ben. Not *you*!"

That was the moment when Ella's expression said she was putting it together. She and Brandon had both been tricked. Of course, the giggle that erupted from Cassie at the same time was a big clue, too. The two girls ran back to the party and had barely sat down before Ella appeared. Cassie and Gracie pretended to be chatting, stifling their laughter as she stood, staring defiantly at them from the other side of the fire. Then she tossed the piece of paper in her hand into the flames and strode off into the darkness beyond.

Long after Gracie had gone to bed, still smiling at the expressions on Ella's and Brandon's faces, a loud banging awoke the Winterses' household. Gracie navigated the stairs down to where her parents and Ben were huddled at the opened front door, talking to some men. She reached it in time to hear one of the uniformed men saying, "Brandon never came home from the beach party. Would any of you happen to know where he might be?"

CHAPTER ONE

DREW SPENCER GOT out of his SUV, parked at the crest of the paved road leading to the main street of the town below. It was the first day of July and a windy, cool one. He zipped up his jacket and lifted the binoculars around his neck up to his eyes. He scanned the long street fronting the small bay and then trained the binoculars east, past a marina filled with a variety of boats, then a sandy beach extending from the edge of town and, finally, to the narrow strip of land leading to a small lighthouse, about two miles away.

So, his tattered copy of the Coast Guard's manual of lighthouses was right. There was a lighthouse here, in this appropriately if unimaginatively named town of Lighthouse Cove. The site wasn't on the spreadsheet he'd found in Gary Hale's computer and Drew wouldn't have included it in the survey but he'd just received an email from his boss informing him that someone from the town had applied for permission to restore the light-house. His boss's email had been blunt. Check it out first but consider decommissioning and demolish. It hasn't been operating for years.

Drew shook his head as he climbed back into the car. Hale had been running the light-house maintenance program as his own little fiefdom until his retirement. Drew had trans-ferred to the Portland Coast Guard office four months after a disastrous sea rescue he had led in the waters north of Southwest Harbor. His thrilling career with the Guard had van-ished overnight. Faced with an administra-tive job that would probably lead all the way to retirement, Drew seized the opportunity to temporarily take over Hale's job in the light-house maintenance division.

Drew had been appalled at the state of the office and was determined to whip the place into shape if he got the permanent position. Which is why this particular assignment in what looked like a poky town was vital.

He'd been traveling along Maine's coast the past four weeks surveying lighthouses—their functionality, condition and so on. Most of them were now cared for by volunteers in the communities where they stood, and he'd attended a few meetings and even one public forum organized to coincide with his survey. With recent cutbacks, there was little government money to cover the total maintenance costs; hence the need to keep volunteers content and committed.

Except for his final report, and now dealing with this last-minute request, Drew's part of the Coast Guard survey was almost done. Although it was a pain to have to investigate some harebrained scheme to restore this lighthouse, Drew figured staying in one place for a couple of days would be a nice break before his return to the Portland office.

He shifted the SUV into gear and headed down the hill toward the businesses and bureaucratic-type buildings strung along the main street aptly called Main Street. Dead center in the arc of waterfront buildings was a four-story hotel, complete with Victorian gingerbread trim and a sweeping veranda. The sign hanging over the street from the hotel's top story read The Lighthouse Hotel. Drew grinned. The place was getting better and better.

There was a parking spot a few yards away from the hotel and Drew spent a couple of seconds debating whether he ought to splurge here or head for the motel he'd spotted up on the highway. The expense could be justified if he planned to stay only a night or two and if Human Resources objected, he'd make up the difference. A couple of days, he thought. How much more time than that would he need for the inspection? He got out of the car and headed for the hotel's front door. The minute he stepped inside Drew knew he'd made the right call.

The lobby was a model of Victorian decor and architecture, with a magnificent central staircase, chandeliers and wood-paneled wainscoting. The marble floor gleamed in the sunlight breaking through tall, narrow windows fronting the street. Drew strode to the sleek oak reception counter. A young woman in a tailored skirt and blouse stood in front of a computer and flashed a welcoming smile as Drew stepped up. Her fresh, scrubbed face made Drew, at thirty-four, feel ancient.

"How may I help you, sir?"

Drew hadn't been called "sir" for almost a year and had to stifle the instinct to quip "at ease." "I'd like a room."

"Of course. Will it be just for yourself?"

"Yes, and only for a couple of nights."

"I have a single available on the third floor."

"Great." He dug out his credit card and moments later he'd retrieved his duffel bag from the SUV and headed for the staircase, shrugging off the clerk's mention of the elevator at the rear of the lobby.

The room was small as he'd expected and unlike the lobby, in need of a reno. Shabby chic, his mother would say. But at least the bed was a double and not the military-size cot he'd spent too many years lying on, and the window had a half screen so he could have fresh air at night. The adjoining bathroom was tiny but had a shower. In all, the room was nothing special, but it would do. It wasn't quite noon and since he'd eaten a late breakfast, he decided to check out the lighthouse first and then the town.

On his way out, he stopped at the counter again. "Everything okay?" the receptionist asked, her red lips highlighting a set of teeth an orthodontist would be proud of.

"Fine, thanks, but is there a library in town?"

"No, sorry. We're getting one but it's only at the fundraising stage right now. There's a bookstore," she added quickly. "A very nice one I hear. Called Novel Thinking. Just go east on Main Street and make a left at Porter. It's a few doors up from the corner."

"Thanks. Asking for that location was going to be my second question." He smiled and started for the door when another thought struck. "Is it possible to get to the lighthouse on foot?"

She frowned. "The lighthouse at the end of the cove?"

Drew raised an eyebrow. "Is there another one?"

Her face flushed and she gave a half laugh. "Right. No, there's only the one. I've heard there's some kind of path that goes to it, but no direct road."

"You've never gone there yourself?"

"Oh no. Not my thing. Besides, it's supposed to be haunted." Her voice lowered to a near whisper on the last word.

Drew nodded. He'd heard that same descriptor several times during his lighthouse survey. "Aren't they all?"

Her eyes widened until she realized he was teasing. "I suppose that's the myth, but the locals seriously believe this one really is."

"You're not from around here?"

"No! I'm summer help. My home's in Augusta."

"Okay, well, thanks for your help."

As he started toward the main door she

suddenly called out, "Don't go there at high tide. It gets cut off from the shore."

"Thanks for the tip." He stepped out onto the pavement and stared at the harbor across the road. The cove right here was too sheltered to be able to tell if the tide was in or out, but the warning was one he'd keep in mind. He knew only too well how quickly tides could rise up and how easily people could be caught unaware.

Drew glanced at the storefronts along the way to the bookstore, noting they were typical of many small towns with several family-run businesses. A sign in one window advertised a fundraiser for the new library. Coming Soon! it proclaimed, Brought to You by Winters Building Ltd., like some kind of blockbuster movie.

Winters. Wasn't that also the name of the woman who'd sent in the funding request? Grace Winters? Then he remembered the logo below the hotel name on his room receipt. *A home away from home with the Winters family.* Did the family own *everything* in town?

He passed a café that was almost full, making it a promising bet for lunch later on, and glanced idly at the string of shops beyond.

A few were targeted at tourists, their front windows displaying the kinds of souvenirs Drew had seen in many of the coastal towns and cities on his tour. Most of the souvenirs reflected fishing themes with a focus on lobsters, the primary catch in the region, and ranged from the tacky to more high-end merchandise. Everything from tea towels with grinning lobsters and cheesy captions like Trapped at Last or Caught in Your Net to saltwater taffy—The Best in Maine. But an antiques shop featuring old lobster pots and a collection of mariners' instruments from centuries ago caught his attention and Drew took a few minutes to study the display, deciding to return later for a look inside.

When he reached Porter, he noticed the sign perched above the sidewalk a few doors up from the corner. It was an opened book, with Novel Thinking etched where a title would go. Drew hesitated, wondering whether to see this Grace Winters first or go to the lighthouse. He knew she'd been emailed that someone from the Guard would be visiting shortly, but he hadn't contacted her himself to set an actual appointment.

First the lighthouse, he decided. He continued down the street, glancing occasionally at more shop windows on his left and the marina with its assortment of pleasure boats on his right. No actual fishing boats, he noted, as he focused on the lighthouse ahead. The distance was hardly a challenge for Drew's long stride, yet by the time he reached the sandy beach at the end of the commercial section of the town, he'd warmed up enough to unzip his jacket.

Now the residential buildings he passed caught his interest—a collection of modest bungalows and cottages of all shapes and ages seemed to vie with one another for access to the beach. The land rose steeply above the water here and he spotted a hilltop house— an impressive nineteenth-century mansion really—that commanded an unrestricted view of the harbor and town.

He stopped, craning his head back for a better look. The house had turrets at each end along with the requisite wraparound veranda. A wooden staircase led from the veranda down through gardens to a sandy path onto the road and the beach. Motor access to the place was probably from the top at the back of the house. The place was no doubt the abode of some founding father of the town.

The ubiquitous Winters family was Drew's guess.

As he continued on, the mix of houses and cottages gave way to a string of wood-framed cottages. Many were painted in a variety of pastel colors and decorated with window boxes or hanging planters, but some were boarded up and a few had For Sale signs up on the mix of sand and grass that passed for lawns. Drew was beginning to think Lighthouse Cove was a tourist town in transition, which probably accounted for the lack of serious fishing boats in the harbor.

The road and sidewalk ended abruptly at a beach about a quarter of a mile from the narrow peninsula leading to the lighthouse. Drew looked for a way up to the dunes stretching behind and beyond the rows of cottages. Then he spotted a trail leading up from the side of a shuttered cottage. By the time he reached the summit of the dune, he'd removed his jacket and slung it over his shoulder. Below him, the town arced along the cove and ahead, a grassy path led to the lighthouse, perched on a concrete base surrounded on three sides by a jumble of huge rocks. Sprays of seawater flung against them. The tide was coming in and Drew realized if he wanted a closer look, he'd better get to it. It was obvious even from where he stood several yards away that the lighthouse would indeed be cut off from the shore. He'd seen other towers like that, stranded from land by the tides, but none as small as this one. Safety for visitors and volunteer keepers was always a concern for the Coast Guard and another reason to support demolition rather than preservation.

He strode to the end where the sandy trail gave way to flat rock. The concrete base was chipped in places but otherwise looked okay, though one of the two steps up to the door was crumbling. The structure itself was a little more than fifty feet tall, he estimated, with a single stripe for a daymark around its circumference. The daymark, once red, was now a faded pink. The tower's white stucco surface had been weathered away in parts, exposing patches of rust-colored bricks underneath. On closer inspection, Drew noticed that some bricks were missing, leaving gaping holes, and someone had been sanding the peeling paint in another section. Grace Winters? Impatient to get started without official recommendation? Well, he'd see about that.

The tower was topped by a typical gallery, but its copper cap was an iodized green now and the gallery's storm panes so coated with grime, bird droppings and sea spray that Drew doubted any light—if there was even a working one anymore—could penetrate it. He walked up to the door and noticed it was locked with a salt-encrusted padlock. It looked like no one had been inside for a long time. Not even Grace Winters, Drew guessed.

As a lover of lighthouses, Drew felt a pang of sadness about the lighthouse's condition. Obviously, the town and the harbor no longer needed a working beacon—in fact, not many in the whole state of Maine were used for marine safety anymore. But generally, single towers and lighthouse stations with their surrounding outbuildings were maintained with affection and respect by the people who lived near them. This was a lighthouse abandoned by time and by the town itself.

A splash of water against his shoe as he stood on the lower step jolted him back to the moment—the tide was coming in. Heading back along the grassy path, Drew noticed a wilting bunch of store-bought flowers resting on a small mound of other floral tributes, long decomposed. He stared at the heap, thinking that at least one person—again, the Winters woman?—hadn't forgotten about the place.

Right then a cloud crossed the sun, throwing a shadow on the lighthouse, and a sudden chill breeze swept over him. Drew shivered. The moment passed as quickly as it had risen. He turned around and marched briskly toward town and the bookstore.

The glass-paned front door was stenciled with the store name and below it, Henry Jenkins Prop. Drew recalled the name from the email his boss had forwarded and wondered who the store's actual owner could be. Winters or this guy? Well, he'd soon find out.

He pushed the door open, setting an interior bell tinkling. The place was long, narrow and dark. Plate-glass windows on either side of the door provided the main source of light and the other came from a lamp midway down the store. Drew paused to let his eyes adjust before walking farther, past shelves of books and a couple of metal spinner racks. He passed a cozy reading corner with a worn leather couch and an armchair to see a high wood counter where a woman was sitting, staring at a laptop screen. A Tiffany-style lamp at her elbow illuminated a head of tousled dark hair that, in spite of the door's warning bell, rose up only when he was standing right before her.

The jet eyes focused on him expressed surprise and her smile was hesitant. She closed the laptop. "Can I help you?"

Drew gave her his best smile. "I hope so. Grace Winters?"

She tilted her head. "Yes?"

"I'm Drew Spencer, from the Coast Guard office in Portland." Her frown leaped quickly to a wide smile as he clarified, "About your request to restore the town's lighthouse?"

"Oh my goodness! This is wonderful. We only sent it in a week or so ago. I can't believe it's happening so quickly."

She was making a whole bunch of assumptions, Drew was thinking, and he really hated to erase that smile because it was transforming. "Um, well, I'm here to make an assessment and submit a recommendation."

That qualifier didn't seem to slow her down. "Of course, I suppose you have to follow a procedure, right?"

"For sure. Anyway, I've been out to take a look at the lighthouse and it's in pretty bad shape."

"Yes, which is why it needs to be restored."

"Frankly it's not worth the bother or the expense. Though I noticed someone's already been working at it—scraping the peeling paint off at the base."

She reddened slightly, maybe due to the reproving tone he couldn't resist. "Well... Henry and I figured we might as well get a start at it."

"That would be Henry Jenkins? The volunteer keeper? Is he also the owner of this store?"

"Yes. I mean no. He's retired and I...that's to say, my father...owns the store. I'm the manager. And yes, he's also the volunteer keeper."

"Also retired from that?" He couldn't resist the dig.

The color in her face deepened. "He's had terrible hip problems the last two years."

Or maybe decades, Drew added under his breath. "Okay, well, I've checked into that hotel down the way for a couple of days. I'll come by later this afternoon and maybe you could arrange for Henry to be here, too. I assume he has the key to the tower?"

She nodded, her pitch-black eyes fixed on his.

Drew had to look away from that gaze. There was something raw about it that was unsettling. Pretending to make a note in his cell phone, he said, "We can go over your application, as well. I'll have a better picture of its viability once I get inside."

She was still staring at him when he tucked his phone into his pants pocket. "How long will all this take?" Her voice was less exuberant now.

"Probably not too long." He knew he could announce the decision right then and there if he wanted to. Interviewing Jenkins and reviewing their application would just be going through the motions as far as Drew was concerned. But he hesitated to further dampen that burst of happiness he'd had a glimpse of moments ago.

"Okay. What time do you think you'll come back? I'll need to let Henry know."

"Say about three?"

Another glum nod but then she seemed to rally. "Henry can tell you some wonderful stories about the history of the lighthouse."

"Great. Do you have any books on it?"

"Not on the Cove lighthouse, but I have a couple on other lighthouses if you'd like to see them."

Drew stood aside while she moved past, a faint scent of flowers trailing behind her as she led the way to a section of books near the sitting area and, stooping to a lower shelf, she pulled out two hardcover tomes. One Drew recognized instantly because it sat in the bookcase in his childhood bedroom in Iowa. If he knew his mother, it was probably still there, waiting for him to finally claim it. The other was devoted to one of Maine's most famous lighthouses, the Portland Head Light in Cape Elizabeth.

"These are great," he murmured, holding them reverently. "I have my own copies at work and at home." He suddenly noticed her peering up at him, smiling as if she, too, had caught that glimpse of his childhood bookshelf. Drew handed the books back.

She replaced them, sighing slightly as she rose to her feet, standing close enough for him to realize exactly how petite she was. Their size difference somehow made her vulnerable, in need of protection. Drew shook himself out of that distracting image.

"All right then, I'll get some lunch and come back at three."

She pursed her lips. From worry or impatience? Of course, he'd follow protocol. Ask questions, listen politely and investigate onsite. Or perhaps she'd already figured out that he was going to disappoint her. For some rea-

son that bothered him. He decided to relieve
some of the tension he was feeling in the
room as he went to the door.

"I heard the place was haunted," he quipped.

A slight gasp caught his attention and he
turned around. She ducked her head but not
before he caught a glimpse of the saddest expression he'd seen in a long time. Drew hesitated, loath to shrug off her unhappiness.
But his lifesaving days were over and he proceeded out the door.

CHAPTER TWO

THE WORDS TUMBLING out of Julie's mouth might as well have been gibberish as far as Grace was concerned. They carried no meaning beyond the first few which were, "So I connected with this guy on one of those dating sites..." because that was the precise moment when that overbearing control freak from the Coast Guard stepped inside Mabel's Diner.

Grace immediately ducked her head to stare at her roasted beet and kale salad as he stood in the doorway, scanning the room for an empty table. There was one a few tables down from where she and Julie were sitting.

"Hey, are you with me here, Grace?"

Grace risked a quick glance at her best friend, whose back faced the diner's door. "Sure, it's just that—" she lowered her voice "—someone has come in and I don't really want to have to talk to him."

"Is this someone you met online?"

Julie started to crane around but Grace hissed, "Don't! He's looking our way." She picked up her fork and stabbed at a chunk of beet, keeping her head down but catching movement out of the corner of her left eye as he walked toward the empty table.

"What's going on?" Julie started to turn her head.

"I said don't look." Grace poked the tip of her friend's shoe under the table.

"I don't have to 'cause now he's sitting four tables down on your side, facing me." Julie paused. "And he's super cute. Are you holding out on me, my friend?"

Grace felt her face heat up. "I just met him this morning. He's from the Coast Guard, about my lighthouse project." She leaned across the table, keeping her voice at a whisper. "I wasn't impressed. He seemed like a bit of a jerk."

"Well, he sure doesn't look like a jerk. What's the story then?"

"Too long to go into now and besides, I don't want him to think we're talking about him."

"Right now he's reading the menu. Maybe he didn't even notice you."

"Good." Grace set her fork down, knowing there was no way she could finish her salad.

"When do I get to hear the story?"

"Soon enough, don't worry. Look, I can't sit here while he's eating his lunch. Can we go?"

"I'm not finished." Julie pointed to the remnants of quiche on her plate.

"C'mon, don't give me a hard time. I don't want to have to talk to him right now. Besides, I'm meeting Henry at the store in half an hour."

"You still have half an hour. Maybe you're making a big deal out of nothing."

"I don't want to get friendly with him. He's here to discuss my idea with Henry and me and…and I don't like the way he makes me feel. I mean," she rushed to explain after seeing Julie's worried expression, "I just got a bad vibe from him about the whole thing."

"A bad *vibe*? You're a throwback, Grace Winters. You know that, right?"

Julie could always read her, ever since senior year in high school when Grace's life was on hold. Julie and her mother had just moved to the Cove and she and Grace soon became best friends. In fact at the time, Julie had been Grace's only friend.

"Please?" Grace pleaded.

Her friend tossed her napkin onto the table. "Fine. So, how do we do this?"

"I'll go first. It's your treat today, right?"

Julie nodded.

"Then I'll keep walking out the door while you pay at the cash register."

Julie sighed loud enough for the couple next to them to glance their way. Grace stifled a curse and hastily got to her feet, grabbed her purse and aimed for the front door. She heard Julie push her chair back and follow her.

When they were out on the sidewalk, Julie caught hold of Grace's forearm. "That whole scene was something out of high school, Gracie. What's come over you?"

"He just...okay, he came across like he'd already made a decision and that got my back up." She didn't mention his comment about the lighthouse being haunted. Although Julie had probably heard the story when she moved here—*who hadn't?*—Grace had never talked to her about it. All Julie knew was that Grace wanted to restore the lighthouse as a memorial to her cousin and that the project was a secret.

"Sounds like you might be jumping to conclusions. I bet his coming here is just a formality. Your project's a good idea and there's no point stressing over some hypothetical problem. You know you tend to do that."

Grace knew her friend was right, but she couldn't admit it. That last sentence was something her older brother, Ben, would say. She was tired of people making assumptions about her responses to life's problems as if she were too sensitive or timid to deal with them on her own. Frustration flared unexpectedly. She jerked her arm sharply enough for Julie's hand to slip off.

"I'm sorry if I seem paranoid but that's the way I feel. Don't worry, I plan to keep my cool when I'm dealing with him."

Julie shrugged. "Sure. I was just…you know…trying to point out that even if he acts like a jerk, it doesn't mean he's going to hassle you about the lighthouse. Don't give up on the whole thing."

"I'll never do that!"

Julie raised her eyebrows. "Yeah, I see that. Okay, well let me know how the meeting goes."

"For sure." Grace watched her friend head down the street and, as she turned to go in the opposite direction, happen to glance through the diner's large plate-glass window. The Coast Guard guy was staring right at her. She wondered if he'd witnessed the uncomfortable goodbye with Julie. Then she thought, *What does it matter? His opinion about me has nothing to do with his decision about the lighthouse. At least it better not!* She marched toward the bookstore and her meeting with Henry, determined to put up a strong front against any objections to her project that some Coast Guard bureaucrat might pose.

DREW HESITATED OUTSIDE the door of Novel Thinking. It was exactly three o'clock and though punctuality was a requisite of his training, it didn't always apply to civilians. He'd made a plan during lunch while watching the odd behavior of the Winters woman at the diner: the constant whispering to her friend and sidelong glances his way; the hasty exit followed by what looked like a spat outside. He didn't have to be an expert in communication to figure out some of that drama was connected to him. But *why* he had no idea.

No matter. He'd have a look inside the lighthouse, get Winters and the volunteer keeper to outline their scheme and leave town as soon as possible. Although he'd paid in advance for two nights at the hotel, one would be enough. Thankfully he wouldn't have to give his decision in person. A short email in a few days or so about the demolition would suffice.

He pushed his camera bag farther up on his left shoulder and opened the door, its tinkling bell alerting Winters, who was handing change to a customer. Drew stood aside for the woman as Winters approached. She gave him a curt nod and asked, "How long do you think we'll need?"

He frowned.

"I mean, should I set the time for an hour? Two? More?"

When she held up a sign featuring a clock with two movable arms, he understood. "Uh, well, I thought the three of us would have a talk, go have a look inside the tower and take some photos. So, maybe an hour?"

She tightened her lips. Unhappily, he thought. "An hour and a half?"

She nodded, moved the little clock arms to four and six and hung the sign on a hook just inside the door. "Henry's at the back," she said, turning to lead the way.

Drew followed like some well-trained

dog. It had taken her mere seconds to gain the upper hand and he didn't like the feeling. Never mind, he told himself. A couple of hours and she—*heck, the whole town*— would be history. As they neared the sitting area, Drew spotted a partially balding, white head bent over a book.

"Henry?"

The man craned round and slowly got to his feet. He was almost as tall as Drew but stooped and as he moved slowly forward, his right hand extended, Drew noticed he clearly had joint issues. He took care not to grasp the man's hand too firmly.

"Mr. Jenkins? Drew Spencer."

"And is there a military attachment to that name?"

"Well, yes, except I don't often use it. It's lieutenant, though Drew works for me."

"And Henry works for me, too. Yet it still took Gracie here a few weeks before she made the transition from Mr. Jenkins." He chuckled and gestured to the armchair opposite his. "Have a seat, please."

Drew liked him instantly. Here was a friendly face, as opposed to the stern-looking Grace Winters pulling up another chair. As they sat down, Drew noticed some papers scrawled with handwriting and a few sketches on the round coffee table and wished he'd thought to bring along a pad and pen, rather than rely on his cell phone for note-taking.

"Gracie? Do you want to start?" Henry prompted.

She flushed and reached for the papers. Coughing a couple of times, she began to speak, her voice wobbling at first.

Drew puzzled over this, trying to connect her obvious nervousness to the serious woman who'd met him at the door. Even more, to the clearly flustered person he'd witnessed having what looked like a set-to with a friend outside the diner. He realized he'd have to be more careful about reading her. *Gracie.* A childhood nickname he presumed.

"I've made copies so you can take these with you," she said, handing him a sheaf of papers. "But I'll go over some of the details anyway." She peered down at her own notes. "Henry and I have made up a rough plan and budget. I mean, in case our project gets the okay."

Drew shifted uncomfortably in his chair. Should he speak up now? He noticed the older man beaming fondly at her. *Okay, give them their five minutes, Spencer. It's the least you can do.*

"I don't suppose there's a chance of getting some money from the Coast Guard for this?" she suddenly asked, her voice faint enough to suggest she already knew the answer.

Drew bit back the cynical reply poised on the tip of his tongue. "Sorry, but that would be a very remote possibility. Cutbacks. This is how it will work," he explained, realizing they had no idea of the process. "After my inspection, I make a decision to decommission the lighthouse or not. Then there are two options. Theoretically, the lighthouse would be sold or torn down. In this case, demolition is the logical choice."

"But tearing down wouldn't be necessary," Grace quickly pointed out, "because we want to restore it. And we'd buy it."

"Not if the structure isn't sound. If the site's unsafe," Drew stressed.

"It just needs some basic repairs," she went on, her voice rising.

"More than a coat of paint."

She flushed, biting her lower lip.

Maybe he could soften the blow and let them have their say. "Okay, so to be clear, you want to restore both the inside and outside."

"Yes," she said.

"Does the lamp work?"

"Not anymore," Henry said. "The glass outside is pretty dirty, too—you maybe noticed that when you went to see it. The bulb and even the lens might have to be replaced. Our goal is to get the light working again. We figure that a good cleaning, fresh paint and some minor repairs should do the trick."

It would take a trick all right, Drew thought. *A magic trick.* He peered down at his papers again, giving the impression—he hoped—that he was considering their ideas. He skimmed through the notes but lingered on the sketches. They were good. Someone had an eye for detail and a steady hand at drawing. One particular drawing held his attention. It showed the lighthouse from the path leading down from the dunes and featured what seemed to be a rock cairn holding a plaque.

"Are these sketches yours?" He looked across at Grace, who nodded. "They're very good. I see a plaque in this one. A dedication or something?"

A look passed between the two that Drew couldn't interpret.

"Yes, it'll be a dedication of some sort but we haven't finalized the wording yet," Henry said.

Drew noticed Grace staring at the papers in her hands. *Her trembling hands.*

"Not that it matters," Drew went on, "because once the tower is decommissioned, it's no longer our concern. I'm just curious." After another moment's silence, he added, "I suppose we should go take a look inside and see how it bears up structurally. We can continue our discussion afterward." He figured it was the least he could do but knew seeing the tower inside wouldn't change the ultimate decision.

"Good idea," Henry announced, laboriously getting to his feet.

Drew noticed him raise a questioning eyebrow at Grace.

"You two go ahead. I'll reopen the store," she said.

This arrangement had already been decided between them, Drew guessed. He gathered his papers and shoved them into his camera bag. Grace went ahead and Drew heard Henry shuffling from behind. After she opened the door, Drew caught her sneaking a peek at her cell phone.

He paused in the doorway. "If there isn't

time to meet after I've seen the site, I can email you my findings. Then I'll submit my report to my supervisor. The whole process might take a week or two."

Her whole face tightened at what he'd meant as a conciliatory gesture, but her dark eyes held his. "Please do whatever you can to help us save this lighthouse," she said quietly.

Drew swallowed hard, knowing disappointment would soon replace the pleading in those eyes.

"Shall we walk there or drive?" he asked Henry as they left the store. "I have a car we can take most of the way."

"Walk. Absolutely!" the older man blustered.

Drew checked the time on his cell phone. Three thirty. No wonder Grace Winters had such a sour expression as she closed the door behind them. The meeting hadn't taken anywhere near as long as she'd obviously anticipated.

Sunlight glinted off the water as he and Henry walked along the concrete boardwalk fronting the marina. Henry pointed to the collection of boats moored at the docks. "You can see most of them are pleasure craft," he muttered, shaking his head. "Twenty years ago, there'd be nothing but trawlers here."

"Was the place always a fishing town?"

"Yep—mainly lobster—and really a village back then, albeit one of the larger communities along this part of the coast."

"What accounted for the change? Decline in the lobster industry?"

"A bit." He shrugged. "But more like a decline in the desire for a simple life. Young folk wanting something else. Something only a city can offer."

Drew could relate. Growing up on a farm in Iowa, he, too, had wanted something more than a rural future. Not a city so much as an ocean. An expanse wider than the eye could see. But he understood what the older man was getting at, knowing how some Midwest towns had also shriveled up, abandoned by younger generations in search of more opportunities.

They came to the end of the boardwalk and climbed the few steps there to the sidewalk leading to the residences beyond. A narrow beach at their right curved in a sweeping arc to the rocky tip and the lighthouse, which Drew noted was inaccessible from the beach area. Just as well, he thought, considering the pile of large, jagged rocks around it.

There were people scattered about the beach—mostly mothers and children, sunbathers and a few beach walkers. Henry stopped to gesture to the hilltop Victorian that Drew had spotted yesterday.

"That's the Winterses' place. Gracie's great-grandfather bought the land and began the house, but it was finished by his son, Desmond—her grandfather."

"Lobstermen?"

"The old man most definitely was! The work was good then and he was a saver. Avoided investing in the stock markets and the like. But lobstering was—and still can be—a hard life. I think he encouraged Desmond to go into something more reliable. Like construction."

Like Winters Building Ltd. Drew recalled the billboard as he pulled off the highway. "Who runs the company now?"

"Gracie's father, Charles, is the head honcho." He shook his head. "For the moment anyway."

"Oh?"

"Charles had heart surgery a little more than six months ago. He's recovering well but slowly. His only son, Ben, came back from Augusta then and was followed by Gracie, shortly after."

"And before?"

"Before what?"

"I mean Grace. Where was *she* before?"

"She was in Augusta, too," Henry said, "working as a librarian."

"Ah. That explains the bookstore."

"Yep. I was considering retiring and Charles got wind of that, I suppose, 'cause Gracie had only been back a month when he made me an offer on the store. At least his lawyer did." Henry chuckled. "As the saying goes, it was an offer I couldn't refuse. I was living above the store, which is where Gracie lives now, and the stairs were getting to be too much for me. And to be honest, I think it might have taken me a long time to sell the place. Not as a bookstore anyway. Not with those big chain ones just down the highway to Portland."

"Convenient timing."

"Charles Winters has always been ahead of the game when it comes to timing. That's what's made him so successful hereabouts. In Portland, too."

"I meant convenient for Grace."

"Would seem so on the surface, but I'd bet money on Charles making it convenient for himself. His wife needed help and he was bedridden. He got his son to run the company for him and what better way to get his daughter to stay than to buy her a business?"

Drew was still pondering this insight into the Winters family dynamic when they reached the end of the road. He stared at the lighthouse.

Henry followed his gaze. "It's not striking like other lighthouses hereabouts, but it's all ours."

"Grace told me there are no books on its history."

"Not yet, but I'm working on one."

"Oh? I'm curious because to tell the truth, I hadn't even heard about it until very recently."

"Well, it's been here since 1918, but construction started the year before."

"Tell me about it."

"The Cove wasn't much bigger than a village at the time," Henry said, "and a lot of the younger men had gone off to war. Old Man Winters was still in the lobster business then and maybe he had some concerns about safety for the few who were still setting out traps. When you get to the site, you'll see those rocks extend quite a way into the bay. People were anxious about the surf in stormy weather—and we get a lot of that here—so Winters got up a petition to request a beacon."

"He'd have gone through Lighthouse Service."

"Yeah?"

"They were in charge of lighthouses until the Coast Guard took over. Thing is, I'm surprised the request was granted for such a small place."

Henry nodded. "Maybe the war had something to do with it. People in power thinking about the security of our coast. Plus, I think the old man had some influential friends."

"Even then?"

"He was still lobstering, but not personally. Had a fleet of trawlers and was the wealthiest man in these parts."

"Makes sense." After a moment, Drew asked, "So how's your book coming along?"

"Slowly. Writing isn't as much fun as researching."

"I'm interested in seeing some of your notes. There's not much information about the tower in my field guide."

"That so?" Henry frowned. "Forgotten?"

"Seems so." Drew flashed a look Henry's way, catching the man's expression, and quickly added, "For a long time. Not just recently."

"I gotta admit, it's been a while since I've been able to take care of it. My hip. Other things." His voice drifted off.

Drew knew the fault wasn't entirely Henry's. A responsible officer of the Coast Guard had messed up, too, and now it was up to him to put things right. "I can go back for my car," he offered, realizing the climb up the dunes might be a challenge for the older man. "Maybe we can reach the tower from the highway."

Henry waved a hand. "You can only get to it on foot from there anyway. And don't worry. Nothing's wrong with my heart. It's only my dang hip. A bit of pain but nothing life-threatening."

His bark of a laugh didn't fool Drew. The man was clearly struggling. Henry was definitely not going to be able to work on any restoration project. Both he and Grace had high and unrealistic expectations.

"If you give me the key, I can go check it out myself."

He took a few seconds to finally agree, confirming for Drew that he was both proud and stubborn. Drew pointed to a couple of weathered Adirondack chairs under a tree at the front of the shuttered cottage nearest them.

"That place looks deserted. I'm sure no one will mind if you sit there."

"That's the old Fielding place. Poor Violet Fielding's been in a nursing home in Portland for several years. Dementia." Henry sighed. "All right, then. But let's keep this between us. Gracie was hoping I'd give you the history of the place while showing you around."

"You can do that when I come back. It shouldn't take too long, right?"

"Maybe not." Henry thought for a minute. "Just that…the place is very important to Gracie. To the whole family but most of all to her."

The emotion in the man's face and voice suddenly took Drew back to the bookstore when he was leaving it yesterday and Grace Winters's expression. What was it about this lighthouse?

CHAPTER THREE

DREW SPENT A few frustrating seconds using the key Henry had given him until he managed to pull the old padlock free, but the tide was low and there was no rush. Henry was sitting comfortably in the shade and Drew could explore the tower by himself. In the months since he'd taken on the lighthouse maintenance program, he had yet to inspect a site on his own. Usually the volunteers hovered, awaiting his comments or recommendations until his reassurance that all was good set them at ease.

As soon as Drew pushed hard on the weather-beaten door, a hundred years of history stopped him on the threshold. He coughed, clamping his hand over his nose against the swirl of dust motes that enveloped him on their way out the door. This lighthouse was young compared to many in Maine, but its oversight—heck, *neglect*—made it unique. There obviously wasn't enough land here on the end of the spit to build a complete light station with outbuildings. Besides, the village hadn't required one. Lighthouse Cove wasn't an actual port and likely never had been due to its proximity to Portland. The only ships coming into the town's natural bay would have been fishing boats and pleasure craft.

All of that made the tower's construction a small miracle. The Winterses who got the project started must have been very persuasive or had some clout with politicians. As far as Drew was concerned, the tower's lack of historical or architectural distinction as well as functionality made it a solid candidate for a teardown. He stepped cautiously into the watch room on the ground floor, spotting a wide crack in one of the bleached wooden floorboards. Traditionally used for storage of supplies, it was a smaller area than a typical watch room would be in bigger towers. There were no gaps in the walls that he could see, which meant the missing bricks he'd spotted outside were from the exterior layer. A few shelves had been drilled into the red brick inner walls and they held some curious items—a flashlight thick with dust, some candles that had been nibbled by rodents next to a cheap cigarette lighter and a dented thermos. Left behind by Henry?

Drew hesitated at the bottom of the wood spiral staircase leading to the lantern room, peering upward to assess its reliability. Well, he wouldn't really know how stable it was until he tested it. He grasped the railing and began to climb, one creaky step at a time. When he reached the top, he was perspiring. No wonder Henry had given up his duties, though why he hadn't handed the job over to someone else was a mystery. It wasn't as if he'd been receiving a salary.

The lantern room at the top was a tad smaller than Drew's bathroom at The Lighthouse Hotel and his soft chuckle echoed down and up the tower. When Henry told him the tower was functioning by 1918, Drew knew its light source would be an incandescent light bulb and sure enough, there was one thousand-watt bulb, long dead by the look of it, screwed in place along with the reflector and a basic Fresnel lens. He figured when the light had been working, the beacon was most likely a fixed one rather than revolving, due to the tower's location. Hence the smaller size of the lens, too.

He sidled around the whole apparatus to

the windows, but the storm panes were so filthy he could barely see the water below. No doubt the tower had served its purpose at the turn of the twentieth century, if in a limited way. Now it even lacked the quaintness that would have made it a tourist draw. It certainly wouldn't generate any income for the town and was far enough off the state's lighthouse tour route that few people would stumble upon it by chance.

After snapping a dozen photos inside and out, Drew locked up to head back to Henry. His initial judgment yesterday was confirmed. Given that the tower no longer served the community in any realistic way, its precarious stability and especially that its historical value was dubious, Drew knew there was no point in putting it up for sale. He doubted even National Park Service, which had purchased a number of lighthouses in the country, would bother with it. Demolition was the only option.

Treading carefully along the pebble-strewn path, he noticed again the wilted flowers. He figured they'd been left by Grace. Henry had said the place was important not only to the family, but especially to her. He thought of the plaque in the drawings he'd seen earlier.

Was the tower's renewal meant to be some sort of family tribute?

He reached the crest of dunes and saw Henry sitting below. Now was his chance to get some answers. The light tumble of sand at his footfall caught Henry's attention. He craned round and smiled as Drew held up the thermos that he'd grabbed at the last minute.

"Hah! Wondered where I'd put that thing. Been a few years since I've seen it."

Drew smiled at his sheepish face. "I also noticed an old flashlight and some candles. Someone been camping out?"

"They've been there from before my time volunteering. Maybe kids hanging out."

"Kind of a dangerous place for that." Drew sat in the chair next to Henry's. "How long have you been volunteering?"

Henry pursed his lips. "About half a dozen years or so. The fellow before me gave it up long before that and for a few years no one else took the job until I stepped up."

Drew nodded. Due to automation, the tower really didn't need someone to look after it, other than to keep the storm panes clean or change the light bulb. General housekeeping. Clearly even that hadn't been done in some time.

"Tell me more about the place. It's in pretty bad shape. I'm puzzled why you and Grace would want to tackle a restoration. What's the payoff for you?"

"No payoff for me, except maybe to make up for my neglect." He averted his gaze again. After a moment, he said, "I guess you'll hear the story anyway, so it might as well come from me 'cause I doubt Gracie will be keen on telling it."

Answers were finally coming. Drew sat back in the chair.

"It must be about sixteen, seventeen years ago. Gracie was just a kid. Well," he clarified, "a young teenager. Maybe fourteen or fifteen. And when I say young, I mean that in more ways than years. She was different from the other girls in town. More protected. I don't think Charles allowed a lot of independence. I still had the bookstore then. In fact, had it many years before that summer. Gracie loved to read, and the town had no library. Still doesn't." He snorted. "So, Gracie was a regular customer, especially in the summer holidays. She usually came in with friends when she got her allowance." His face crinkled. "Can't recall their names, but one of them was Cassie Fielding." The smile gave way to a frown as he glanced briefly at the derelict cottage behind them.

"Anyway," Henry continued, "it happened on Labor Day weekend. The local teens as well as the ones vacationing here had a beach party up in the dunes." He gestured behind him. "One of the boys—Gracie's younger cousin, Brandon—left the party early for some reason and went missing. No one knows exactly what happened but there were plenty of rumors." Henry shook his head. "They found him on the shore next morning, not far from the lighthouse. Drowned." His voice trailed off as he stared out across the water.

"An accident?" Drew finally asked.

"Most likely. There was a bit of a police investigation because he'd been reported missing the night before. Then a few weeks later there was an inquest and the ruling was accidental drowning. Figured he'd been caught at the lighthouse in high tide."

"Didn't the kids know about the tides?"

"'Course they did! Kids here learn about the dangers of that place as soon as they're old enough to start going off on their own." He paused, the indignation in his voice fading. "The tragedy shook up all the Winterses. Brandon's father, Fred, was Charles's younger brother and his family was never the same afterward. Fred took to drink and that eventually ended his marriage. His wife, Jane, took their daughter and moved to Bangor. They came back when Fred passed away but only for a couple of days."

"Did they ever learn why Brandon was at the lighthouse?"

"Nope. As I said, just lots of rumors and gossip. Things small towns are famous for." Henry gave a cynical harrumph. "I don't repeat them," he added, facing Drew. "No point. What good could come of spreading stories?"

The question was rhetorical, but it interested Drew. Clearly there was much more to the tragedy, but it wouldn't be coming from Henry Jenkins. He thought suddenly of Grace, her anxious expression when he dismissed the tower's potential for restoration— her whispered "please" and imploring eyes.

A slight unease flowed through him. Maybe this detour to Lighthouse Cove wasn't going to be as uneventful as he'd thought. Even more, maybe his recommendation wasn't going to be as easy to make. Her project was obviously meant to be a memorial for this cousin, but why now, after all this time?

GRACE WAS ON the verge of flipping over the open sign and locking the door when Drew Spencer appeared. She noticed two things right away. He'd changed his jeans and T-shirt for khaki slacks and a short-sleeved cotton striped shirt—*as Mom would say, he cleans up nicely*—and he was smiling. That simple expression made all the difference to her initial calculation of his age as somewhere in the early forties. *He's not much older than my thirty-two years*, she decided, *and with fewer gray strands in his hair.*

"I'm not planning to make your workday any longer," he began as soon as she opened the door, "but I thought you might be interested in hearing my observations."

His returning to talk surprised her because she'd guessed he wouldn't bother. She'd learned from experience that bad news often arrived via email. Maybe his appearance was a good thing. Plus, he *was* smiling.

"Yes, of course. Come in."

"If you're closing up, would you like to go for a coffee? Or maybe even a drink? To talk about your proposal," he added quickly.

Grace hesitated, unsure if this was a good sign or not. Was he hoping a drink might catch her off guard or lessen the blow of a rejection? She had a sudden image of her brother wagging his finger at her, telling her she was overthinking things as usual. "Um, sure. Come in while I finish up."

He brushed past her, wafting a light scent of aftershave and soap. "Take a seat," she said, pointing to the area where they'd chatted earlier.

"Okay to browse? Bookstores are one of my favorite places."

"Along with lighthouses?"

His smile was even brighter, a fact that pleased her for some unknown reason. Julie was right. He was cute. Super cute, as she'd said. Not that it mattered.

"Definitely. Not sure which comes first though. But considering it was a book about lighthouses that got me into the Coast Guard, maybe they tie for first place."

It was her turn to smile. "I won't be long." She closed down the computer, checked that the rear door was locked and reviewed her calendar for the next day. A shipment of books was due and the family was meeting with her father's specialist in Portland. It would be a full day and one she hoped wouldn't be marred by bad news from Drew Spencer.

"All set," she announced, pushing her purse over her shoulder.

He was perusing a book and his head shot up. Almost startled, Grace thought with amusement. As if he'd forgotten she was even there.

"Great." He replaced the book on the shelf and headed for the door, stepping out onto the sidewalk while she locked the door. "So, what's it to be then?"

"Well, if I have a coffee, I'll be up all night. And it is just past five so…"

He grinned. "A woman after my own heart. Beer? Wine?"

"If you'd prefer a beer, there's a nice pub up the street."

"Lead the way!"

Grace had never been good at small talk and she lapsed into silence almost at once. Normally she felt awkward in these moments, keeping quiet while others talked. It was a holdover from high school. She'd always been on the fringes, hanging around the popular girls but never actually part of the group. That's why her friendship with Cassie had been so important. *And look where that got me.* She pushed the unhappy memory aside, focusing on the easy saunter of the man at her side who didn't seem bothered by her silence.

The pub was cool and dark inside. It was a Wednesday and early yet, so only a handful of people were scattered around the main area.

"Live entertainment?" Drew nodded toward the small raised platform at the far end of the room as they sat at a table.

"Fridays and Saturdays. Usually only local talent, though sometimes performers come from Portland."

"What kind of music?"

"All kinds. The pub posts a monthly calendar of acts online and in *The Beacon*."

"The Beacon?"

"Our local paper. It's only a weekly."

"Is everything here lighthouse related?"

Grace laughed. "Of course! That and lobsters."

The waiter appeared before he could comment and they ordered beer for him and a glass of white wine for her. "Any snacks?" the server asked.

"What've you got?" Drew looked across at Grace. "Lunch seems a long time ago."

Grace felt her face heat up, recalling the silly scene with Julie outside Mabel's. She wondered briefly if he'd intended the remark to prompt an explanation from her but decided from his absorption in the menu that she was overanalyzing again.

When the waiter left, Drew glanced around the room. "It's nice. Neither trendy nor kitschy. No dartboards at least. No loud music, thank goodness."

"Not until Friday night anyway."

"Guess I'll miss it then."

"How long are you staying in town?"

"I took my room for two nights."

"Are you in town or in a motel up by the highway?"

"Here. At The Lighthouse Hotel. Another example of the town's obsession with themes." He smiled.

She leaned against the back of her chair, enjoying the moment simply for what it was—on the surface at least. A casual drink after work with an attractive man. "The hotel's convenient though I hear it's seen better days," she said.

"Perhaps. My room is definitely on the basic side but I like the place. Reminds me of the grand old hotels in movies."

Grace smiled at the fitting comparison. "My cousin runs it."

His face faltered for a second and from the way he said, "Your *cousin*?" Grace realized he might have heard about Brandon. From Henry?

She picked up her wineglass, taking a sip to cover her surprise. Then she realized perhaps it was better he'd heard the story from Henry rather than her. She didn't trust her emotions enough to recount that weekend. Plus, he'd find out when they discussed the memorial aspect of the project.

"Yes, my cousin—Suzanna Winters. She and her husband have been managing it for a couple of years now."

"Do the Winterses own *everything* in town?" His tone was teasing.

"Just about," she said in all seriousness.

Their order arrived and for several minutes they dug into the nachos that were surprisingly delicious. They had a brief debate about whether they ought to have chosen the ground beef topping as opposed to the melted cheese.

"Decadent," Drew said. "Definitely would have put them over the top."

"I agree. Without is better."

For a few minutes the only sounds were crunching ones until he asked, "What was it like growing up in a small town like this?"

"Okay, until my teens."

"And then?"

"Then it seemed *too* small. Everyone knew your business."

"I can relate to that. I grew up on a farm and got my driver's license as soon as I legally could to escape whenever possible."

"Where was that?"

"Iowa."

"It's a long way from Iowa to Maine. How did that happen?"

"When I was about twelve, I got a book on the Portland Head Light for Christmas. The same one you have in your store as a matter of fact."

"And that's all it took?" She smiled at the way his face lit up.

"That's all it took. But it remained a secret passion for several years and after I graduated from college, I joined the Coast Guard."

She thought of her own path to librarianship, taken more by default than choice. She'd always been a reader and loved books. Why not be a librarian? Unfortunately, the logic in that decision had been flawed because the job had never been as interesting as the idea.

She sipped her wine, feeling her earlier tension ease. For a moment she could almost believe they were having a night out like some of the other people in the pub and that thought was troubling. This was a business meeting.

"About the lighthouse," he said.

Grace set her glass down. The way his voice dropped and his eyes flicked from hers to some point beyond her told Grace all she needed to know. So, it actually is a business meeting, she was thinking, scarcely listening to his comments about the tower's structure, safety and something about broken floorboards but only focusing on three words— *tear it down.*

"Wait!" she interrupted. "You spent what? Ten or fifteen minutes inside and this is what you've decided?"

He reared back in his chair as if she'd struck him.

Grace glanced around, noticing the bartender shoot a curious look their way. She lowered her voice. "Of course, it's in bad shape. It's been neglected for years. That's why we want to repair it." She waited for him to continue but he just kept staring at her. She picked up her wineglass but her hand was trembling so she set it down again.

"Look," he said, leaning forward to make his point. "I understand what the lighthouse must mean to you and your family. Henry told me about your cousin's death there when you were a teen."

The eyes fixed on hers were almost soothing, but she peered down at the table, afraid the sympathy she saw in them would bring tears. And she had shed enough of those over the years.

"When we decommission there are two options, as I told you earlier. Selling—often to National Park Service, though unlikely in this case—or tearing down. We clearly can't sell it in its present condition. It's unsafe. Therefore, the only option is to pull it down."

Grace raised her head to protest.

"But," he went on, holding up his hand, "you can still use the site afterward as a memorial to your cousin. I believe that was the intention of the project, wasn't it? The plaque in the drawing?"

She nodded, unable to speak.

"And considering what happened to your cousin, perhaps keeping the lighthouse would be too painful. Maybe the plaque alone would be a more fitting reminder."

Grace felt the room close in. She wanted to defend her side but was afraid the truth would come out to this man—*a stranger*—

whose assessment of the lighthouse was based purely on cold hard facts. How could she prove having the lighthouse was a way to keep Brandon alive? That tearing it down would essentially delete him from memory, not only hers but the town's?

"I'm sorry but…uh… I have to leave," she stammered. "There's somewhere I have to be."

He set his half-empty pint of beer down. "You—"

"I'll think about what you've said and get back to you." She reached for her handbag on the floor and stood. "But remember this—all acts have consequences. Do you want this town to bear the consequence of no memorial for a young teenager because you're obviously too stubborn or nearsighted to see another point of view about the lighthouse?"

He was staring up at her, his face a map of confusion.

"Thanks for your input," she said as she headed for the door.

CHAPTER FOUR

SLEEPING IN WAS a luxury Drew hadn't enjoyed in many years. He rolled over and stared up at the ceiling, its blotchy surface a puzzle at first until he remembered he was at the hotel in Lighthouse Cove and not his apartment in Portland. Perhaps waking at nine didn't count as a sleep-in if you didn't actually get to sleep until well after midnight. He almost wished he could attribute his grogginess to a hangover, but no. One beer and a platter of soggy nachos accounted for his rumbling stomach but not for the cloud in his head.

He simply didn't understand Grace Winters. He'd intended the invite as a friendly gesture—a way to ease the impact of her inevitable disappointment. They could talk freely over a drink and perhaps discuss options for her memorial idea. If he'd known she'd get up and walk out, he'd have had the talk at the bookstore. And his humiliation didn't arise from the curious heads turned his way or at the frown on the waiter's face when he appeared at that exact moment to ask if everything was okay. *What do you think?* Drew had been tempted to ask.

No. It was how she'd reacted. Except for the instant flush of red and the hint of an emotional struggle in her face, she'd kept her cool. She'd managed to put him in a place he hadn't been since his training days. Her "thanks for your input" was the clincher. As if he were some kind of consultant rather than the person making the decisions.

He sat up, rubbed his face and contemplated the day ahead. Although he'd booked a second night, he realized there probably was no point in staying. Any contact with her would best be made by email, that safety net for people who hate face-to-face confrontation. It had been his default mode of communication for a while, especially since the tragedy that had propelled him into a desk job.

Drew sighed. He hadn't thought about that day in ages and hadn't awakened in a cold sweat from tormenting dreams in weeks. As the therapist he'd been ordered to visit had said, *grief is a long process.* His immediate response at the time had been to protest that the family of the man he'd failed to save—his wife and children—would know all too well about that. But eventually he'd accepted that grief and guilt were sometimes linked, merging almost amorphously so that one was indistinguishable from the other. Yet there were days and nights when reality struck like a punch to the gut and he knew he'd never be able to put that judgment call behind him. He'd never really forget.

He stood, still unsure about his next steps but knowing movement was the best antidote to bad memories and difficult decisions. By the time he'd shaved, showered and dressed it was past midmorning. His appetite had bounced back and he was ready to tackle the day in all its brightness and potential. Just what the doctor ordered, he was thinking, as he made his way across the hotel lobby to the front door and a hearty breakfast at Mabel's Diner.

A tall attractive woman heading his way stopped to say, "Good morning," and then added, "Are you enjoying your stay at our hotel?"

"Um, yes, thank you," Drew noticed the small badge on her dress. Suzanna Winters, Manager. Grace's cousin and sister of the boy who drowned? He wondered what she thought about Grace's plan to restore the tower as a memorial to her brother.

"Wonderful," she said. "And if there's anything you need help with, please feel free to contact me. I'm usually in the office behind the reception desk." She gestured to the far side of the lobby. "And of course, there's always someone at the counter, too."

When she frowned suddenly Drew glanced across the lobby. The same young woman from his check-in yesterday was on duty, her head bent over her cell phone. Some trouble there? Drew wondered. Maybe the summer help wasn't working out. "Sure, thanks."

He was about to walk on when she added, "Will you be staying with us long?"

"I leave tomorrow."

"Ah, too bad. There are some lovely sights in the Cove, as well as possible day trips from here to Portland and other smaller places. Have you seen the Portland Head Light in Cape Elizabeth? It's an iconic lighthouse here in Maine."

"I have seen it and you're right, it's unforgettable. And you have a lighthouse here, too."

Her smile disappeared. "Yes, we do, but it's

not very accessible to tourists." After a brief pause, she added, "Well, enjoy your day," and headed to the reception counter.

Enjoy my day. I dearly hope to, but the odds are against me right now, Drew was thinking. After breakfast he'd stop in at that antiques store he'd seen yesterday and then consider his options. Leaving early was at the top of his list but only after seeing Grace Winters one more time. Why that was suddenly important, Drew couldn't explain. Perhaps he wanted to show that her melodramatic exit last night hadn't bothered him at all. Or perhaps he simply didn't want to leave town on such a negative note.

The diner had few customers midmorning and there were plenty of tables. Drew automatically aimed for the one he'd been sitting at the day before. He preferred facing outward whenever he ate alone so he could indulge a favorite pastime of people-watching. Besides, he figured sitting the other way would imply a desire for isolation that wasn't in his character. He wasn't an extrovert, but he liked people and being around people. He was finally moving on from his self-imposed solitary life last year. His therapist would approve of that at least.

He'd just ordered eggs Benedict and was sipping his coffee when the diner door opened and Grace Winters stepped inside, paused briefly, spotted him and walked his way. Drew suddenly lost his appetite.

"May I?" she asked as she pulled out the chair opposite his and sat down before he could set his coffee mug onto the table.

It occurred to Drew that unless Mabel's was the only diner in town, he and Grace must be on the same wavelength, turning up at the same time in the same place two days in a row. If their last meeting had been more amicable, he'd have made a lame joke like "we can't keep meeting like this."

"I was at the corner down the street when I saw you come inside," she began. "I'm sorry to interrupt your—" she stared at the empty table space in front of him "—breakfast? But I wanted to apologize for yesterday."

Drew tilted his head slightly, as if he didn't know what she was referring to.

"I was taken aback and disappointed. Unfortunately, I often let my emotions get the best of me." She uttered a small laugh. "My family has been pointing that out to me since I was little."

He felt an unexpected twinge of sympathy for her.

"Last night I had time to…uh…reflect on what you said—or *tried* to say." She took an audible breath, glancing briefly at the wall behind him. "Before I interrupted. Walking out like that—" she briefly bit down on her lower lip and then continued "—was very childish and unfair to you. I didn't even think to leave any money for my share."

Her eyes met his and something in Drew thawed ever so slightly. He had to put her out of her misery. "Look," he said before she could continue. "I understand how important your project is for you and for Henry, too. I get it. Families don't recover from tragedies like that." He had to stop, his mind flooded again with the memory of last year. The waiter showed up with his order, giving him a few seconds to focus on something else.

"Can I get you anything?" the waiter was asking Grace.

"A coffee please, with milk."

She looked at Drew, her expression slightly puzzled. Had she noted the change in his face just then?

"Please," she prompted, "go ahead and eat. Their eggs Benedict are delicious and should be devoured immediately. With gusto!" she added, her voice pitching.

He tucked in, but kept his eyes fixed on hers, waiting to hear the real purpose of her dropping by.

After her coffee was delivered, Grace said, "Henry and I thought maybe you'd be interested in seeing more of the town and hearing its history before you leave."

Drew swallowed his mouthful of egg and ham.

She held up a palm before he could get a word out. "Don't take this as another pitch for the lighthouse or an excuse to reopen the debate. Just that it would be a shame for you to leave a place you'll probably never return to without really seeing it. Do you know what I mean?"

He did, but he also believed the invite *was* another pitch. Albeit a last-ditch one. Still, he was interested and as she said, it was highly unlikely he'd be coming back. "Okay, that would be nice."

"That's great! Can you drop by the store in about an hour? I'll let Henry know." She pushed back her chair and stood. "I'll let you enjoy the rest of your breakfast." She started to leave but turned quickly around, her smile a gift after yesterday's meeting. "Oops, almost forgot."

She was digging around in her purse when Drew realized what she was doing. "Please. The coffee's on me and…um… I'll see you in an hour."

Her "thank you" was breathless and happy. Drew watched her walk out the door before picking up his fork. For some reason, he wasn't as hungry as he had been. In fact, the faint gnawing in his stomach was from dread about disappointing her again.

HENRY WAS WAITING outside Novel Thinking. Grace had called him first thing in the morning with her idea. Maybe if Drew Spencer saw the whole town and heard some of its stories he'd understand the importance of the lighthouse to the community. "Can't hurt," Henry had said but his tone was skeptical.

"Well?" he asked as she arrived at the door.

He could have gone inside, Grace knew, because he still had a key, but she also knew he'd never take liberties, not even as the former owner. "Sorry to have kept you so long but when I got to the hotel, I found out from the receptionist that he'd already left. Then

I happened to see him go into Mabel's so thought I'd catch him there."

Henry chuckled. "You mean *corner* him there."

Grace's laugh was slightly embarrassed. "Well, it's true he had little chance of escape. Anyway, he's interested. Are you still up for playing tour guide?"

"I'll stick it out as long as my hip allows."

She had a twinge of guilt then. Knowing Henry would do almost anything for her wasn't really playing fair when she also knew he had mobility issues.

"But not to worry." He smiled, patting her forearm as she unlocked the door. "I'll lead him right back to you when I've had enough."

As she unlocked the door, Grace was glad that Henry couldn't see her expression. So far, her success at communicating with Drew Spencer was at zero and she doubted she could improve that score. She seemed to self-destruct every time she tried to counter his reasons for a teardown. She had a habit of overreacting but knew there was something more afoot. Maybe some doubt about the project itself? No, she wouldn't go there. She'd already spent far too many sleepless nights over it. Last night's restlessness was solely due to her childish behavior at the pub. Her reaction was not only embarrassing but excessive, given the circumstances. The idea of a tour of the Cove came to her about daybreak. She knew instinctively this might be her one and only chance to persuade him to reconsider.

"Okay," she replied as she tucked the closed sign behind the door and walked ahead to flick on lights. Official opening time was ten, but she'd delayed today by going to find Drew. Hopefully any disappointed customers would return.

Henry headed for the reading area and eased into an armchair. "Tell me again where you think I should take him?"

Grace sighed inwardly. His hip wasn't the only thing failing Henry these days. "Basically, a short tour of the town center, the square—"

"The statue of old Hiram?" Henry's eyes twinkled.

"Can't miss it I guess." Grace had often been teased by schoolmates about the bronze tribute to her great-grandfather, a lobster pot at his feet and his eyes fixed on a distant horizon. It had been commissioned by her grandfather. "Were you able to contact anybody from the Historical Society?"

"Leonard Maguire says he can spare some time before lunch. And Betty Anderson from the Information Center has a break at two."

"That's sounding like a full day. He'll be here sometime after eleven. What time do you think Leonard would be available?"

"I arranged to meet him around noon at the Society's office in Town Hall."

In the past all fifteen members of the Cove's Historical Society had met monthly in the town's elementary school for lack of a community center or library, but soon other community groups had competed for evening space with the Society, which recently had negotiated a temporary room in the town hall. Grace's mother was a member of the Society, though she rarely attended meetings anymore due to Charles's health problems. Just as well, Grace figured, because she didn't want to reveal her restoration idea to her family until it was approved.

Henry settled in with the latest copy of *The Beacon* and Grace busied herself setting up the store for the day while waiting for Drew.

"Say," Henry called from his armchair,

"don't you and the family have a meeting with your father's specialist today?"

Grace looked up from the computer. "Yes, but not till four."

"In Portland, right? Want me to take over here for you?"

"I thought I'd close early."

"Gracie, don't do that unless you absolutely have to. You shut the store down yesterday while we met with Drew and opened late this morning. Customers are going to think your hours are unreliable. They'll stop coming."

Grace flushed. "I know it's not a good idea, Henry, but this is important. Drew Spencer is only here for a day or two and I have to convince him my plan is a good one. Once he leaves, the whole thing will be forgotten. Anyway, this is the only bookstore in town."

"But plenty in Portland, a short drive away."

"I know." She sighed. Henry was right but there was too much at stake. She had only hours to change the man's mind and she had a feeling that Drew Spencer was the kind of man whose mind resisted changing. "All right. If you're finished showing him around by three, then yes, please come and take over for me."

"Good. You know, I had an idea, too. Not sure if it would work out but…"

Grace glanced up from logging in to the computer. "What idea?"

"Did he say he lives in Portland as well as working there?"

"I…um… I can't remember. Maybe."

"If he were to spend a few more days here, he'd need a place to stay. It's the holiday weekend and the hotel might be fully booked."

"And?" She called up the store's accounting program while keeping an eye on the time.

"Just that I've got a specialist appointment myself on Tuesday in Portland and I'd been thinking of spending a couple more days there, see my sister. Her health hasn't been good lately and I think she'd like some company."

"Uh-huh." Grace's fingers worked at the keyboard, checking yesterday's receipts.

"Well, if we can persuade Drew to extend his visit, he could use my place. I was going to take Felix with me, but I could leave him behind. It'd be a reason to offer my cottage if he wouldn't mind cat-sitting for a day or two."

Grace raised her head and smiled. "A very good reason, Henry."

"Think that might be a plan, then?" He winked.

"I do, Henry." She laughed. "I think that's an excellent idea."

The tinkle of the front doorbell caught their attention.

THEY WERE PARTWAY up Porter when Drew remembered he ought to slow down. Henry couldn't keep pace, especially once the street started its climb up to the center of town. He'd felt surprisingly let down that Grace hadn't joined them, though he realized his expectation had been a tad unrealistic. She did have a business to run and possibly her budget didn't extend to hiring part-time help.

When he arrived, Drew gathered from their furtive glances that they'd been discussing either the tour or him. Probably both, he concluded, since the obvious purpose of showing him the town was to persuade him to change his mind. For some reason the idea that they'd been talking about him rankled. Since he'd begun this survey a month ago, he'd had a couple of confrontations with volunteer keepers, usually around upkeep or funding. Lighthouses were expensive to maintain and he doubted Grace Winters had considered that aspect of her project.

While he waited at the next corner for Henry to catch up, Drew wondered why he was spending so much time thinking about a woman he'd known less than forty-eight hours. He couldn't even rationalize his preoccupation as attraction because she wasn't his type at all. Tall blondes with outgoing personalities had always been the draw for him.

A flash of Emily tumbled into his mind and Drew sighed. Thoughts of his ex-fiancée seldom arose anymore. He couldn't exactly pinpoint when that part of his life ended—sometime in the weeks after the botched sea rescue—but he did remember the morning when he woke up and realized she wasn't ever coming back. The moment was memorable only because he realized at the same time that he didn't actually care.

"Sorry, Henry," he said as the older man came closer. "I was lost in thought and forgot I was with someone else."

Henry waved a dismissive hand. "Happens to us all." He took a deep breath and pointed to his right. "The main square is that way and we're meeting the chair of the Lighthouse

Cove Historical Society, which is located in our town hall, at twelve."

"A historical society? Great." Drew checked his watch. "In half an hour then? We might have some time to kill."

"Maybe. If so, we can always grab a coffee. There seems to be plenty of those places around these days."

"Even here in Lighthouse Cove?" he teased.

"Yes, sir, in spite of the older generation's efforts to stave off…what's it called?" He frowned.

"Gentrification?"

"That's the word. We'd have called it modernization. Same thing. Habits and customs change with the times. Not too long ago there was one tea shop in town and coffee at Mabel's. Now it seems like there's a coffee shop in every block."

"My parents complain about the same thing."

Henry stopped walking to look at Drew. "Where do they live?"

"On a farm in Iowa, outside a town bigger—but not by much—than Lighthouse Cove."

"Good heavens! What's an Iowa farm

lad doing in Maine, working for the Coast Guard?"

Drew smiled. "My folks were just as incredulous, Henry. Although they did have an inkling I was drawn to a world beyond the farm when my Christmas wish list one year had a single item on it—a book about the Portland Head Light."

"How about that! So that's what sparked your interest in lighthouses?"

"My folks had no idea what that one book would lead to."

"How did they feel about you moving East?"

"Well, that's a story over a couple of cups of coffee," Drew said with a small laugh. "In short, their disappointment eventually led to acceptance."

"The path many parents take."

His sigh prompted Drew to ask, "Are you speaking from experience?"

"Well, I have no children. Never married, in fact. Let's just say I had a similar confrontation with my own folks, but it didn't lead to my leaving Lighthouse Cove. For that, I'm grateful," he announced as he continued walking.

Drew let Henry take the lead, studying his

shoulder-backed gait with its slight limp and his head jutting forward as if he were tacking into the wind. There were old-timers like him back home in Iowa, too. Proud men with their own stories. Perhaps one day he'd be like that and the sad story in his life right now would be just one of many. He hoped so.

The street suddenly gave way to an open square edged by an assortment of buildings, many from past eras constructed typically with red brick. Dead center at the top end of the flagstone plaza stood an imposing three-story stone structure complete with clock tower. A wide expanse of concrete steps led up to a pair of tall wood doors.

"Wow!" Drew stopped at Henry's side.

"Something, isn't it?"

"The town hall I assume?"

"Our one and only. Building began in the last part of old Hiram's life and finished by the end of Desmond's. Then his son, Charles—Gracie's father—had the steps re-done about fifteen years ago. Concrete." He sniffed. "His granddaddy would disapprove."

As did Henry, Drew thought, hiding his smile. But he got the man's point. The steps simply didn't fit in.

"Must have taken a lot of work, not to mention money, hauling all those stones from wherever when red brick was readily available."

"Yup. That Winters determination most likely started with old Hiram himself." He pointed to a construction site at the opposite end of the square. "That's the library... well...it's going to be but it's behind schedule for some reason. Used to be a magnificent movie theater there. Now everyone has to drive to one of those malls in Portland to see a movie." He sighed.

Drew recalled the sign he'd seen advertising its future arrival as he took in the scaffolding, tarps and hoardings.

They waited for the red light at the intersection before crossing over to the pedestrian-only square. Beds of flowering bushes and plants broke up the expanse of gray flagstone and two impressive rows of oak trees lined the main walkway leading to the front of the town hall. It was almost noon and people sat on a scattering of park benches eating lunches. Employees from the nearby businesses, Drew guessed. There were women pushing strollers with youngsters toddling behind, older kids breezing by on skateboards and a few gray-haired men hunched over chessboards that appeared to be painted onto concrete tables.

Henry waved to one of the men. "That area was built this past spring and it's full almost every day. In fine weather, of course."

"Another Winters family project?"

"Nope. In fact, I think Charles would have opposed it but at the time his heart trouble was keeping him away from council meetings."

"He's on the council?"

Henry snorted. "There's always been a Winters on council here in the Cove."

Drew looked from the chess players to Henry. It was the first time he'd heard the man refer to the Winterses in even a mild negative tone. "Oh?"

"Don't get me wrong. I'm not bad-mouthing the family. They've been here as long as the Cove itself. Had a lot to do with its very beginnings, like I told you yesterday."

"But?"

Henry shrugged. "Just that they've always got their way it seems. Some people are like that, you know." He turned to face Drew. "Needing to be in control."

For an uncomfortable second Drew thought the man was referring to him until Henry added, "Charlie Winters has always been one."

"I guess you know him well, since this is a small town."

"Went to school with him," he muttered as he resumed walking.

That apparently summed up the matter, Drew thought, following along until Henry came to an abrupt halt several yards ahead. Drew realized he'd have noticed the statue sooner had he not turned his head to look at a bird in a nearby tree branch. His identification of the statue was much quicker than that of the bird. A Winters, no doubt. He read the etched plaque at the base of the bronze.

Hiram Frederick Winters, 1890-1950
Fisherman.

"The founding father?"

"The very same." Henry stared thoughtfully at the statue as if seeing it for the first time.

"I'd have expected a more eloquent epitaph," Drew commented.

"It's what he wanted. That's the story anyway. He took great pride in his humble beginnings as a fisherman."

"But he was more than that, from what you've told me."

"Much more. A visionary."

"He died young."

"Lived hard," Henry said.

Those two words said a lot, but Drew figured "hard" could be taken many ways. The statue wasn't a work of art by any means, but the unnamed sculptor had managed to capture an interesting expression in Hiram's face beneath the hand up to his brow. Obviously, he was meant to be staring out across the water, the lobster pot at his feet symbolizing his occupation. But Drew decided the man could just as well have been surveying his small empire—Lighthouse Cove.

"Shall we go inside?" Henry asked.

CHAPTER FIVE

THEY CROSSED THE street wrapping around the town square and mounted the steps up to the massive wood doors of Town Hall. Drew ran his hand across them. Oak, he guessed.

"Handmade," Henry said, "but I can't recall where. Len would know. Charles wanted to replace them with a steel and glass set. For security, he said. But the motion was defeated, thank heavens."

"Are you on the council, too?"

"Not anymore, but I go to most of the meetings now that I'm retired. It's good to stir the pot once in a while. Ask uncomfortable questions. Keeps the local politicians on their toes."

Drew smiled at the sparkle in Henry's eyes. The man reminded him a bit of his grandfather. He clasped one of the etched brass doorknobs and tugged.

"Push," Henry prompted.

The door creaked open into a large central

foyer lit by an enormous chandelier. Polished wooden staircases on each side of the entry hall curved gracefully upward, meeting on the second floor. Drew tilted his head back to see that two more traditional staircases led to the top. The country and state flags stood like sentries across from one another at the base of each staircase.

There were only a few people walking purposefully up the stairs or across the foyer to the inner hallways and various offices. The lunch hour was Drew's explanation for the quiet. He circled around a large granite table holding a crystal vase of flowers and only then noticed a reception and information counter on the far right. A man and a woman sat behind it and adjacent to the counter, a burly security guard.

"We're here to see Leonard Maguire," Henry announced. "In the Historical Society's office," he added at the woman's slight frown.

"Your name?"

Drew saw Henry roll his eyes.

"Henry Jenkins," he barked.

She keyed into a computer and, looking up with a smile, said, "Right. You know where it is?"

Henry uttered a curt "Yup" and, without a thank-you, veered off to his left to head for a small set of stairs in a far corner of the foyer.

Drew tipped an index finger and said, "Thanks," following the older man down into what he presumed was the basement, feeling a stab of disappointment that they were not going to be ascending that grand staircase.

Henry was waiting for him at the bottom of the stairs. "Guess I should have been more polite there," he muttered, "but I've been coming here for council meetings—plus lately, several Society meetings—for nigh on fifteen years and haven't had to do more than wave a hand as I walk by that counter. Now they've got these young people and that stone-faced security guard who make me feel like they're going to be asking me for some formal identification anytime soon."

"Change is always a challenge," Drew said.

Henry glared at him. "It's not *change* I'm objecting to. It's the fact that no one knows anyone anymore. This is the Cove! Not too long ago you couldn't walk a block without stopping for a chat or a hello at least but now…"

Drew understood. He'd heard his grandparents complain about the same thing whenever they'd returned from a trip into town.

With a low harrumph Henry continued along the narrow hall to a wooden door almost at its end. He gave it a sharp tap and opened it. "Leonard," Drew heard him say as he followed him inside.

The short balding man rising out of a chair looked a few years younger than Henry, whom he clapped on the shoulders before extending a hand to Drew.

"I hear you're interested in our town," he said after introductions.

"Uh, yes," Drew began and was about to add specifically the lighthouse when Henry interrupted.

"I've told him a bit of the history and thought you could show him some of our collection."

"Of course! I've pulled out a few photos already." He turned to the long table in the center of the room. There were at least twenty chairs around the table, sets of filing cabinets along one wall and a counter with a coffee urn and supplies against the other.

The room was surprisingly spartan for a club's meeting place and Drew wondered if it was meant to be a temporary location.

As if reading his mind, Leonard said, "We're in transition. We had a room at the local school but it got too busy with other community groups so Ev Winters arranged a move here. But as you can see..." He gestured unhappily at the basement room with three small windows set up so high on the exterior wall they barely emitted any light.

"Where will you be moving to?" Drew asked.

"The library!" Both men answered in unison.

"Whenever that happens," Leonard grumbled.

"Problems?"

"A few. Some planning issues and—" he gave a loud sigh "—funding, of course."

Drew nodded, thinking again of Grace's plan to raise money for the lighthouse. Not the best timing and one more check mark against selling.

He joined the other two men at the table and Leonard's display, patiently listening to him summarize the Cove's history—mainly repeating what Henry told him—until a brief pause in his account gave Drew the chance to ask, "And the lighthouse? Any early pictures of that?"

"Sure." He flipped through some pages. "I apologize for these albums. Our archived collection has been curated appropriately but it's in storage until we move into the library."

"If," Henry intoned.

Leonard nodded agreement. "Okay, here are a few taken by some local citizens years ago. We have some of its construction but they're—"

"In storage," Drew finished for him as he thumbed through the few pages featuring the lighthouse. The photos had been taken years before, judging by the pristine exterior of the tower and the red daymark was bright and fresh. The storm panes of the gallery atop the tower sparkled. The images reinforced Drew's conclusion that the lighthouse had been long abandoned, even by its keeper— Henry—and a rush of sadness combined with irritation overwhelmed him. If Grace and Henry wanted a memorial so badly, why hadn't they been looking after the place?

Leonard was rummaging through a box of loose photographs and pulled out a wrinkled one of a serious-looking man in old-fashioned clothes, which he handed to Drew. "Augustin-Jean Fresnel," he said, "an eighteenth-century physicist and the inventor of the Fresnel lens that made lighthouses so much more effective as lifesaving structures."

Drew gazed at the photographic reproduction of a portrait of the man he'd read about in college, nodded politely and passed it back to Leonard. "You have a nice Fresnel in the town's lighthouse. Sized appropriately for the height of the tower and with a fixed beacon."

"Ah, you're a lighthouse buff I take it. And you've been *inside*?"

Henry cleared his throat. "Uh, well, Drew here isn't a tourist. He's from the Coast Guard. Doing an inspection of lighthouses."

The expression in the other man's face ranged from surprise to something that almost was disbelief. Drew had assumed Henry had already explained to Maguire why he was in town. He was about to ask if there was a problem with him going inside when Henry interrupted again. "Apparently these inspections happen more or less as routine."

"I can't even remember the last time when someone came to check ours," Leonard declared.

Drew opened his mouth to speak when Henry stepped in again. "Guess we were off the Coast Guard radar," he said, chuckling. Then he looked at his watch. "Uh-oh, we're due to go see Betty Anderson at the Information Center."

He got up from his chair with more agility than Drew had seen in him thus far and shook Leonard's hand. "Thanks for this."

Drew added his thanks and followed Henry along the shadowy corridor, up the stairs, across the foyer with a quick wave to the trio at the reception counter and outside. He stopped at the top of the steps, blinking against the brightness. When his vision settled, he turned to Henry as he drew up beside him.

"Sorry for rushing you out," the old man muttered. "Just that no one knows about Gracie's plan and she wants to keep it that way until it's approved."

When were these two people going to understand there wasn't going to be any project? But "I see" was all Drew could muster.

HENRY GOT BACK to the store minutes before Ben was supposed to pick up Grace for the drive to Portland.

"How did it go?" Grace asked, as she met him at the door.

He pulled out a business card from his trousers pocket and handed it to her. "He said to please call him. He'd like to take you to dinner tonight if possible."

"Did you ask him about staying at your place?"

"I did and he said, 'Thank you, I'll think about it.'" Henry turned at the sound of a car. "Here's your ride, Gracie."

"But the tour? Did you show him everything?"

"Betty was home sick today, so we skipped that part and had lunch instead. I'll tell you more later."

A light tap of a horn. Ben was behind the wheel of their father's car and pointing to his wrist.

"Okay, thanks, Henry. I don't know when we'll be back so just close up. You've got your key?"

"I do. Off you go, then."

She dashed out to the car, getting into the back beside her mother.

"Busy day?" her father asked from the front seat.

It always seemed to be the first question he posed when they were together. Either that or "Slow day again?" Grace wondered if he regretted buying the store for her to manage. She thought some people in town—including Henry—believed Charles had purchased the store to get her to stay but in truth, it had been her idea.

She knew after a month back home with her parents that she'd never be able to stay for as long as they wanted unless she had something to do and her own place to live. Henry's mention of retirement came at the right time for both of them. She moved into his apartment above the store and he bought his bungalow with the sale money. But four months after taking over the store, she was beginning to wonder if she'd made a mistake. Business was slow and people were always asking for Henry, as if he were on a holiday somewhere and would soon be back.

"Is Henry filling in for you, dear?" her mother asked, giving Grace's hand a quick squeeze.

"Uh-huh."

"He's very generous with his time."

"I think he's still adapting to retirement."

"That explains it," Ben commented from the front.

"Explains what?" Grace asked.

"I've seen him in the neighborhood around the store a few times recently. Just this morning actually, coming out with some guy."

Small towns! Grace shook her head, thinking that didn't take long. Her second thought flashed to Drew Spencer, clearly the "guy" Ben was referring to and someone she didn't want to talk about.

"And what were you doing hanging around Porter Street may I ask—in the middle of the morning on a weekday?"

When Ben sneaked a quick glance at their father, Grace smiled. She'd intended the tease as a diversion, but it ended up as a dig. Her brother had admitted a week ago that he needed to escape from the office occasionally. "For my peace of mind," he'd said.

A month after his own return to the Cove to help out after Charles's surgery, Ben had pressured Grace to do her part supporting the family. She'd resisted at first. Not because of the job—leaving the reference library in Augusta had been on her mind for some time—but returning to Lighthouse Cove was an emotional obstacle and one she'd struggled with since she'd left for college fourteen years ago.

Three long years after that summer. Grace's eyes welled up and she turned to gaze out the window, silently swearing. *This is why I shouldn't have come home. No matter how hard I try, something or someone will trigger that memory. It won't ever go away until I lay it to rest.*

"Everything okay, honey?"

"Sure," Grace murmured, waiting until her eyes cleared before facing her mother.

"Don't worry about the store," her mother whispered. "Businesses have these slumps. We've been through it ourselves."

Unlike her mother, Grace was skeptical about better days ahead, but gave her a reassuring smile. Evelyn Winters—along with Henry—was the bonus in coming home. Her mother's sweet personality had often been a buffer against her father's unbending sternness and Grace hoped never to have to shake that faith in her.

The trip to Portland gave her a chance to contemplate Drew's invite to dinner. Was it simply a thank-you for the afternoon tour but if so, wouldn't he have treated Henry? Or was it another attempt at easing the blow of a refusal—a repeat of the drink invitation last night? She hadn't seriously believed a couple hours of sightseeing would change his mind, but she'd meant to pique his interest in the community.

If she could persuade him to stay through

the July Fourth weekend at Henry's, she could show him the rest of the Cove and introduce him to more old-timers who had memories of the days when the lighthouse was functional. Even her peers remembered when the beacon switched on at dusk, shooting light past the harbor onto the dark waters of Casco Bay. But Grace would never ask any of her former friends to talk about the lighthouse. She couldn't trust what they might say.

By the time they reached the specialist's office, Grace had come up with a rough plan for the next two days if Drew Spencer agreed to stay on. And when they were leaving Portland an hour later—stopping briefly at a drugstore for her father's prescription—she'd decided to accept the dinner invitation in order to lay her ideas out on the table. Sometime between now and then she'd have to summon enough enthusiasm to make her pitch convincing.

No one spoke on the way back to the Cove. Charles's doctor had been firm in his caution against a return to work and blunt with his prognosis. *You've got at least another ten years or more if you follow instructions.* Exercise, diet and no stress.

Right, Grace had thought. The first two were easy because her parents had always followed a healthy lifestyle, but Charles's condition was genetic—his father and grandfather had both died of heart attacks at fairly young ages. The single important factor was stress. Luring her father away from the family business, even now that Ben was home to temporarily take over, would be the biggest challenge.

When Ben pulled up in front of the store, Grace saw that Henry had already locked up. She didn't blame him. It was almost five thirty and although she stayed open until six on Thursdays, Grace figured he must have been tired after the sightseeing. She'd have to wait until tomorrow to find out more about the afternoon.

"I see the place is closed already," Charles muttered.

Grace stifled a sigh. Fortunately, her mother saved her from having to reply.

"Well, if you're free, dear, why don't you come for dinner? I've got a pot roast in the slow cooker and it's more than enough for the four of us."

Grace saw her brother wink as he caught her eye in the rearview mirror. Her mother's pot roast was legendary for its dryness.

"Thanks, Mom, but I've other plans for dinner tonight."

That got Ben's full attention. "Anyone I know?" He met her gaze again in the rearview mirror.

"Frankly, dear brother, I stopped having to answer that question from you when you left the Cove for college."

He flushed and looked away. Grace felt a tiny bit of satisfaction as she climbed out of the car. They'd never talked about that summer seventeen years ago, a time when Grace wanted desperately to confide in her older brother. But when he went off to college, he left the Cove for good until six months ago. He'd also left her behind to deal with the pain, the confusion and the whispers. *And the guilt.*

As soon as the car pulled away, she dug her cell phone out of her purse.

CHAPTER SIX

HIS QUALMS THAT he was making a huge mistake vanished the instant Drew saw Grace Winters crossing the hotel lobby. She was wearing a filmy turquoise dress that billowed in her wake, as if she were floating across the marble floor. She waved when he stood up from the chair he'd been sitting in, waiting for her ten minutes earlier than they'd arranged. The dinner invite had been impulsive, but she and Henry had gone to some trouble to give him a sense of life in Lighthouse Cove. The truth was though, he was reluctant to leave town without seeing her again.

"I hope I'm not late," she said as she drew closer.

"On the dot. I...uh... I came down a bit earlier to check out before the morning."

Her bright smile wobbled a bit but thankfully she didn't start in on the questioning. Drew's intention was to enjoy a friendly dinner with her and outline his thoughts about the lighthouse. He'd had time after leaving Henry to hike back to the site to confirm his thinking. The return walk along the shore and the marina, watching the gulls wheeling overhead and diving for scraps littered on the footpath, had filled him with a sense of peace but also purpose. He just hoped she'd view his decision as a good compromise for everyone.

"This was a surprise," she said, "but a very pleasant one."

"I wanted to thank you for organizing my walkabout with Henry."

"Maybe he should be here, then, instead of me."

Her tinkling laugh seemed to bounce off the walls. It was the first spontaneous happiness Drew had seen in her. "No, I'm taking the right person out," he said. "But I did get a recommendation from Henry."

"Oh?"

"A place on the waterfront. He said it's casual, but the food is excellent."

"The Daily Catch?"

"You know it, of course. I suppose there are a limited number of places in a town this size."

"True enough but I haven't been to the Catch in years."

"So it's an old establishment?"

"Owned and operated by the same family for a couple of generations. In fact, I went to school with the current chef, who's also one of the owners."

"Sounds like a good choice, then. Shall we go?" He placed a hand on the small of her back to guide her around the grouping of armchairs. His palm fit nicely into the small curve at the base of her spine, as if it belonged there. He was thinking how he liked that almost protecting sensation, when a voice behind them brought Grace to an abrupt stop.

"Gracie?"

The woman Drew had encountered the day before was heading their way. The warm smile she aimed at Grace shifted to confusion when she recognized Drew.

"Oh hi, Suzanna."

"I haven't seen you in a while," the other woman said. "Guess that means we've both been busy and a good thing for us, right?"

Drew was curious about the hint of nervousness in the other woman's light laugh and even more, at the unyielding posture in Grace. Weren't these two cousins?

"I guess so," replied Grace.

Suzanna turned her attention to Drew. "I see you're still with us, Mr.—"

"Spencer. Yes, but I'm leaving tomorrow."

"Oh."

He waited for Grace to offer some explanation about him but when none came, he said, "Guess we should get going."

Grace didn't speak until they were outside on the pavement. "I should let you know that my cousin and her family are kind of on the outs with my family. It's a long story and if you don't mind, I'd rather not spoil the evening."

Light from the hotel and street reflected off the dark eyes staring up at him. Drew would have promised her anything in that moment. "Of course," he said and followed her down the steps onto the boardwalk that paralleled the marina.

When they entered The Daily Catch, tucked into an alcove on the boardwalk, Drew knew he'd found a treasure. It was a small wood-framed building—some would call it a shack, he thought—with a single large room strewn with mismatched tables and chairs, checked tablecloths and walls decorated with fishing nets, oars and the occasional lobster trap. At first glance it might have appeared kitschy, but Drew saw the artifacts were genuine. Candles shoved into empty wine bottles provided the main lighting but toward the rear, Drew could see a modern galley-style kitchen, its stainless-steel appliances and counters gleaming under fluorescent lights. Two men and a woman in white chef jackets were at work, bent over plates and pots.

A young woman greeted them and escorted them to a corner table after plunking down two pieces of paper no larger than a shopping list.

"Sandy will be right with you to take your drink order," she said as she returned to the door to welcome more people.

Drew glanced down at the sheet of paper in front of him and the three or four lines of writing on it. "This is the menu?"

"The *daily catch*?" she prompted, smiling.

He got her point. "Ah, yes. But tell me, considering the small number of fishing trawlers I've seen here, where does this daily catch come from?"

"Nowadays the catch is trucked in from Portland, but it will be fresh, caught this morning and shipped on ice directly here. When I was growing up though, everything here was caught in the waters of Casco Bay, way out there." She gestured with her head toward the open windows and the gentle swishing of seawater against the break wall.

"Has the town changed much since you were a kid?"

"Well, it's grown a lot. Spread out to the highway as you probably noticed on your way in. Newer stores have replaced old favorites and some people in town, like Henry, regret that but—" she shrugged "—change is inevitable. Isn't that what they say? The only predictable thing in life is change?"

"Personally, I'd side with Henry on that issue. I accept that change is inevitable as you say, but is it always for the good? That's the part of change I have a problem with."

"You love old things?"

He hesitated, unable to tell from her voice where her own preferences lay. *But what did it matter?* he asked himself. *This is a one-time dinner with a woman I know I'm going to disappoint. That was definitely inevitable.* "Some things," he said.

"Like lighthouses?"

There was a sparkle in her eyes that Drew knew didn't come only from the candle. Fortunately, the arrival of their waiter to take their order saved him from tackling that topic just yet.

After a brief consultation of the wine list and Sandy's insistence that the house special that night—the striped bass—was a must for both of them, Grace asked, "What was the highlight of your walking tour with Henry?"

Drew thought for a minute. "The town hall was pretty impressive, but I think the real highlight was Henry himself." He smiled. "He had a story for everything we saw, and his obvious love of this town was refreshing."

"How do you mean?"

"Well, getting back to our talk about change. At first glance, you might mistakenly pigeonhole Henry as—"

"An old curmudgeon?"

She was smiling so Drew knew she thought otherwise. "Yeah. But that would be a poor assumption. He's someone who stands up for what he believes and if that includes clutching on to the important parts of the status quo in defiance of change, well, good for him."

The glow in her eyes made Drew grateful for the arrival of their wine and crab cake appetizer. He was beginning to realize dinner in a place like this, with a woman who looked like her, might derail his plan to discuss the lighthouse demolition. Oddly enough, that didn't bother him.

They were waiting for their main course when a man in a white jacket approached the table. "Gracie Winters?"

She turned around and gave a huge smile. "Tommy! I heard you and your brother had taken over the place."

"Yet you're only showing up now, months after coming back home?"

The pink in her face and brightness in her eyes were a giveaway, Drew thought with a slight tinge of envy. This man had been—or perhaps still was—someone special.

She shrugged. "I've been busy, setting up a new business. You know how it is."

"I do. Yeah, I heard you'd taken over old man Jenkins's place. How's that working out?"

"Slowly, slowly."

"Tell me about it." He looked around the room. "Things are picking up here now that summer's finally arrived." His eyes fell on Drew, as if noticing him for the first time.

"Oh," she said, "um…this is Drew Spencer. Drew, Tom Nakamura. As I told you, his family has run this place forever. And how is your family, Tom? Parents okay?"

"Everyone's okay, thanks." He glanced at Drew again.

Waiting for further information, Drew thought, which Grace evaded providing.

Instead she asked, "Have you seen Ben yet? He's moved back home, too."

"I have. He came in here a couple of weeks ago for lunch. We had a great time catching up." A clatter from the kitchen caught his attention. "Okay, best get back to work. So nice to see you, Gracie. Don't be a stranger." As he walked away, he turned around to say, "Dessert's on the house."

"The school friend?" Drew asked.

"He was actually in my brother's class." She smiled. "He was always around our house. I had a teenage crush on him."

"My older brother often had girls around, too. One of the few perks of being the youngest."

She grinned. "For sure."

Then he added, "It must be nice to come back after a long time away and meet old friends."

A shadow crossed her face but before Drew could follow up, Sandy brought their main courses.

Grace exclaimed, "That looks amazing."

The fish was perfectly cooked. Drew couldn't remember the last time he'd eaten such a meal and he was content to savor every mouthful, avoiding any talk more serious than comments about the quality of the meal and some more small talk about Drew's visit to Town Hall. There was a brief lull while plates were taken away and wine replaced by coffee while they debated whether they ought to share a dessert.

"We only have two tonight so get one of each and share them," Sandy advised. "Besides, Tom says they're on the house so…"

Drew caught Grace's eye and grinned. "Half and half?"

"Definitely."

When Sandy left to get the desserts, Grace said, "Tell me about yourself."

"I told you I grew up on a farm in Iowa?"

She nodded.

"My parents still live there but my brother and his family run the place now. We've always had soybeans, rotating with corn. A few chickens. It's not a big place but big enough to make a living."

"Were your parents upset about you joining the Coast Guard?"

"Disappointed rather than upset. Fortunately, my older brother was there to take over when the work became too much for my father."

"It seems disappointment in a child comes with being a parent."

Drew remembered Henry's comment about Charles Winters—the allusion to the man's overbearing nature—and wondered how a woman like her could possibly cause a parent any disappointment.

"Sometimes," he said, softening his voice, "but I'm sure that feeling doesn't last. It's natural for people to let down their loved ones. It's just part of the normal ups and downs of a family."

After a long pause, she murmured, "Perhaps."

He wanted to reach across the table and take her hand, bring back that smile of a moment ago. Her sigh also piqued his curiosity. "Henry told me you were a librarian in Augusta, before coming back here to help take care of your father. Was it difficult for you, leaving town and your family when you went to college?"

"No! It wasn't difficult at all. I had no choice but to leave."

Sandy's arrival with their desserts was

well-timed because Drew sensed that Grace Winters had no intention of explaining the vehemence in those last few words. After some small talk about the artistry of their desserts, the mood changed again. Drew carefully cut his chocolate cake in two exact halves and then caught Grace popping a whole strawberry into her mouth.

"Hey," he protested. "There was only one berry on top of that—whatever it is." He pointed with his fork to the large white blob on the plate she was eating from.

"Pavlova," she said as she dug into it again, running her tongue along her spoon after she swallowed.

Drew couldn't take his eyes off her—the full lips bright red from the berry, the satisfied murmur as the spoon poised over the dessert for a second mouthful.

"Strictly speaking, half of that huge strawberry was mine."

She beamed. "Too late now."

He wanted to reach over and dab the fleck of whipped cream in the corner of her mouth. With his finger, not his napkin. *What's happening here, Spencer?* Then he told himself, *Don't question it, just enjoy it.* The food, the soft glow of candlelight, the beautiful woman across the table. Life—his recent life in particular—hadn't been this pleasant in a long time.

"What do you think about Henry's invitation to spend this weekend at his place? The town will have some wonderful July Fourth events."

Drew sensed the light moment was gone. Of course, he'd recognized Henry's invite as a ploy right away. Not that he had anything against cats, but seriously? Henry could probably have taken the cat with him.

"Um, it was very generous of Henry to offer his place, but I really ought to get back to Portland and file my reports. I've been out of office for a month now and—"

"Sure," she interrupted, glancing away but not before Drew saw the disappointment in her face.

He finished his half of the cake, chewing and swallowing without any pleasure and when she politely refused the other half, claiming she'd had too much pavlova, he knew the evening was drawing to an end.

He signaled for the bill and minutes later they emerged onto the boardwalk. The stillness of the evening fell over them like a cozy comforter. The lights from the street above bounced prettily off the shallow water in the marina, but Drew knew only too well how frightening the dark sea beyond could be. He shivered in spite of the balmy night air. When they ascended to street level, he asked, "Can I walk you back to your place?"

She hesitated long enough for him to think she might be misinterpreting his suggestion. Or perhaps she wanted to end the evening right then and there. His response to her question about staying through the weekend had been a conversation stopper and he regretted that.

"If you like." Her voice was almost a whisper.

They walked silently in the opposite direction from the hotel toward the bookstore. Henry had told him Grace lived upstairs in his former apartment.

When they reached the front door of Novel Thinking, Grace fumbled in her purse for the key. Drew wondered if she'd have asked him inside if his answer about staying for the weekend had been different. If he hadn't broken the magic of the evening.

"Listen," he said as she unlocked the door. He couldn't walk away knowing he might be able to fix things.

She swung around.

"I do have to get back to the office tomorrow but…uh… I also don't have plans for the weekend."

She didn't speak, looking up at him with eyes that now seemed to glimmer with hope.

"I…uh…maybe I could take you and Henry up on your offer. It would be nice to spend the holiday in a smaller place, like the Cove."

"He…*we*…would like that. Thank you. I'll let Henry know." She extended her right hand. "And thank you for this night. The dinner. It was lovely."

Drew held on to her hand tucked into his as long as possible. He realized he hadn't mentioned the lighthouse at all. Just as well, he thought. Grace Winters had had enough disappointment for one night.

CHAPTER SEVEN

THE DRIVE TO Portland was a blur. Not due to speed, but to his own inattention. Thankfully most of the traffic was against Drew as people were leaving the city for an early start at the holiday weekend. He'd left Lighthouse Cove right after a quick breakfast at Mabel's, disappointingly uninterrupted by another appearance of Grace Winters. He'd sent her a brief text asking if she'd arrange for him to meet Henry at the bookstore at ten on Saturday morning but hadn't yet received a reply.

Somewhere between Portland and the Cove he asked himself what he hoped to gain by going back. He didn't need to see Grace to reiterate why the tower had to be torn down. That could be done by phone or email. The holiday ahead could be filled—*endured*, he amended—in Portland with his usual weekend routines of a jog around the seafront, brunch at his favorite café and a night of TV with a curry takeout. And he certainly didn't need to enrich his life by cat-sitting. So, he didn't *need* to see Grace, but he *wanted* to.

He parked his car in his usual space in the Coast Guard headquarters parking lot and retrieved his laptop from the trunk. He'd finished writing up all his findings, tying them collectively into a summarizing report, after walking Grace home last night. Except for the tower at Lighthouse Cove. For that, he decided to send a separate memo to Jim Pitarokilis, his commanding officer.

Jim had been a mentor since Drew's transfer to the administrative job in the Portland office eight months ago. His calm and patient manner had guided Drew through the transition from living with regret and guilt to a renewed sense of purpose and hope. When it was obvious that his desk job was hindering more than helping Drew recover from his trauma, Jim had assigned him to temporarily take over the vacant lighthouse maintenance program and encouraged him to apply for the full-time position.

Drew carried his gear across the lobby, through security and up to the second floor. He shared a small office with Ensign McNaught, whose tasks included acting as an assistant to Drew but who primarily spent a lot of time on his cell phone with his current girlfriend. When he strode into the office, Drew saw that the room was empty, a used take-out coffee cup on the other desk the only indication that at some point in the day Mc-Naught had physically been there. He sighed but rationalized that it was the start of a holiday weekend and with luck, he, too, would be gone shortly.

He unpacked his work and booted up his laptop to type up his thoughts on the Cove lighthouse. When he finished the descriptions of the exterior and interior of the tower, he began work on the section that would sell his idea—or not. He summarized the history of the town and the tower's own story, omitting the past tragedy that had occurred there, which, he decided, was irrelevant to the present request. He included a brief picture of the Cove in transition from a prosperous fishing village to a satellite community of Portland. A growing town but one longing to retain the symbols of its humble past. He concluded by referring to Grace and Henry and their solid commitment to restoring and preserving the tower for their community. His recommendation was, rather than tear the tower down, to offer to sell it to the town contingent on a pass from a structural inspection.

He was taking a big risk, knowing that Jim was expecting the decommission and demolition process to be initiated. But Drew had lain awake long into the night after leaving Grace. He thought about her efforts to convince him to change his mind and the faraway, almost pained expression in her eyes when she talked about the lighthouse. The demolition was inevitable because he doubted the tower would be sound enough to sell to the community. Better to have that bitter disappointment come from his supervisor now that Drew had committed himself to the holiday weekend in Lighthouse Cove. Perhaps an extra few days would give him the chance to temper the blow that would eventually come when the tower failed a safety inspection.

The fact that he might not be making this conciliatory gesture if someone other than Grace was requesting a sale wasn't lost on Drew. But he reasoned that his report wasn't a change in direction so much as a postponement—one that would at least give him more time with Grace Winters and perhaps even take some of the edge off his role as the messenger of bad news. He read his email once more and hit Send.

Half an hour later, as he was finishing a memo to McNaught to input the survey data onto a spreadsheet, Drew's cell phone chimed. He snatched it off the desk and saw two words that gave him an ominous feeling. See me.

He walked down the hall and tapped on the door at the end, opening at the loud "Enter."

Jim Pitarokilis looked up from the papers he'd been reading. His smile was reassuring but his gesture to sit suggested Drew was going to be there for longer than the simple "Okay" he'd been anticipating.

"Good trip?" Jim asked.

"Very."

His boss nodded. "Great. So, this memo you just sent me." He pointed to the screen on his desktop monitor. "I've read it over a couple of times and frankly, I'm puzzled."

"Sir?"

"Everything you've written, up to the last paragraph, indicates the obvious conclusion of a teardown. And that's what your assignment was." He shook his bald head. "I'm not seeing any evidence of the tower's viability. Just the opposite. The fact that it hasn't had a functioning beacon in who knows how many years is proof enough. Then you go on to recommend a structural inspection, which will no doubt confirm the site is compromised." He stopped looking at the screen, meeting Drew's steady gaze. "What was your thinking?"

Drew stifled his impatience. Hadn't he made all that clear in his report? He paused, forming a response that would persuade his boss rather than rile him. "The Cove tower is unique, sir. As I wrote, its construction was begun in 1917 when the place was a thriving village dependent on its fishing industry and finished a year later. The wartime situation and perhaps fears of a coastal invasion led to its construction agreement from Lighthouse Service, but the tower was basically built at the request of one of the founding fathers of the community. The Hiram Winters I mentioned."

"I get that, Spencer. That's not my point. Even if it passed an inspection, does this proposal from—" he peered at the computer screen "—Grace Winters, a descendant I gather, have community support? Because if not, unless she's an independently wealthy woman…"

"Other community members seem to be on board, sir." At least two others, he silently added, thinking of Leonard Maguire and Henry. "And as long as the tower passes inspection, won't responsibility for it rest with the buyers? I mean, how the town finds the money for it isn't our problem."

After a long uneasy moment, Jim gave a loud sigh. "You haven't convinced me, but I see that you're all gung ho on this. I'll okay the funds for an inspection but that's it. If there's a hint of doubt about its soundness..."

Drew jumped to his feet. "Got it, sir." He was partway out the door when Jim asked, "Did you get your application in?"

"Yes, and thanks for the reference."

"Anytime. We'll be lucky to have you on board. Though I should tell you there are a couple of excellent applications in from officers outside Portland."

The sobering reminder that the promotion wasn't a done deal had Drew pause in the doorway. "Thanks again, sir, and I'll make sure the right decision is made on that tower."

Grace Winters's face suddenly came to mind and Drew realized at that exact moment how vital his decision would be. He returned to his office and began to pack up the

material he needed to take with him for the
weekend. He had three days ahead to discuss
his report with Grace and Henry and set an
inspection in motion. The inspection would
likely prove what Drew had been attempting
to tell them—that the tower should be demol-
ished. But at least he'd be back in a beautiful
place with a beautiful woman. He had a few
days grace before reality hit.

GRACE ENJOYED A rare sleep-in. Usually the
store was open on Saturdays but because
today was July Fourth, she'd closed it until
Monday. She puttered around her upstairs
apartment, happy to be alone in her own
space. Henry had bought the entire building
many years before and when he decided to
retire, he'd considered renting out the store
and staying in the apartment. But as much
as he loved what he affectionately called
his aerie, the stairs had become an issue for
him. He'd found a cute bungalow two streets
up from the beach road and had taken up
bird-watching. A win-win for everyone because six weeks back in the Cove had proven
that adult children living with aging parents
wasn't an ideal situation.

She'd resisted the move home for weeks,

agreeing to return only days before her father's surgery. Receiving a layoff notice from the Augusta library service due to budget cutbacks had been a factor but Ben's admonition to "step up to the plate" was the deciding argument. She'd protested that he himself had only made irregular visits after he'd gone off to college, but he'd played the mom card, using Evelyn's rheumatoid arthritis condition as leverage. Grace wouldn't refuse to help her mother and just as Grace had predicted, the temporary move had somehow segued into semipermanence.

Now she was living above an old bookstore that had weathered the years better than the lighthouse. After Brandon's death, few residents ventured near the site. Since Henry's hip troubles began, his keeper's visits stretched from once a month to every six months and finally to once a year. If that.

But Grace had no right to judge. Until a month ago, she hadn't stepped a foot on the path to the lighthouse since that night seventeen years ago when she and Cassie had hidden behind some shrubs to witness the meeting between Ella and Brandon. Over the years, Grace had struggled to block all thoughts of that night. She'd avoided the general area because that was where Brandon had drowned—*all because of her*.

It had been Henry who'd persuaded her to take the first step. She still didn't know why he'd bothered and wondered if his concern that she visit the place where Brandon had died stemmed from his own guilt over the neglect of the site. When she finally agreed, she'd managed the walk along the grassy path until a few feet away from the lighthouse door when she froze, picturing Brandon standing there, bracing to tackle the high tide to get to shore. No one knew exactly how he'd drowned, but Grace had stored that imagined scene in her mind since that night.

Henry had clasped her hand in his as they walked almost to the steps at the lighthouse base. She'd stood there as Henry pointed to areas where the structure seemed to be crumbling and while he rambled on about fixing it up. But what had really held her interest was a bunch of dead flowers lying nearby. Later that night, as she lay awake for hours, Grace had wondered about the flowers. Who had brought them and why? Obviously someone who was remembering Brandon. That was the moment that she decided to help Henry fix up the lighthouse as a memorial to Brandon.

It would be a chance to make up, if even in a small way, for what she'd done.

She sighed, coming back to the present. *It's summer, it's a holiday and a good-looking man is headed your way.* Because the day was going to be hot, she opted for a cool dress rather than shorts. Studying herself in the mirror, Grace thought of the smile on Drew's face when he'd watched her cross the hotel lobby Thursday night. It had been a long time since a man had greeted her like that and she had only herself to blame. There had been a few relationships in college and after, but none for long. The beginnings were always good, until Grace realized serious commitments would involve disclosure. She'd become very adept at handling endings.

She had no idea how the weekend was going to play out as far as getting Drew's agreement to sell them the lighthouse, but since their dinner at The Daily Catch, Grace knew she could handle spending more time with Drew. Time that didn't have to pertain exclusively to the lighthouse. She grabbed sunglasses and her summer straw handbag on the way downstairs, locking the interior door leading to her apartment behind her just as someone knocked at the store's front one.

"On the dot as usual," she teased, letting Henry inside. "You could have come right in."

"Ah no. It's your place now. Having an extra key is only for emergencies or the like."

"You look nice, Henry."

"I clean up well," he said, smiling. "Isn't that what your mother says?" He handed her a set of keys. "I was surprised by your message that our young Coast Guard officer had taken us up on the offer." He paused. "Must have been a successful dinner."

Grace felt her face heat up but ignored his teasing. "I was surprised, too, Henry."

"Tell him Felix has plenty of food and water for the day so no need to check on him till later. I left a note on the kitchen table with any information about the place he might want. And let him know I left some windows open, so he won't worry that someone's broken in."

No one would need to at that invitation, Grace thought. "Have you heard that there have been some burglaries recently?"

He waved a hand. "It's the Cove, Gracie. Was a time when we didn't even lock our doors at night."

"Things are different now."

"Maybe in Portland or in that new housing complex up by the highway, but not down here."

Grace knew better than to argue. Henry and change were incompatible.

Henry lay a hand on her shoulder. "Gracie, do me a favor, will you?"

"Yes?"

"Just enjoy the weekend. Forget about the dang lighthouse and live it up a little. That fella—he's a nice guy. Whatever he decides, I'm sure it'll be for the best. Don't fret about it. Have fun." He turned around and was out the door before she had a chance to reply.

Grace teared up, watching Henry limp toward his old Chevy parked outside. The man had been a lifesaver for her all through her teens, suggesting—or buying at her recommendation—all kinds of books for the store. He'd always taken an interest in her. Not as a Winters, but simply as Gracie, the girl who came by once a week for a book.

The nostalgic moment vanished as a black SUV pulled up in front. Grace waited inside the door as Drew Spencer climbed out. He caught sight of her and waved, smiling broadly as he walked around the vehicle to the sidewalk.

"Hello," he said when she came out the door, locking it behind her.

The greeting was casual, but not the glance that swept over her. Grace felt her pulse quicken.

"You look nice," he said.

"So do you."

They laughed together. "All right, niceties aside," he said. "Have I missed Henry? Cause I see you've locked up."

She held out the keys. "These are for you and he said to tell you that Felix has been fed and watered and there's a note on the kitchen table for you."

"Felix?"

"His cat?"

He laughed again. "Right. Why I'm here."

"I hope that's not the only reason."

He seemed as surprised at her tease as she was, and a bigger grin was his reply.

"Here's the day's agenda," she said, slipping on her sunglasses and pulling a flyer out of her handbag. "The parade starts at eleven from Town Square and comes down to Main Street, right there—" she pointed to the corner "—follows all along Main to the top of the hill where you probably drove in off the highway and that's where it disperses. Meanwhile stalls will be setting up in the square along with some food trucks plus a couple of kiddie carnival rides."

She felt his eyes on her as she read and tried to keep the piece of paper steady in her hand. "There are various activities around town. A rubber ducky race down at the marina, a pie-eating contest outside the Tasty Bake Shop at one o'clock, music in the park—that's the green area at the bottom of the square—at two, a strawberry shortcake festival at the church opposite Town Hall, all afternoon for that—"

"Or as long as supplies last," he broke in.

She laughed. "I'm already worn-out just reading this." She shoved the flyer back into her handbag. "Of course, there will be fireworks after dark, about nine or so."

"Sounds like a full day."

"We've missed the pancake breakfast at the other church in town, two streets over from here. Sorry." She giggled and immediately hated herself for doing so.

"Maybe we can do breakfast together tomorrow morning," he murmured, his gaze holding hers.

Grace took a calming breath. She felt a sudden tug into the past and all of her failed relationships. Then Henry's parting words popped into her head. *Have fun.*

"Sure." She cleared her throat and managed a smile. "Where to first?"

"I think the parade," he said and reached for her hand.

CHAPTER EIGHT

DREW HAD SEEN countless July Fourth parades, but even before the bandmaster raised his baton high in the air to signal the start, he knew this one was already memorable. But only because Grace's hand was tucked into his. He gazed down at the top of her head, barely reaching his shoulder, and smiled. In fact, he hadn't stopped smiling since he got out of his SUV and saw her standing in the doorway of Novel Thinking.

Well, he corrected himself, until he'd spotted that brief shadow in her lovely face minutes ago, as if she were lost in thought or in another place. Had it been something he'd said? It came and went so quickly he thought he'd imagined it but no, he decided. It happened right after he'd joked about having breakfast together next day. Had she inferred some other meaning in his remark that accounted for that unreadable expression? Or was it him, completely misinterpreting her smiles as interest in him?

When the drum majorettes pranced by, he bent to ask, "Were you one of those once upon a time?"

"Nope. I couldn't keep the baton in the air." Then she quipped, "Now if the auditions had involved balancing an armful of books while walking with my nose in one at the same time, that would have been another story."

"But I'm sure you went on to bigger and better things in college at least."

"In college for sure. But high school, that was a whole different game." She turned back to the parade but not before he glimpsed that far-off look again. He wondered for a second if she was remembering a high school crush. Maybe the one she'd admitted to the other night—the chef at the restaurant. What intrigued him was the fact that most people got over their high school crushes.

By the time the volunteer fire department had marched past, along with the local Rotary club and then a float featuring a giant lobster and a cookpot, Drew was ready to head for the food vendors. Fortunately, Grace agreed.

"Parades never seem to change. Same costumes, same bands and music year after year," she said as they walked toward the outside perimeter of the square where the stalls had been set up.

Drew laughed. "You sound a bit jaded. I thought you liked old things. Aren't traditions part of that?"

"Of course, and I do like the tradition of parades. But I wish whoever's in charge would ramp it up a bit. It's always the same."

"How many times in the last few years have you seen the July Fourth parade here?"

Her pink face was the answer. "Okay, you've got me. Maybe three or four times."

"In how many years?"

"This is getting embarrassing. I left for college at eighteen and I'm thirty-two this summer."

"A handful of times in fourteen years?"

"Probably. Are you saying I've no right to complain about the parade?"

"I'm teasing, Grace." He squeezed her hand. "My track record watching parades back home isn't much better."

They'd almost reached the first row of stalls when he impulsively asked, "But I'm curious. It sounds like you didn't go home a lot after leaving for college. Why was that?"

Letting go of his hand was the first sign

that she hadn't liked his question. The second was the stiffness in her voice. "I don't think that's unusual. College, summer jobs and then a real job…all kept me busy. Plus, I was in Augusta."

"Sure." He could have pointed out that Augusta wasn't so far away or that he'd gone to college in Des Moines, half a state away from the Spencer farm, and still had managed visits home. But he wasn't about to spoil the moment, much less the day. He was beginning to wonder if she had a moody side or a touchiness about certain subjects. If only he could second-guess what they might be.

The first stall they came upon had a cluster of children around it. Drew stretched his neck to see what was on sale. "Candy," he told Grace. "Little chocolate lobsters, candy floss, caramel corn and saltwater taffy."

"If there's fudge…"

He peered over the heads in front of him again. "Um…yes… I see fudge." Then he slowly worked his way through the crowd until he reached the edge of the long table where he realized that most of the kids were gawping rather than buying. That eased his conscience about butting in. One of the harried-looking vendors asked, "Help you, sir?"

and seconds later he was handing Grace a wedge of chocolate fudge while clutching a small bag of caramel corn for himself.

"It was either this or maple walnut."

"You made the right choice." She bit off a corner. "This is one tradition I hope never changes."

They strolled along the line of stalls, glancing at the tables but content to walk and munch. The mood blip earlier was forgotten. *Unless I put my foot in it again*, Drew thought.

The crowds around the edges of the square were thick now and Drew was relieved when Grace suggested going down to the harbor. "I'm not a fan of hordes of people," he said as they left the square. "Maybe it has to do with growing up on a farm. All those big open spaces with very few people."

"The Cove was smaller when I was growing up and you could hardly walk a block without meeting someone you knew, but still it seemed different back then. I found the busyness of Augusta overwhelming at first, until I grew to like the anonymity of a bigger place."

"True. That can be refreshing."

"And appealing."

"We agree on some things, then."

"More than just 'some,' I hope," she said. She stowed the rest of her fudge in her handbag and took his hand again.

He pressed it gently as they strolled down toward the harbor. Drew was happy to find the waterfront less crowded. "Ah, this is better," he said, taking a deep breath of salty air.

"Totally." She suddenly pulled him toward the steps leading to the boardwalk below the street. "I think I see the rubber ducky race. C'mon." She dropped his hand and strode briskly to a group of adults and kids standing at the water's edge.

Drew smiled, thinking at least there was something here that excited her. By the time he caught up to her she'd managed to wriggle through to the front. She waved for him to join her, but he shook his head. He was content to stand back and watch Grace. The group was cheering on at least twenty or more rubber ducks of all shapes and sizes. A couple of older teens on Drew's right seemed to have a betting pool going as the ducks bobbed randomly toward the shore. Drew noticed a skiff about fifteen feet out where they had probably been set into the water. A raucous mix of cheers and groans greeted the first ducks to arrive at the finish line, a long rope tied between two buoys.

Grace worked her way back through the crowd, a grin in her face.

"I see this event is a winner for you."

"I entered it almost every year from the time I was seven or eight till I was twelve."

"Ever win?"

"Never!"

Her laugh caused a few heads to turn and Drew impulsively hugged her. She was gazing up at him when a voice behind them got their attention.

"Gracie?"

An older couple was walking toward them. The woman instantly reminded Drew of Grace and as they got closer, his guess was confirmed.

"Mom? Dad?" She didn't sound pleased.

"Your father and I were just talking about you, wondering if you'd make it to some of the events."

"Well, here I am."

Her mother's gaze passed quickly over Drew, then back to Grace. The father studied him longer. Drew held out his hand. "Drew Spencer."

Grace quickly said, "Uh…this is my father, Charles Winters, and my mother, Evelyn."

Drew moved his hand from the father to the mother, who clasped it warmly. He liked her instantly, noting the sparkle of interest in her eyes and a smile identical to Grace's.

There was a lull after the introductions. Drew figured the parents were waiting for some further information than his name.

"Are you new to the Cove, Mr. Spencer?" Evelyn asked.

"No, I'm from Portland. Here for the weekend."

"Lovely," she said. "Is this your first July Fourth celebration here, then?"

"It is."

"Enjoying it?"

"Very much." Drew glanced sharply at Grace, waiting for her to explain something more about him but she remained silent.

"Perhaps a bit smaller than the one in Portland," Evelyn added.

"Um, well, I haven't actually experienced one in Portland yet. I've only been there less than a year."

Charles Winters broke in. "We'd best go, Ev. Ben's waiting."

Drew noticed Grace relax until her mother

said, "Won't you two join us? We're having lunch at The Daily Catch. They've got a clambake organized and Ben's saving a table for us. Please come. It'll be fun."

Grace opened her mouth to speak just as Drew said, "We'd love to, thanks."

He knew he'd made a mistake from the look Grace shot him, but he reasoned she could easily have come up with some excuse. When she didn't, he decided meeting her family might give him some insight into Grace Winters. As they approached the outdoor patio set up on the boardwalk in front of the restaurant, a tall, broad-shouldered man rose from a chair to greet them. He had the same curly dark hair that Grace had though his was trimmed, and his chin and hawkish nose were clearly from his father.

"We bumped into Grace, Ben," Evelyn said, "and this is Drew Spencer. A…uh…a friend of Grace's."

Grace's brother shook hands, giving him a once-over similar to his father's. They sat down as the waiter appeared.

"Oh? Hello again," Sandy said. "Back so soon? I guess we were a hit the other night."

Drew was the only one to return her pleasant smile. After orders of beer, wine and seafood platters were given, Drew felt obliged to explain, since Grace remained exasperatingly quiet. "Grace and I had a wonderful dinner here Thursday night."

Three sets of eyes turned to Grace sitting next to him but only her mother spoke. "How nice. We haven't been here in ages, have we, dear?" She looked at her husband, adding, "I see now why you couldn't make it for pot roast that night." She reached across to pat Grace's forearm, resting on the table.

Drew thought the mother's smile was a mix of delight and amusement. He had a feeling she didn't mind Grace missing the pot roast if dinner with him at The Daily Catch was the reason.

Drinks were delivered and Ben said, "Cheers everyone! Happy July Fourth!" When he set his beer down, he peered at Drew across the table. "So, where did you two meet? In Portland or here at the Cove?"

"Here," said Drew. "I came to—"

"He's a friend of Henry's," Grace interrupted. "I met him through Henry and he's staying at his place while Henry's in Portland. He has a doctor appointment there and decided to spend a couple of extra days visiting his sister. Drew is cat-sitting."

Drew hoped his jaw hadn't dropped because he was having difficulty processing the blend of fact and fiction that had spewed automatically from her mouth. A mouth he'd fantasized kissing a few times over the past twenty-four hours. "Yes, I…uh… I'm looking after Felix for the weekend," was all he said.

The food arrived and was all they talked about while eating a variety of seafood, corn on the cob and fries.

"Do you have family in Portland, Drew?" Evelyn asked at one point.

"No, Mrs. Winters. My family's in Iowa, where I grew up."

"Good heavens! What brought you to the East Coast?"

"A combination of things but specifically childhood books on lighthouses." He smiled at all four faces turned his way.

Grace suddenly piped up. "I heard there's strawberry shortcake at the church. Maybe dessert?"

"I'm absolutely positive I won't be able to eat dessert after this." Evelyn gestured to the platters of leftovers. "One platter would have been enough."

"They'll pack it up for you, Mom," Grace said. "I've had enough, too."

Drew had been watching her peck at the food on her plate and suspected she'd either lost her appetite from the fudge or from her efforts to steer the conversation away from why Drew was in town. At least that's what he guessed she'd been doing.

Charles signaled for the bill and as Drew went to withdraw his wallet from his pants pocket, raised a hand. "No, I insist. Cove hospitality."

"Thank you, Mr. Winters—and Mrs. Winters." Drew looked Evelyn's way and was rewarded with a smile. He wasn't quite as certain about his reception from the father and brother. They were definitely interested and curious, too. Not that he blamed them. His introduction had been sketchy to say the least.

They prepared to leave after the containers of the lunch leftovers were brought to Evelyn. Drew saw her take Grace aside and speak quietly to her.

At the same time, Ben asked, "So what's your job in the Coast Guard, Drew? Are you there as a civilian or officer?"

"An officer. I was in search and rescue but now—" He happened to glance across at Grace, shaking her head at him. "Now I'm in admin." Drew found himself both annoyed and mystified. What was her problem?

Ben nodded. When he noticed his father rising shakily from his chair he rushed to his father's side. "Dad, let me help."

Evelyn Winters walked over to say good-bye. "I've invited you and Grace for Sunday dinner tomorrow. Please persuade her. We'd love to have you both."

Drew smiled. "Thank you, Mrs. Winters."

"Evelyn, please." She tucked her arm through her husband's and gave a small wave.

Drew sensed Grace coming up beside him as they watched the three slowly make their way along the crowded boardwalk.

After a moment, Grace spoke. Her voice was cheery—falsely so, he thought. "Where to now?" she asked.

He looked into her dark eyes. "Someplace quiet," he replied. "Where we can talk."

To her credit, she didn't play coy with him and simply said, "Why don't I take you to Henry's place? It's away from all this activity."

"Fine. Let's collect my car and drive there. I assume his place has road access? Or is it too close to the beach?"

"It's on the first street up from the waterfront, running parallel to the beach road. There's parking."

"Okay then, shall we go?" He didn't reach for her hand, no longer sure if he ought to. Were they simply two people negotiating a possible business agreement or, as he'd almost begun to imagine hours ago, something more? Perhaps after their talk, she wouldn't be as enthusiastic about spending the rest of the weekend with him. Of course, he could always go back to Portland. Then he remembered the cat. *Well, if Grace no longer wants my company, the least she can do is take the cat until Henry gets home.*

They worked their way through knots of chatting adults and children running frenetically here and there to where Drew had left his car. He swore softly, noticing that the street had now been blocked off at one end and there were so many people crossing back and forth that he couldn't risk making a U-turn.

"I don't have much stuff," he said. "Looks like we'll have to leave the car here and hike it. Is it far?"

She shook her head. "I can help."

He removed a small backpack, his laptop and a cloth bag of assorted food items. "Nonperishables," Drew explained. "Coffee, a loaf of bread, peanut butter. My go-to emergency rations. I wasn't sure what Henry would have or what would be open this weekend."

"That was a good idea, though I bet Henry left something for you. He thinks like that."

Drew handed her the cloth bag, hoisted the backpack over one shoulder and grabbed hold of the laptop. "Will the car be okay here till tomorrow? What about parking enforcement?"

"It's pretty relaxed on holidays. You can leave it here until you go back to Portland if you want. Whenever."

He noticed her glancing up at him but busied himself adjusting the backpack on his shoulder. There was no point making a commitment about when he'd be leaving Lighthouse Cove. They still had much to talk about after those awkward few minutes with her parents. Drew suspected the impression that he'd finally begun to know Grace Winters might be all in his imagination.

They set out for Henry's, navigating through the swarm of pedestrians and making a wide berth around the pie-eating contest on the sidewalk in front of a bakery. Drew noticed that most of the contestants were teen-age boys and chuckled.

"Some things haven't changed here," Grace said. "The rubber duck race was my thing but this was always Ben's and…"

"And?"

"Brandon's," she finally said.

"I admit to loving church potluck suppers back home," he said, filling in the silence that followed. "There were no eating contests but always lots of homemade pies and other treats."

"I remember some of those social events, too." She sighed. "It's funny how childhood attractions lose meaning once you're an adult."

That observation might have led to a good discussion, Drew was thinking, if they were somewhere else rather than on a side street filled with July Fourth revelers. They finally emerged onto the far end of Main Street, past the marina where the paved road reverted to sand and the public beach.

Grace turned onto a street leading up from the beach road. As he followed, Drew caught sight of the solitary lighthouse, detached from the town's festivities. Henry's bunga-low was the third house in from the corner and although it faced the water, there were other one-story dwellings in between. It was a pretty wood-framed bungalow with a pale gray painted exterior set off by cobalt blue shutters, door and window trim.

"Nice," he said as he stepped up onto the small porch with an overhang and two wicker rocking chairs. He pictured Henry sitting there, pondering the world and all its problems. He dug into his jeans pocket for the key and handed it to Grace. As soon as she opened the door a gray-and-white object streaked between their legs.

"Uh-oh," Grace muttered.

"Felix?"

She nodded glumly.

"Guess that talk will have to wait," Drew said. He couldn't be sure, but thought her expression brightened a bit.

CHAPTER NINE

"Is he an indoor or outdoor cat?"

Drew looked worried so Grace put him at ease. "Indoor, and he's escaped before. I'll leave some water on the porch, but I bet he'll be mewing at the door when he's hungry."

"Okay."

He sounded doubtful. "There's not much road traffic up here. He'll be fine," she added.

Grace stepped inside and moved from the small entryway into the cozy living room, where she whisked back the curtains Henry had left closed to keep the place cooler.

"Make yourself at home," she told Drew as she carried his bag of food items into the kitchen. She picked up the note Henry had left on the kitchen table and returned to find Drew studying Henry's collection of Civil War toy soldiers in a glass display cabinet mounted on a wall in the living room.

"I see more evidence of Henry's interest in history as well as bird-watching." He gestured to the stack of books on the small table set between a recliner chair and a two-seat sofa.

"I think he's taken up cooking, too, because he was asking me about cookbooks last week." She held out the note. "Here's his info about the cottage. It's a pretty basic place so I don't imagine you'll have any trouble finding things. He made up the bed in the guest room down the hall."

He took it from her but didn't read it. Instead he kept his eyes on her.

"Do you want a quick look around or..."

"Maybe the talk and then we can enjoy the rest of the day," he said as he sat down on the sofa.

Grace hesitated. She felt a bit like Goldilocks. The big recliner was too big—she pictured herself disappearing between its fake leather arms—while the small sofa was definitely too intimate. "Maybe outside on the porch? Where we can get some fresh air?"

His indifferent shrug almost prompted her to ask him to forget the talk entirely and go back into town for some fun. She suddenly thought of Cassie Fielding and Ella Jacobs from that long-ago summer. They would have said exactly that.

He followed her out onto the porch, and for

a few minutes they sat quietly, taking in the salty air tinged with a hint of decomposing kelp and the sound of waves crashing onto the beach beyond the rows of cottages and bungalows across from Henry's. He was waiting for her to begin. She liked that. It made him seem calm and unhurried. Something she herself wasn't feeling at that moment.

"My family doesn't know about my plan."

He looked from the view to her but said nothing.

"I imagine you figured that out pretty quickly."

That brought a brief nod. Grace stifled a rise of irritation. As much as she hated being grilled by her father, this patient silence was almost as maddening. "I haven't told them because I didn't see the point, considering it may not happen. The memorial I mean. And yes," she went on, seeing he was about to interject, "I know that I could still erect a plaque at the site even without the lighthouse. But I don't want to do that."

"Why not?"

She gazed across the street and at the bay beyond. "Nothing can bring my cousin back. No memorial plaque and not even the lighthouse restoration can ease the pain and grief my family—especially Brandon's—have suffered." She took a deep breath and turned to face him, hoping she could hold back the tears. "His family will never forget him."

Another breath. "Brandon drowned because he went to the lighthouse and got trapped by the tide. It should be kept as a symbol for him." She slowly enunciated her last words. "I want the town to remember where and how he died." What she didn't add was her own need to see that tangible reminder of Brandon.

"I get that," he eventually said in a low voice, "and perhaps this is a good time to tell you what I recommended in my report. The lighthouse is no longer a viable beacon in the Cove, but it obviously has a place in its history. We're going to definitely decommission it and if it passes a structural test by a qualified engineer, it won't need to be torn down. The Guard could then offer it for sale to the town or to a group in town."

Words and worry tumbled out from her. "That's wonderful, Drew! I'm so happy and Henry and the whole Historical Society will be thrilled. Thank you so much."

"Well…uh…look…it has to pass the test. That's a big 'if.'"

"I'm sure it will. Do we organize that, or what?"

"The Guard will. We have people who inspect the towers and lighthouse stations fairly regularly. Though obviously not this one," he added with a light snort.

"How long will all that take? The inspection and so on, once you've made your official report."

"A few weeks for the first part but as for the start of any restoration—assuming it's okayed—that could take several months. And to reiterate, Grace, I think you should be prepared for the very real possibility that it won't pass."

Her dismay must have been obvious as he quickly added, "As for the time span after a possible approval, the job would be outsourced to private contractors."

"Like my dad's company?"

"Um, I don't know about that. It's not up to me who they hire for the job."

"But they could do it. I mean, they're right here in town. They could even do the inspection. I can talk to my brother and—"

He put his hand on her arm. "Best not to get ahead of yourself, Grace."

She knew he was right. In fact, she was

now cursing her breathless rush of excitement. But it was hard not to show what she was feeling about his decision. "Of course," was what she said, but what she was thinking was a whole other matter.

"Do you want to get settled now and then maybe we could meet up for dinner?" Grace got up.

"Speaking of dinner. Your mother invited me for tomorrow night."

Grace sat back down. She had a feeling what he was about to mention. "Um, yes. That's right."

"Are you planning to tell them about the lighthouse beforehand?"

"I…um… I haven't thought about that. Does it matter?"

"Actually, it does matter. To me. I don't want to be put in the kind of situation I was in earlier today, having to watch everything I say or avoiding any reference that might tie me to the lighthouse."

When she didn't reply, he asked, "Are you worried about their reaction?"

How could he know me so well, after mere days? She nodded.

"It's your call, but what difference would

it make whether you tell them now or in a week or so?"

"It's hard to explain."

"Try."

She wanted to, but there was so much she couldn't—*wouldn't*—tell him. "I'd rather wait until everything's approved. I don't want to upset them unnecessarily."

"Don't you think enough time has passed since your cousin's death? Maybe they'll be pleased about a memorial to him."

"Maybe." She paused. "The other problem is that I don't know how Brandon's own family will react. His sister and mother. As I told you, our side doesn't see much of them."

"Okay, but as I said, I'm not willing to be part of any cover-up. If someone asks me directly about why I'm here, I'll have to be honest. Are you prepared for that?"

The excitement she felt minutes ago fizzled out. She didn't know how she'd field any awkward questions at dinner tomorrow, but now she knew how Drew would handle them. She respected his integrity. Perhaps he was one of those people who viewed circumstances in life as good or bad; right or wrong; black or white. If so then she knew for certain she'd never be able to reveal everything about Brandon's death. It was a story she could barely recount to herself.

Drew was grateful for a chance to be alone. After the uncomfortable conversation with Grace he needed to sift out his impressions from hard facts. They'd come to some kind of agreement, although he was beginning to think understanding Grace Winters was in itself a paradox. She was basically incomprehensible.

But she'd agreed that if any questions about his presence in the Cove or his occupation arose, she would do the explaining. He wasn't happy with that compromise—felt it was totally unnecessary—but he realized it was important to her. He guessed that there was a lot more to the parents' upset than Grace was admitting and wondered when—or *if*—he'd ever know the whole story.

Drew aimed for a lighter note as Grace was getting ready to leave and he asked if they could have dinner later. Her eyes lit up briefly, though she still bore a troubled expression when she said goodbye. He stewed about that frown while he unpacked and familiarized himself with Henry's place. He fed Felix, who'd returned and had accepted his presence as no big deal.

That got Drew thinking about the other places he'd visited and people he'd met during the past four weeks on the road. There had been polite and friendly discussions, even when Drew had to point out management shortcomings. Not a single interview or inspection had been a big deal. So why this drama? he asked himself. What was there about the tower here in Lighthouse Cove that accounted for the tension around it? And it wasn't just between him and Grace. There'd been odd reactions from others—the guy from the Historical Society, for instance. Not to mention the cousin, Suzanna, and even Henry to some degree. There was a mysterious unspoken narrative about the tower. One that he wondered he'd ever get to hear.

By the time he'd showered and changed into casual trousers and shirt, Drew was no closer to answers than before. But he figured Grace was the reason he hadn't simply driven out of the Cove by now. He left a light on for Felix and locked up. Dusk was creeping up on the July Fourth events and Grace had suggested dinner outdoors, at a rib-fest in Town Square.

The day's crowds were thinning as he made his way along the beach road to the board-walk. Except for a few noisy clusters of teen-agers, most of the children and their families had clearly yielded to exhaustion and gone home. Grace was waiting for him outside the bookstore. She, too, had changed, trad-ing her sundress for jeans and a pullover. The evening air would be cool, she'd reminded him, although cool wasn't what he was feel-ing when she waved and walked toward him, her smile erasing all doubt about why he was still in town.

"I got tickets for us," she exclaimed, hold-ing up two strips of paper. "But seating is on a first-come basis so we should get over to the square right away."

"Sounds good," he said. This time he didn't reach for her hand. He'd wait to see how the evening played out.

"Did you get settled in okay at Henry's?" she asked as they headed up the street toward the square.

"I did, thanks. And fed Felix, who didn't seem to question my presence at all."

"He's a very chill cat," she said.

"Aren't they all? Cats, I mean."

"I guess. We never had cats because my brother is allergic to them."

"Dogs?"

"No pets at all. Too much bother, my father always said."

"Too bad. Pets are good for people, especially kids. We always had dogs because my mother wasn't a cat person. Sometimes cats would turn up at the farm, but they were almost always feral and stayed in the barn."

"Do you miss the country? It must be so different from Maine."

"I spent most of my teens fantasizing about leaving so no, I don't really miss it. Though it's always nice to go home for a few days at holidays."

"Sounds like me and the Cove. But as I told you, when I went off to college, I swore I'd never come back."

"And you never did?"

"Well, except for special occasions. And now because of my dad's surgery."

"But you've made a commitment to stay, I presume, since you're now manager of a bookstore here."

"Manager is the key word, as opposed to owner. My commitment is temporary."

"Do your parents know that?"

"Honestly, I don't know. I think they might be guessing but don't want to admit it."

Something else she hasn't discussed with her family, he thought. Communication didn't seem to be her forte. While he was glad she wasn't the type to prattle, a bit more openness about herself would help him understand her more.

They heard the music and smelled the smoky aroma of barbecue before they reached the square. Lights were strung along the outer edge of the pavilion and a large space had been cordoned off where Drew could see picnic tables with checked tablecloths. Most of them were already full of people eating. There was a line of ticket holders in front of the entrance to the area.

"A good thing you got tickets," he said as they got in line.

"My friend Julie advised me to." Her first reference to a friend, he noted, other than the chef at The Daily Catch.

"How was it coming back home and reconnecting with former schoolmates?"

"Well…um… Julie's the only one I kept in contact with. She moved here when we were both in senior year and she went to college in Augusta, too."

"And yet you both ended up back here."

"Julie came back to take care of her mother. And yes, another comparison between us. Though in my case it was helping my mom look after my father."

"Is she the friend you were with the other day? In Mabel's?"

"Uh, yes," she mumbled, and she turned away as the line moved forward.

Minutes later they were seated at a long communal table, enjoying the rib-fest dinner, shoulder to shoulder with strangers. Any conversation more serious than small talk couldn't have happened even if Drew wanted it to. Frankly, he thought, it's just as well. He was reluctant to have such a beautiful evening turn serious.

It was cooler once the sun had set, and the light ocean breeze carried a tang of salt and seaweed, blending with the roasting meats on the industrial-sized portable barbecues. Drew studied Grace across the table, the way she delicately licked her fingertips before dabbing them with her napkin or dipped each French fry into the daub of ketchup on her paper plate. Her small hands worked steadily at the food and he smiled at the enjoyment in her face.

It was a rare moment of uninhibited pleasure and he knew he wanted to see more of
these snapshots of Grace Winters. *Gracie*, he
amended, for right then she seemed more like
that young version of herself. As he set the
last rib down onto the small pile of bones on
the spare plate between them, Drew caught
Grace's eye and smiled.

"That was really amazing. I didn't think I'd
be able to finish it all, but as you can see..."
He pointed to his empty plate.

"I'm done, too," she announced, crumpling
up her napkin. "But I still have one small rib
left."

He shook his head. "No way. I can't."

"Come on! You can do it."

He held up his hands. "Okay, okay. If you
insist."

Her laugh caught the attention of some of
their table partners who smiled. "That was a
fast capitulation," she said.

He nibbled at the rib, aware of her gaze
fixed on his every bite until he tossed it onto
the pile of bones and she clapped her hands.
"Told you!"

Her dark eyes never left his while he cleaned
his hands, finished off the rest of his beer and
plunked the empty glass onto the table with a

satisfied sigh. He was about to reach across the table to clasp one of her hands when a woman came up behind Grace, tapping her on the shoulder.

"Bet you're glad you took my advice."

Grace craned round and smiled. "Hey! Have you eaten already?"

"Of course. I came when it first opened."

"Um, this is my friend Julie. And Julie, this is Drew Spencer."

"Aha, the lighthouse guy." She gave Drew an appreciative once-over. "I'm meeting someone for a drink," she said, turning back to Grace. "Would you two care to join us?"

Someone else besides Henry knows about Grace's project was Drew's first thought and his second was that from Grace's sheepish face, she'd made the same connection. *So why the big fuss about telling her parents?*

"Uh…"

"I think I've had my share of drink tonight," Drew swiftly put in. He didn't know what Grace was about to say, but he did know he wanted to spend the rest of this special night alone with her. Not in some bar.

From the smile Grace directed at him, he'd made the right decision.

Julie shrugged. "Okay, well, if you change

your mind, come to The Lobster Claw. Oh, and don't forget the fireworks down at the harbor, just after nine." She gave a quick wave and disappeared into the groups of people milling around the tables.

"The Lobster Claw?" Drew smirked.

"It's a pub. I told you this town could almost qualify as a theme park. But thanks for the rescue. I think the fireworks will be a lot more enjoyable than a noisy pub on July Fourth."

"I'm with you. Shall we?" He gathered up the empty plates onto a tray and stood. By the time he deposited it on a nearby holding station, Grace was waiting at the entrance. The light bouncing off her eyes from the Christmas decorations was no match for her smile.

"Shall we stake out a spot for the fireworks?" he asked as he draped an arm across her shoulders and led her away from the bustle of the square into the dark streets beyond. When they reached the harbor, Grace tucked herself into his side as people also walking to where the fireworks would be viewed pressed against them. Drew's arm tightened around her and he was beginning to think the pub might have been less crowded.

"I know where we can watch them without anyone around," Grace shouted over the clamor of voices around them. "Keep walking till we get to the beach road and I'll tell you where to go from there."

Most of the crowd lingered around the harbor area while some continued on to the beach. Despite a bit of jostling, Drew managed to keep Grace under his arm all the way to where the boardwalk and paved road merged into the sandy beach road.

She stopped suddenly, pointing to her left. "See that clump of trees? There's a set of stairs in the middle of it."

He looked beyond the cottages and houses leading upward from the road until he spotted a light way above, shining like a tower's beacon. "Your parents' house?"

"You've seen it before?"

"Henry pointed it out to me when we went to the lighthouse."

A sudden explosion caused them to swing around. Tentacles of red, white and blue streaked down from the dark night sky.

"They've started! Come on." Grace pulled Drew by the hand and they ran to the bottom of the staircase.

The fireworks were in full force by the time they'd climbed midway up the stairs to a landing with a long wooden bench. "My dad built this when we were young, so we could have a resting place on our way up from the beach," Grace said as they sat on the bench overlooking the beach and beyond it, the bay.

Drew pulled her against him as the sky filled with color. When she glanced up at him, her eyes sparkling in the afterglow of fireworks, he felt a burst of emotion that he couldn't quite identify. Something more than pleasure or satisfaction. Was it as big as joy? Or did it even matter whether he could name it or not? He only knew that he wanted to kiss this woman leaning into him.

He ran his finger along the curve of her cheek down to her mouth, along her lips that were already parted and lowered his mouth to hers. What began as a friendly kiss became something more as he pulled her close enough to feel her trembling against him. Her arms reached up around his back and Drew had a fleeting sense of the fireworks exploding above and Grace's lips on his until he lost himself in a long, breathless moment.

CHAPTER TEN

"NO NO NO! This is not a good idea, Gracie. Think about it."

Grace watched Ben pacing back and forth in her living room. "I have, Ben. All night long. That's why I asked you to come over this morning so I could explain everything before dinner tonight. In case...well, in case the subject comes up."

He stopped to stare at her. "Why would it come up unless you raised it yourself?"

"I just want your support."

"I don't get why you want to do this after all these years."

"Please, sit down so we can talk." Grace could see he was still processing what she'd told him. She hadn't seen him this upset since that night seventeen years ago when the police came to their door to say that Brandon was missing. The details of that night were etched in her memory. One in particular that had always puzzled her had been the moment

Ben had handed over to the police the note she and Cassie had sent to Brandon. She'd been stunned, wondering how he'd gotten hold of it until he'd said he'd met Brandon near the lighthouse after deciding to go to the bonfire after all. That had shaken Grace. What if he'd turned up just as Ella was meeting Brandon? Yet if he had, the whole tragedy might never have happened. Grace sighed. It was too late now for thoughts like these.

He was still shaking his head in disbelief when he sat down on her sofa.

"When I came back home five months ago, I realized that as much as I'd tried over the years to deal with what happened that summer—to make it all simply a bad thing that happened in our family—I couldn't. Every time I go to the beach or walk along the harbor or go anywhere down near the water, I see that lighthouse. It's a constant reminder."

"Then why not go along with the proposal this Drew guy gave about tearing it down? Get the blasted thing out of all our lives."

"Cut it out, Ben. He's not 'this Drew guy'! You met him. You had lunch with him. Don't do that." She saw a flicker of surprise in his face. Her big brother wasn't used to heated words from her. "Brandon shouldn't be forgotten. He was fourteen years old. He deserves to be remembered."

"He hasn't been forgotten, Gracie, and he never will be, certainly not by his mother and sister. Do they know anything about this scheme of yours?"

"No, but—"

"The least you can do is pass it by them first. See if they're willing to support it. If not, then you should scrap the whole idea."

"I need to know if you're on my side." She watched him lower his forehead onto his palms, his fingers rubbing the top of his head. He always did that as a kid. Taking a break from an argument—usually one with their father—to think and compose himself.

Grace had to smile. He was a whole lot more like Charles than he'd ever want to admit. Each of them had their mother's naturally curly black hair but while Grace also inherited Evelyn's sculpted nose and cheeks, Ben had received their father's stern brow and his need to run the show.

"I'm always on your side. You should know that by now."

She saw the slightly injured look in his eyes. He'd always been on her side in the past, but he might not be again—if he knew everything about that night.

"And what's going on with you and Drew?"

He'd changed tactics—another typical Ben move. "I don't have a clue what you mean."

"Don't be so obtuse, Grace. First Mom and Dad and I encounter you two on the waterfront yesterday and—"

"We met to discuss his recommendation."

He waved a dismissive hand. "Then I hear you had dinner with him at the rib-fest—"

"What! How—"

"I bumped into Julie Parker at The Lobster Claw."

This was precisely why she'd avoided the Cove all these years. "First of all, where I go and what I do is none of your business. And second, you yourself told me coming back here would be a lot nicer if I reconnected with friends and assimilated into the community. Right?"

"Grace."

She knew that tone. Another gene from their father.

"Don't digress," he said quietly. "Julie knows, too, doesn't she? Because she realized I didn't know what she was talking about when she mentioned 'the guy here about the lighthouse' and she clammed right up. Why is our family the last to know your plans?"

Her teenage self might have started crying at this point, but that girl was long gone. "Drew has become a friend. I like him and I hope I continue to see him when all this business is wrapped up. As to our family? We're not very good communicators. You know that. No one talks about Brandon, no one conjures up any old stories about him. No one tries to keep him in alive in our minds. It's time we gave him that respect."

"And Aunt Jane? Suzanna? What about their feelings?"

"You're right. The people closest to Brandon should be consulted and they will be when I know it's definitely going to happen."

"So that brings us back to my original question. What if they don't want it?"

"I don't know, Ben. I really don't. But I need to try to make this happen."

He got up. "Look, I have to go. I'll be at dinner tonight but all I can promise is that I won't say anything against the idea." On his way to the door, he turned to add, "I'm sure Dad will have enough to say about it anyway."

"We were all affected by what happened

to Brandon, including you, Ben. Think how different our lives might have been if that night hadn't happened. You left and never came back until Dad's surgery. You married Jen when you might have—"

"No, Grace, don't go there."

She saw the hurt in his pale face. "I'll see you tonight," he muttered as he closed the door behind him.

She plopped onto the sofa, exhausted by their talk. Ben had changed so much from the teasing, often indulgent, older brother she'd adored. Now he always seemed so constrained. She knew in her heart that he'd be a completely different person if the dreams and hopes of that summer had come true. He'd never spoken Ella Jacobs's name aloud since she and her family left the Cove at the end of the Labor Day weekend. *And it was all Grace's fault.*

Grace might have sat there the rest of the morning, ruminating over the past but the chime from her cell phone got her off the sofa. It was a text from Drew. Felix has escaped again. I'll text when I've found him so maybe meet at the marina a bit later?

Just as well, Grace thought, as she quickly replied ok. She'd have time to pick up snacks for their boat cruise and get in line for tickets. When Drew had walked her to her door last night, there'd been one of those awkward moments. His kiss had taken her by surprise but at the same time, it hadn't been completely unexpected. She couldn't pinpoint when the shift from business to friendliness had occurred but suspected their light banter over dessert at The Daily Catch had been the beginning. Last night he'd placed his hand on her back to guide her through the crowd and casually draped his arm across her shoulders as if it belonged there. The sensations running through her then had little to do with friendliness.

She hadn't been truthful when she'd told Ben she and Drew were just friends. The kiss hadn't been a kiss between friends. That realization struck home sometime in the middle of the night. She was broaching the danger zone—that transition from friendship to relationship—and knew it was time to step back. As much as she'd enjoyed his kiss and snuggling in his arms, there was no possible future for them. Drew deserved someone untainted by the past. And she needed to focus on her goal—buying the lighthouse and establishing Brandon's memorial. If losing a chance with Drew Spencer was the price she had to pay, so be it.

Getting the family on board without admitting her part in that awful night would require a balancing act. In spite of Ben's doubts, Grace believed she could do it.

DREW SWORE. He'd stepped outside to snap a photo because the early morning light over the water was breathtaking. The fire-red of daybreak had morphed into rose-colored streaks against a cobalt sky and there, at the end of its rocky promontory, was the lighthouse, spotlighted by the rising sun. If he hadn't been gawking at the spectacle, Drew might have noticed Felix casually stroll between his legs onto the porch. Before he could shout more than a "hey," the cat was gone.

But he didn't run after it because he'd already figured out that Felix was a cat who knew what was best for him. He'd accepted Drew's presence unequivocally, wrapping around his calves just long enough for Drew to get the message and refill the stainless-steel dish on the floor next to the fridge.

He shot a few more photos and was about to set his camera down when the sudden appearance of a distant figure near the lighthouse prompted him to zoom in. He couldn't be certain, even with the telephoto, who the person was but the skirt flaring up in the off-shore breeze suggested a female. Drew rotated the lens, trying to get a clearer image. There was no one else around and the lighthouse wasn't exactly on the tourist trail. He snapped off pictures until the woman disappeared behind the dunes. Perhaps Grace would recognize her. *Unless it was Grace?*

No, Drew thought, but decided to text her about Felix right then and suggest meeting a bit later. Last night Grace had suggested a boat cruise around the outer bay for today and either pack a lunch or eat out afterward. He'd have agreed to anything that involved spending more time with her, even though his stomach lurched at the idea of the cruise. He hadn't been on a boat of any type since that day a year ago and he had no idea how he'd handle himself. Yet for some reason he didn't feel ready to talk about it with Grace. He hoped he would be able to someday, but for now, he didn't want anything to tarnish the image of the confident Coast Guard officer he'd worked so hard at presenting.

He took his camera inside and set out on foot to look for Felix. Although the cat would eventually come back, Drew was reluctant to go on the cruise without at least trying to find him. If he couldn't, he'd leave water outside and there was shade from the porch overhang. He headed down the street toward the beach road and the dunes, thinking if he didn't see Felix on the way, he might encounter the mystery woman from the lighthouse. The air was cooler when he reached the beach and as he walked, Drew glanced left and right for the cat. When his phone chimed, he saw Grace's reply—ok. So likely not Grace, he thought. *But then who?*

By the time he reached the deserted cottage where he'd climbed with Henry a few days ago, Drew decided to continue on to the lighthouse. There was no sign of the woman—or the cat—on the way. She must have taken the route on the other side of the dunes. Drew stood for a few minutes, his back to the sun, scanning the expanse leading away from the lighthouse path. The dunes ended at a handful of cottages on the outer edge of the residential area where Henry lived. From there, the town connected to a paved road leading up to the highway and the new housing development. Whoever the woman was, she'd vanished.

Drew decided to go on to the lighthouse before returning to Henry's. It wasn't long before he guessed why the woman had been there. A fresh bouquet of flowers rested atop the rotting pile he'd noticed days ago. He drew closer and spotted something new. A small flag, the kind children wave at parades, lay beside the flowers and next to it, a package of mini firecrackers. *Someone had already established a memorial for Brandon Winters.*

He wondered if Grace knew about this makeshift remembrance. *Grace.* He dug out his phone and texted her that he was on his way. If Felix had returned, all the better. As he turned onto Henry's street, he spotted the cat waiting patiently at the front door and breathed a sigh of relief. The cruise was going to be stressful enough without worrying about Felix. When Grace had suggested it, his immediate impulse was to flatly say no way. Then she'd told him some story about always wanting to do it when she was a kid but the opportunity never arose. He hadn't paid too much attention because his mind was far away, out on a stormy sea, and the first queasy rumbles had begun in his stomach.

By the time Drew was waving to Grace,

standing in line at the marina, all thoughts of the lighthouse, the mystery woman and his stomach had gone. He felt like a schoolboy with his first crush—breathless and giddy at the same time—unsure for a second where to place his hands in greeting when he came up beside her. Shoulders, for a quick hug? Waist, for a more intimate one? She solved the problem by placing a hand on his forearm and beaming up at him.

"I was getting worried. Trust you found Felix?"

He took her hand, intertwining their fingers. "Safe indoors, with plenty of food and water."

The line moved forward as a crew member checked tickets. Drew looked anxiously at the boat as they walked up a metal gangway. It appeared sound enough but still his heart rate picked up. The boat was a typical tourist version of a fishing trawler: open-sided with a canvas canopy and two sections of benches for passengers with life jackets stowed beneath. The boat's pilot stood at the wheel inside a small cabin, watching his passengers take their seats. He was well past middle age and Drew wondered if he was a local man, familiar with the waters of Casco Bay. He had no choice but to rely on faith and that thought took him to the men in the sinking boat off Bar Harbor. Nausea roiled in his gut and a cold sweat broke out all over.

Grace rushed ahead to get an outside place on a bench midway down the length of the boat and when Drew finally joined her, she placed a hand on his arm. "Is everything okay?"

The boat's engine revved and Drew's attention shifted to the crew untying the lines and pulling up the gangway. He craned round as the boat reversed, moving away from the dock. As it chugged out of the harbor, he was relieved to see the waters of the open bay were relatively calm with no visible whitecaps. He realized Grace was looking at him, waiting for an answer.

"Sure. Why?" He ran his finger along the inside of his shirt collar.

"You seem a bit tense."

"Nope. But…uh…isn't the captain going to have us put on our life jackets?"

"I don't know." She peered around at the other passengers, pointing at things on shore or snapping photos with their cell phones. "I suppose safety is a big issue for someone in the Coast Guard though. Do you think we should put ours on?"

"No one else is. I guess it's okay." He swallowed hard.

The boat was motoring toward the rocky spit at the end of the cove and beyond, open water. Drew tried to get his mind off the sea ahead. "I was taking some pictures earlier this morning when I saw a woman up there," he said, gesturing to the lighthouse as they cruised past it.

Grace turned sharply. "A woman?"

"Looked like a woman. For a minute I thought it was you."

"It wasn't me."

"You sound as if that would be an impossibility." He managed a smile, in spite of his queasiness.

"Well...uh... I was busy all morning."

"I walked out to the tower when I was looking for Felix, but there was no sign of her by the time I got there."

"Hmm," she murmured, gazing indifferently out to the bay.

"But I did see something interesting."

She turned back to him again. "What?"

"I guess you've noticed that someone has been placing flowers on the path."

She nodded.

"This morning someone—it must have been that woman—put a small flag and a packet of firecrackers by the flowers."

Her eyes grew big in her small face. She swiveled round to stare at the lighthouse until the boat made a slow, wide turn toward the outer bay and left it behind.

Drew was interested in her reaction. She'd known about the flowers but hadn't seemed very curious about them. As if she already knew who was bringing them? He was about to ask her when the sea breeze picked up and the boat rolled gently into oncoming swells. Drew gripped the edge of the bench.

"You're not seasick, are you?" She was peering down at his hands.

He might have laughed at the incredulity in her voice if he wasn't feeling so nauseous. "Not exactly," he mumbled.

"You don't look as if you're enjoying this." She touched the side of his face. "Do you want some water?"

He cleared his throat. "Um…sure… thanks."

She opened a plastic bottle and handed it to him, watching him take a couple of long swigs.

"Thanks. That's better." Except it really wasn't and Drew prayed the cruise boat didn't go out of the bay. He felt her staring at him. "What?" he asked, trying for a casual tone.

"I'm thinking it's a bit funny that a Coast Guard officer might be seasick."

Drew took a deep breath. "I haven't been in a boat for quite a while. I'm more of a land Coast Guard officer."

"I didn't know there was such a creature."

"We're a rare breed." He aimed for a smile but failed.

She lifted one of his hands off the bench and held it in her lap. Drew's eyes met hers and this time he could smile. As his breathing slowed, he eased his hand out of hers to stretch his arm across her shoulders and draw her close. He looked across the wide bay and relaxed against the back of the bench.

I can do this, as long as she stays right here, close by me.

CHAPTER ELEVEN

"CAN YOU OPEN THIS, dear?"

Evelyn handed Grace a jar of pickles. Her mother never complained about her rheumatoid arthritis, but there were signs when she was experiencing a flare-up: slow, deliberate movements, fatigue or a lack of strength in her joints.

"Sure, Mom." Grace unscrewed the lid and handed the jar back. "Aches and pains?"

Her mother grimaced at the euphemism she'd established with her children years ago when they were little and she sometimes couldn't lift or carry them. She'd developed rheumatoid arthritis after Grace's birth. Fortunately, modern medicine had made a huge difference in the autoimmune disease, but there were times when the symptoms recurred.

"What time did you ask Drew to come?"

"You said six, right?"

"Yes, but I thought you were *both* coming then."

"I thought I'd come early, to help." Which was true, more or less. She'd tossed and turned all night, replaying the day with Drew and his parting words after kissing her goodnight. "Think about telling your parents, Grace. Soon."

He was right. They needed to know but now that she was here alone with her mother her courage was fading. Charles was resting upstairs and Ben had gone into the company office. She wanted to get it over with so that they'd have time to process the news well before Drew arrived. But she was running out of time, she realized, looking at the microwave clock.

"I'll set the table for you," she said, getting up from the kitchen island's bar stool.

"It's already done."

Grace shook her head. Her mother's organizational skills had definitely not been passed down to her. "Have you left anything for me to do?"

Evelyn thought for a minute. "Check the table for me to make sure everything's on it that should be."

Grace headed through the open kitchen,

which had been modernized three years ago, and down the hall toward the dining room. Except for electrical and plumbing upgrades, along with necessary redecorating through the years, the Winters family home had changed very little from Grace's grandfather's time. With five bedrooms, three bathrooms, a formal dining room and two parlors that had been combined into one airy living room overlooking the bay, the house had always been far too big for their small family.

Once when she was little, her grandfather Desmond had rummaged through his rolltop desk and pulled out a large piece of yellowed paper marked with faint pencil lines. "Your great-granddaddy Hiram drew the plans for this house and started its construction," he'd explained. "And I followed his design as best as I could when I finished it." Grace figured old Hiram had anticipated more descendants than he'd gotten.

Now when she watched her mother and father shuffling around, avoiding the narrow stairs leading to the turret bedrooms that she and Ben had once occupied—though Ben was back in his again—and basically living in only a few of the rooms, Grace realized that her parents might have to consider downsizing. As she entered the formal dining room with its gleaming oak wainscoting and massive bay window, she felt a pang at the thought that one day this beautiful home might no longer be in the family. Of course, it would be an inheritance, but realistically neither she nor her brother considered their move back to Lighthouse Cove permanent.

Grace knew that Ben's taking over the family business had been a challenge, mainly because their father couldn't let go. Charles refused to officially retire, in spite of his doctor's—and his wife's—advice, and Ben struggled with having to double-check every action or decision. Grace had no idea what her brother's plans would be after his divorce was finalized because his desire for privacy was almost an obsession. But she suspected that unless he was given full autonomy of the family business, he might not stay beyond the year he'd promised.

As for Grace, her refusal to consider the return home as anything more than temporary was what got her up in the morning. That and the bookstore. Drew's remark at dinner on Thursday night about reconnecting with school friends had been a sobering reminder that, except for Cassie and her summer friend,

Ella, Grace had been pretty much a loner in high school. Especially after that summer when everyone was speculating and whispering about what had happened on Labor Day weekend.

She strolled around the table, set the way her mother liked it. Not too fussy but fancy, with the Winterses' collection of china, crystal and silver. Then she paused to recount. There were six places rather than five.

"Mom?" She headed back to the kitchen, where her mother was tossing a salad.

"Yes, dear?"

"Is someone else coming besides Drew? There are six settings."

Evelyn placed the salad tongs on the island counter. "Suzanna is coming."

"Seriously?"

"Your father and I feel this rift between our families has gone on far too long."

"But why now?"

"His heart condition has resulted in some self-reflection, I think. We thought this would be a good opportunity for the family."

"Isn't her husband coming?"

"Apparently he had other plans." Evelyn pulled a face. "I think there might be some trouble with their marriage."

"How do you know all this?"

"Suzanna and I have been in touch these past few months. She reached out to me when your father had his surgery. We've chatted a few times on the phone, about how her mother is doing in Bangor, the hotel and so on. Once when we were speaking, she implied her husband might be having an affair."

Grace was speechless, trying to process this information and realizing how out of touch she'd been with her extended family.

"You know the family story, I'm sure," Evelyn was saying but the only narrative in Grace's mind at that moment was her plan to tell her parents the real reason behind Drew's arrival in the Cove. "Your father and his brother fell out not long after your grandfather died. Fred always thought it was unfair that Charles got the business. He felt he was stuck with the hotel that never brought in nearly as much money as the construction company. And to be fair, he had a point. Then after Brandon died..." Evelyn shrugged.

Everyone knew how that story ended, Grace was thinking. And maybe now was a good time. "Speaking of Brandon," she began. Her mother's puzzled face caused Grace to falter briefly but she thought of her promise to Drew and plunged in. "I'm… I'm sorry, Mom, but I misled you and Dad the other day when Drew and I bumped into you at the harbor."

Evelyn frowned but waited for her to continue. It was a trait in her mother she'd always appreciated, especially as a teen. The ability to listen, without interrupting.

Knowing her mother hated the bar stools, Grace gestured to the round bistro table near the glass sliding doors leading out to the deck. "Why don't we sit over there?"

When they were seated, she took a deep breath before starting. "I didn't meet Drew through Henry as I implied, but we met because of a plan that Henry and I concocted."

Evelyn leaned forward, placing her forearms on the table and fixing her eyes on Grace.

"Drew's work for the Coast Guard has to do with lighthouse maintenance. He's been traveling up and down the coast the last few weeks inspecting lighthouses, but he came here because of a request Henry and I sent to the Coast Guard offices in Portland. We… uh…we asked for funds to restore the lighthouse. We want to restore it as a memorial to Brandon. With a plaque."

Now her mother's eyes widened and sensing she was finally about to speak, Grace rushed on, "Drew came to discuss our request and to check out the lighthouse. Or tower, as he calls it, because there's only the tower and no other building attached to it. Then it would be called a light station."

Evelyn held up a hand.

"Okay, I know I'm digressing."

"Why now, Gracie, after all this time?"

Grace sighed. "That's what Ben said."

"Ben knows?"

"I just told him this morning. Since I've come home, everything that happened that summer has come back. I see the lighthouse almost every day and…and it makes me feel sad. I thought that maybe if it could be a positive reminder of Brandon for all of us that we might feel better. That it would be a kind of—"

"Don't say that word," her mother warned.

"What word?"

"Closure. I dislike that word. There's no such thing as closure. There's only acceptance."

"I think looking at a memorial every day would give us a warmer feeling than just seeing the lighthouse as a place of death. And yes, it would also be a kind of acceptance for us."

"Who are you referring to, Gracie, when you say 'us'?"

"Well, all of us. The family."

"What about Brandon's immediate family? His mother and sister?"

Grace felt as if she were in a time loop, the same questions arising over and over but with different people posing them. *Perhaps there's a reason for that*, she thought. *I've been conveniently overlooking the most important part of the whole equation. Aunt Jane and Suzanna.*

"I intend to ask them how they feel about the idea, Mom, but the problem is that it might not happen at all. Drew says the lighthouse will be decommissioned and after that, it could be sold or torn down. But it can't be sold unless it passes a structural inspection, to see if it's stable and can even be repaired. So…" She stopped, noticing her mother's head shaking.

"Grace, please don't tell me you hope to purchase the lighthouse."

"Well, not me personally. But we would fundraise for it. Get the whole town on board."

Evelyn ran her fingers back and forth across her forehead. Thinking what to say and how to say it, Grace thought. Her mother was far more circumspect than she had ever been.

"When were you planning on discussing this with Suzanna? Or Jane?"

"I wanted to tell you and Dad today, before Drew came."

"Does he know all about this…this family situation of ours?"

"A bit. He suggested I confer with everyone as soon as possible."

"I'm pleased to know he's sensible as well as nice." Evelyn smiled. She thought some more before adding, "You can't ambush Suzanna with this tonight over dinner. It's not fair. She needs time—and privacy—to consider the whole idea and what it would mean to her and her mother."

"I'm afraid the matter might come up."

"You'll simply have to make sure it doesn't, Gracie. Do your best. Without any more misleading statements."

Grace smiled. Her mother had always been low-key, even in her scolding. "What about Dad?"

"Let me deal with your father." Evelyn

stood and glanced at the time. "Would you set the wineglasses out on the dining room sideboard, please? Our guests will be here soon." She opened a cabinet door and began to take out serving dishes. Their talk was over.

Grace went to the dining room china cabinet for the wineglasses. Some of her nervousness about the dinner had disappeared, but she knew this was only her first step back into the past. The next one—if she ever had the courage to take it—would be much more painful.

DREW KNEW SOMETHING was up when Grace met him at the front door of her parents' house and said in a low voice, "I told my mother and she's going to speak to my father but just to warn you, my cousin Suzanna is coming, too." She tucked her arm into his, leading him inside.

Drew could only nod, overwhelmed by the greeting. He wondered if there was always this much drama with Grace and could someone like him, who preferred an even keel in life, grow to tolerate it? But looking down at the mix of worry and pleasure—at seeing him, he hoped—in her lovely face, Drew knew right then he wanted the opportunity to do just that. To discover *all* the sides of Grace Winters.

"And Mom thought it isn't fair to drop the news on Suzanna like this, so I've decided to contact her tomorrow and tell her."

"You don't have to explain your actions to me, Grace. I realize what I said last night sounded a bit too much like advice and I'm sorry for that. You don't need to listen to advice from me, much less take it. I'm not the person to give advice to anyone, believe me."

"Maybe I told you all about the family situation and my dilemma because I *wanted* some advice. Besides, I trust you." She smiled, her dark eyes shining. "Come, Mom says to give you a quick tour of the house while she puts the finishing touches on her dessert."

I trust you. No one had said those words to him in a long time and they were nice to hear. He hoped he could live up to them.

Grace led him into the entry hall with its chandelier and staircase that wound up to the second floor. He stopped to look up at the landing where the stairs branched off on either side. "Do those sets of stairs go to the turrets?"

"Yes. There's a bedroom in each one. Dad says they were for servants in my great-grandfather's time. When my father was growing up, he and his brother had them for bedrooms and so did my brother and I. Ben's back up there again, for now."

"His return to town isn't permanent?"

"I doubt it. He promised he'd help out for a year but he's in the middle of a divorce, so who knows?" She shrugged. "I'll show you the rest of the ground floor, but Suzanna will be here soon, and we'll be having drinks in the living room."

The old house was beautiful. As they walked through room after room, Drew gaped at original wood paneling and light fixtures, stained and beveled glass panes above door lintels; a study/library with floor-to-ceiling bookcases; another room that Grace explained had been a bedroom before its transformation into a den with comfy leather furniture and a wall-mounted TV; a small solarium and finally, a powder room.

When he'd driven through the wrought-iron gates at the front of the house, Drew had surmised that the rear of the house overlooking the town would have expansive windows and he was right. The large living room that they now entered had breathtaking views of the harbor and Casco Bay beyond.

"My parents had this room redone twenty years ago. When I was little, this space consisted of two small, gloomy parlors. My father's company did the reno," she said with a sweeping gesture of her arm toward the floor-to-ceiling windows along the length of the room.

A long white multi-sectional sofa sprinkled with colorful cushions was positioned midway down the room, facing the windows. A marble-topped coffee table stood in front of the sofa and a wing chair at each of its ends. At one end of the room there was a fireplace—either gas or electric was Drew's guess—and around it two more wing chairs and a love seat. The end of the room where Drew and Grace were standing held a reading nook with built-in shelves. Two armchairs flanked another marble-topped side table in a corner.

Drew moved closer to examine a collection of porcelain, glass and metal items on two of the shelves.

"Treasures, past and present," Grace said. "When we were little, Mom kindly let us add our own finds there, but I see they've disappeared." She laughed.

"Only put away for safekeeping, dear," put

in her mother, standing in the doorway behind them.

Drew turned around. "Mrs. Winters, you have a lovely home."

She smiled. "I'm happy you like it. So many young people these days prefer new, glitzy surroundings."

"I hope you're not referring to me," said Ben as he came up beside her.

Drew liked Evelyn's laugh—a light tinkle that reminded him a bit of his mother's. And Grace's.

"I've given up on you, Ben," she replied, "and am crossing my fingers for Grace. Your father and I consider this a heritage home, with all that the word *heritage* implies."

Drew figured from their grins this might be a family joke. His own family heritage—the Iowa farmhouse—had been implicitly handed to his brother when Drew left for college. Everyone knew his own future lay miles away, near an ocean.

Voices and a door closing down the hall got their attention. "That will be Suzanna. Charles must have noticed her arrival on his way downstairs," said Evelyn. "Ben, please get the sherry and port from the kitchen and the plate of appetizers. Grace, would you and

Drew bring some glasses from the dining room cabinet? I'm going to greet Suzanna."

When both she and Ben left, Drew glanced at Grace. *"Sherry?"*

She grinned. "Welcome to the Winters family dinner traditions."

A warm glow rolled through him. "I like traditions," he murmured, bending his head to kiss her.

CHAPTER TWELVE

DREW'S REASSURING KISS minutes ago failed to prevent Grace's stomach from clenching when Suzanna came into the living room.

Her cousin hadn't been in the Winters family home in years, but she strolled into the room as if her absence from family events had been mere weeks rather than more than a decade. When Uncle Fred died, Aunt Jane and Suzanna had come from Bangor to stay with them. Grace had come home from college for the funeral and it had been a challenging few days, fraught with reminders of her unintentional role in their family's grief.

Suzanna took after her mother's side of the family. Tall and slender with chestnut-colored hair that she'd worn shoulder length her whole life, she had an aloofness about her that used to intimidate the younger Grace. She once told Ben that Zanna—the family nickname for her—thought she was better than her cousins, but he'd replied she was just myopic and refused to wear glasses. Grace had been twelve at the time and had no idea what myopic meant. She did know Zanna rarely wore her glasses, especially not at school.

"Hello, Grace," she said and when Drew stood up from setting the tray of sherry glasses on the coffee table, added, "Well, hello again!"

"Have you two met?" asked Evelyn, following Suzanna into the room.

Grace was about to reply when Suzanna did. "Mr. Spencer was a guest in my hotel."

"He was?" This came from Grace's father, who was sitting in one of the chairs at the end of the sofa. "I thought he was staying with Henry Jenkins?"

"Not *with* Henry, Dad. He's been cat-sitting while Henry's in Portland," Ben corrected as he returned from the kitchen carrying two bottles by their necks in one hand and a plate of bacon-wrapped water chestnuts—Evelyn's standard appetizer—in the other.

I could be in one of those bad comedies, or a farce, thought Grace as she took in Drew's bewildered face as all eyes were on him. Okay, he's not bewildered so much as amused.

"Ms. Winters," Drew finally had a chance to say.

"Please, it's Suzanna. Since we're meeting again at a family dinner."

There was a momentary lull broken finally by Ben, who was pouring sherry and port in the glasses on the coffee table. "All right, folks, come get a glass and one of these delicious—what do you call them?—bacon thingies."

"Canapés, Ben!" Evelyn giggled, casting her son an adoring glance.

Grace caught Drew's eye and he grinned, as if he knew exactly what she was thinking. Ben had always been the one to receive approval from her parents, especially her mother, whereas with Grace perplexed shoulder-shrugging had often been the norm.

They gathered around the coffee table, sipping and munching while taking in the view. The sunset was behind them but streaks of pink and yellow shot across the sky and over the bay. Grace noticed Suzanna gravitate to Drew's side to speak to him and she watched Drew, hoping he'd signal to be rescued if her cousin asked why he was in the Cove. He'd warned her he wouldn't lie if someone asked and Grace knew it was up to her to make sure that didn't happen.

Using the excuse of passing around the canapés, she reached them just as Suzanna remarked, "I hope your move from the hotel wasn't due to some lack of service on our part." She cocked her head slightly, giving Drew a teasing smile.

"Not at all," Drew said. "It's a great hotel, but Henry Jenkins needed someone to care for his cat while he was out of town and his place was more convenient."

"I've been showing Drew around," Grace put in. "Yesterday we took that harbor and bay cruise."

"Oh, how was that?"

"Terrific!" Drew exclaimed.

Grace looked sharply at him. She bet the terrific part applied to the end of the trip, when they disembarked. His pale face and jittery hands and legs during the two-hour cruise wouldn't have made a good advertisement for it at all.

Then he added, "We got a wonderful view of the lighthouse."

"I'm sure," was all Suzanna said as she turned to Grace, still holding the plate of canapés. "Oh, I haven't had one of Aunt Ev's

bacon thingies, as Ben calls them." She delicately picked up one, removed the toothpick
holding the bacon strip and water chestnut
together and popped it into her mouth.

That ends the talk for now, Grace thought,
as Suzanna moved over to Ben and Charles,
sitting nearby. When Evelyn announced that
they should find a seat at the dining room
table Grace sighed with relief. All she had
to do was find a way to separate her cousin
from Drew. On her way into the dining room
her mother placed a hand on Grace's arm and
said in a low voice, "Be friendly with Zanna,
dear. Talk to her."

"Of course."

Her mother's eyes flashed a warning at the
indignation in Grace's tone. "I know you and
Zanna have never been close, even when her
family was still living here. But she's been
through a lot in the last two years, taking on
the hotel and getting used to being back in
town." She paused a second, adding, "I've
spoken to your father and he'd like to discuss
that matter with you. But tomorrow, not tonight." She patted Grace's arm and motioned
to Ben to accompany her into the kitchen.

Grace knew her father would want all the
details of her plan but thought the word *dis-*

cuss was a bad sign. There was no possibility of discussion as far as she was concerned. She glanced across the room at Drew, taking a seat at the table and gesturing to the empty chair beside his. She headed for it but was suddenly preempted by her cousin. Grace reluctantly sat across from Drew, though she was slightly cheered by his wink.

The meal was delicious, and Grace realized her mother had made an extra effort with it—poaching a whole salmon with vegetable sides and two salads. The bay windows were open, allowing the cool night air into the room and the chandelier had been dimmed to enhance the glow from the table's candles, flickering in the light sea breeze. If Suzanna hadn't been sitting next to the man Grace was beginning to know and like, the evening might have been perfect.

Grace had thought the subject of the lighthouse would be dropped, but once everyone had complimented Evelyn on the meal and spent some time discussing the merits of Atlantic salmon as opposed to Pacific, Suzanna spoke up.

"I remember we had a brief chat about lighthouses when you were staying at my hotel, Drew. Did you ever get to see ours on land, as well as by sea?"

Grace reached for her water glass and took a large gulp.

"I did, my first day here."

"What did you think of it?"

"Well…it's not in very good shape from what I could see. I don't think anyone's been inside for quite a while."

Except for you, Grace thought. She peered down at her plate, her fingers twisting the cloth napkin in her lap, worried that he was about to mention that.

"Henry Jenkins was supposed to be taking care of it."

"He is," Grace blurted, rushing to her friend's defense. "At least, he was. But he's had hip trouble and will likely need a hip replacement. That's why he hasn't been able to keep up with it."

"Well, I've heard he's hardly been there at all in the past couple of years." Suzanna picked up her glass of wine and took a sip.

"I noticed someone has been leaving flowers there," Drew unexpectedly added.

Grace caught his eye and wanted to shake her head, warning him away from any more talk about the lighthouse, but she was afraid her cousin might notice.

But a simple "Oh?" was all Suzanna said.

"Shall we have dessert in the living room?" her mother piped up and Grace knew she was off the hook. *Temporarily.*

DREW CLOSED THE car door and looked at Grace beside him in the passenger seat. She hadn't spoken much during dinner and not afterward when they were eating strawberry shortcake in the living room. Suzanna had done most of the talking, recounting amusing stories about guests at the hotel. Then she and Ben moved away from the group to discuss possible renovations in the hotel while Grace's mother showed him the collection of artifacts on the bookshelves. Grace had sat next to her father on the sofa, picking at her dessert while he dozed.

"It was a nice evening," Drew said as he fastened his seat belt and pressed the ignition button.

She murmured something inaudible over the car engine. He guessed she was thinking about Suzanna's offer to give her a ride home. Grace's hesitation had prompted Drew to quickly say, "Grace and I have plans later."

Suzanna had merely said, "Okay," but Drew guessed he'd confirmed her assumption that they were a couple. Yet now, sitting next to a very subdued Grace, he doubted that. He felt they'd become friends—more than friends, judging by her response to his kisses—but that didn't make them a couple in the true sense of the word.

As they pulled out onto the main road, Grace finally spoke. "Thanks for rescuing me back there. And just to let you know, I do intend to tell Suzanna after I talk to Dad tomorrow."

Drew stifled what he wanted to say—that she always seemed to have a reason to delay. What exactly was she waiting for? "Sure," he said, focusing on his driving.

"You don't sound sure."

He turned at her sharp tone but she was staring out the passenger side window. When they were closer to the bookstore, he said, "Look, why don't you come back to Henry's with me. Maybe we can talk this over and discuss next steps. I have to get back to Portland tomorrow and—"

"I have to open the store, too. I can't afford to close three days in a row."

He struggled to keep his irritation in check.

Was she blaming him for her decision to close the store during the entire holiday? "Okay, so you're saying you'd like to go home instead?"

"Yes," she mumbled.

She hadn't uttered another word by the time he pulled up front of her place. He shut down the car and sat drumming his fingertips on the steering wheel, waiting for some sign from her that would clarify this drastic change in mood. He might have kissed her good-night but she unsnapped her seat belt and opened the door.

"Thanks for the ride. I'll see you tomorrow...maybe." She closed the door and went to unlock the store.

All the way to Henry's he mulled over that last word *maybe*. It was typical of Grace to toss off such an ambiguous remark when he couldn't follow up on it. Did she want to see him or not? If she did, then a smile would have been enough. But given her silence since they'd left her parents, he could only assume she was ambivalent. Not merely at seeing him before he left for Portland, but perhaps about their whole relationship. *Friendship*, he amended.

Figuring out Grace Winters was like playing that childhood game. He couldn't recall the name, something about Simon. *Take two steps forward. Now take three back.* Considering what he was planning to do for her—sticking his neck out by promising a safety inspection—Drew had to ask himself *why?* What was it about this woman that had him going in circles?

CHAPTER THIRTEEN

GRACE HAD A lot on her mind. Last night's dinner that had begun so auspiciously with Drew's kiss had fizzled into disappointment by the time Drew had dropped her off at the store. The back and forth exchanges about the lighthouse had been nerve-racking and the stress of fending off any revelation about why Drew had really come to town had made her stomach churn. How much longer could she continue the charade that the memorial was for her cousin when deep inside she knew it was for herself? That whatever she felt for Drew Spencer was impossible and could only come to nothing but grief for both of them. He was simply too decent a person.

But by morning, some vestige of her normal self returned. She phoned to arrange a visit with her father at lunchtime. Fortunately, she reached her mother instead and didn't have to get into the discussion beforehand. She fretted over the talk, because her father liked information presented to him in point form: no digressions, no embellishments and definitely no irrelevant facts. Ben had mastered the technique but not Grace. That wasn't her style. Never had been.

She hadn't contacted Suzanna. That task picked away at her mind no matter how hard she tried to ignore it. Of course, it couldn't be put off forever, but what was the point in raising painful memories for no reason? Better to wait until the project was a done deal. Which brought her back to Drew's reminder that he'd come by to speak to her about the lighthouse. He'd told her that it would need to pass an inspection and that it wouldn't be sold if it was found to be a hazard. *Fine. So, let's get on with it.*

She got to work in the store—turning on the air-conditioning, opening the blinds and dusting. She booted up the computer to see if any shipments were due that week and reviewed last week's earnings. When she first took over the business, Henry had warned her sales had dropped recently, perhaps due to the opening of a chain bookstore in the new mall on the outskirts of Portland. His advice had been to sell books that were prizewinners or more difficult to find and also to promote local authors whose books might never hit the big stores. "Don't compete—be different," he'd said.

This week she'd invited a former fisherman turned author to talk about his self-published memoir of lobstering years ago when Lighthouse Cove was still a viable fishing community. Henry had recommended the man, a member of the Historical Society, so Grace was assured that at least *some* people would be attending. She'd read the book and found the stories of the hardships and dangers the fishermen faced compelling. She typed a brief email confirming his visit on Friday, flipped over the closed sign on the front door and waited for customers.

Some businesses in the Cove were closed due to Saturday's holiday but most reopened. Midmorning a few passersby noticed Novel Thinking and wandered in to browse. Grace had expanded the children's section from Henry's time, learning from Ben that many of the home buyers in the new subdivision had young families, and had even created a cozy nook with carpet and beanbag seats. The problem was that so far it was being used as a temporary library, with adults and their charges reading but not buying.

Once the library was built… No, she refused to contemplate staying in the Cove longer than a year. She felt some guilt at knowing she'd suggested her father purchase the store, but she also knew it was a good investment for him. Even if it couldn't function as a bookstore, its proximity to Main Street made it prime real estate. With the new development, the town was in transition, evidenced by a shift in the type of businesses from older, established places to trendier ones. Despite Henry's objections to change, it was happening and there was no stopping it.

She was reading the reply email from Terrance Langford, the author, when the front doorbell tinkled. Her mixed feelings at seeing Drew walk through the door were heightened by the animal carry-cage in his hand. Drew was leaving town and really, after her parting last night, could she blame him?

"Hi," she said when he reached the cash counter. "I guess you told Henry you were leaving."

"I have and as you can see—" he gestured to Felix crouched unhappily in the cage "—he's grateful for your offer to take Felix. At least there's less chance of his escaping from upstairs."

He reached for her hand. "I…um… I'm not very good at this but I can't leave without telling you how much the weekend meant to me. Not just getting to know the town a bit more but seeing it through your eyes. Meeting your family. Most of all, spending time with you. Being with you. That was the best part." He pulled her close in a hug.

Grace pressed the side of her face against his chest, his heartbeat pulsing at her temple. She wrapped her arms up and around to his back, and when he tipped her face up to kiss her, she knew she was making another big mistake. But then all thought of anything more than his lips on hers vanished and she let herself sink into the kiss, letting it flood all her senses, until he finally pulled away.

"Wow." His laugh sounded a bit shaky. "I'm tempted to suggest closing the store and going somewhere—anywhere—so I can be alone with you."

We could, Grace wanted to say but didn't dare.

"But I should get back today," he went on, "and start the ball rolling on my recommendation. I have an idea… I have some days off coming to me—not many, maybe three or four—but I'd love to come back to…well…

um, see more of the town and—I'm sounding like a teenager here, aren't I?"

Hope soared. "Go on."

"You're not letting me off the hook, are you?" He shook his head in mock resignation, his eyes shining. "I really want to be with you—and that could be anywhere, really—to get to know all about you."

"That sounds good to me." Though it didn't really. She didn't want him to know *all* about her.

Their eyes locked for a long moment and as Grace was thinking another kiss might happen, Felix gave a loud, plaintive meow. "Okay, Felix, we get the message." She bent down to unlock the cage and scoop up the cat.

"Right." Drew sounded disappointed. "And just to clarify, I'm recommending a sale rather than a teardown and will organize the structural inspection, okay? It might take some time."

Too overwhelmed to speak, Grace could only nod.

"I'll contact you about coming back. Maybe toward the end of the week? Does that sound good?"

"Anytime. Soon, I hope." She watched him head to the door, glad that she was holding a cat and unable to run after him for one more hug or kiss. The bell sounded as he left. She stared at the closed door as if expecting him to change his mind about leaving and come back to her. But he didn't. She let out a long sigh. "All right, it's just you and me now, Felix. Although you're going upstairs and I'm staying here until lunch. And Dad."

GRACE CALLED OUT a "hello" as she opened the door of her parents' home and headed to the kitchen. Her mother was putting the finishing touches to a salad at the island counter and looked up when she walked into the room.

"Just in time, dear. Lunch is ready so why don't we sit at the table?" Her mother pointed to the bistro set by the opened sliding doors. "Or we could sit out on the terrace."

"Too sunny for me," Charles complained as he sat down at the table.

"That's fine. Grace, will you get glasses and the pitcher of iced tea from the fridge."

During lunch, Grace focused on the salad and her mother's butter biscuits but felt the tension rising inside. When her father mentioned a desire to get back to work, she jumped at the chance to forestall the planned discussion. "Has your doctor okayed that,

Dad?" She caught her mother's head shake but ignored it.

"I'm sure he will. I'm feeling better than ever. There's a town planning meeting coming up at the end of the summer and I hope to attend."

"What's the meeting about and why do you want to be there?"

"Budgets for the coming year." He glanced quickly at Evelyn. "Our plans aren't finalized yet but there's more land up by the highway available for expansion."

"Charles, you know very well Ben wants the company to assess the risks involved."

The unexpected tension in the room interested Grace, who worried her father's sour expression at this unexpected reprimand from her mother might jeopardize her plea for the lighthouse.

"Why don't we have our talk over tea in the den?" her mother suggested and got up to clear the table.

"So, about my lighthouse memorial idea," Grace began once they were settled in the den. "Drew thinks whatever problems the lighthouse has could possibly be fixed." Well, he hadn't said that, but Grace felt certain that he would once the inspection was completed.

"That isn't the issue though, is it?" Charles asked.

"I'm not sure what you mean."

"The point isn't whether the thing can be fixed, it's whether it ought to be a memorial."

"Surely that's something the town could decide," Evelyn said. "With input from Brandon's family, of course."

"That's what I'm trying to point out," Charles exclaimed.

"No need to get testy, dear. Grace is going to speak to Jane and Suzanna, aren't you?"

"Of course. And frankly I don't see a problem. Why wouldn't they want a permanent reminder of Brandon, rather than that makeshift one someone's established."

"Whoever could that person be, making that shrine?" her mother unexpectedly asked.

"Suzanna?" Grace suggested.

"I got the impression she didn't like going out there."

"There's something else to consider," Charles interjected. "What about the cost of buying the thing? Why the heck would the town want to buy an old run-down lighthouse?"

"We could have a fundraising campaign. Maybe the town council would match what we raise, or at least contribute. I could go to that budget planning meeting, too."

Charles frowned. "I've heard rumblings that money is tight. I doubt the town would have enough for something like a memorial as well as paying infrastructure costs for our proposed subdivision expansion."

Grace's hope for an easy resolution sank. Her father's stubborn streak was a family legend. She was about to get up and leave when he said with a loud and heavy sigh, "Well, go ahead and do what you want, Gracie. You will anyway."

Her jaw dropped. She glanced at her mother, who gave a quick shrug. Grace wasn't about to question that remark. "Thanks, Dad, I appreciate your support."

But his comment about buying the lighthouse was on Grace's mind after her return to the bookstore. The information about the town's budget meeting took the whole issue to another level. Drew had mentioned the inspection process could take a while. She didn't know when the budget meeting was happening, but she ought to have fundraising ideas in place well in advance. Then she got an idea.

"NICE WEEKEND?"

Drew was surprised to see Ensign Mc-Naught at his desk on the other side of the office early Tuesday morning. He set his takeout coffee cup on his own desk and said, "Yes, thanks. You're in early."

"Yeah, thought I'd finish off some stuff I didn't get around to on Friday."

Drew was tempted to ask, "You mean when you left work midafternoon?" but restrained himself. If he got the promotion to take over the office for good, he'd need cooperation from McNaught.

"And here's that complete list of towers and stations in the state that you asked for," Mc-Naught said, crossing the room with a file folder.

Another surprise. Drew had asked for it almost two weeks ago, when he was still on the road surveying the lighthouses. "Great. Thanks."

"Let me know if it's okay. Right now, I'm working on something for Jim."

"Yeah?" Drew sank onto his swivel chair.

"An up-to-date inventory of lighthouses that've been decommissioned and what happened to them."

Drew straightened up. That seemed to be

something he ought to have been told about or even doing himself. He felt a combination of annoyance and confusion, which got him knocking on his boss's door seconds later.

"It's basically a make-work project," Jim explained at Drew's concerns. "McNaught has applied for a promotion out of lighthouse maintenance and into Human Resources."

"What?"

Jim sighed. "I know. Between us, I don't get it. Anyway, I need to assess him and so I dreamed up this task over the weekend. Didn't think you'd mind."

"No, guess not. I was just taken aback."

"While you're here, I've been thinking over what we talked about Friday. That tower in... what's the name of the place again?"

"Lighthouse Cove." Drew had a bad feeling about where this was going.

"Right. Whatever. Anyway, I don't see the point in spending some of my budget on a structural assessment. Money's tight and about to get tighter from what I hear. You've said it would take a lot to get the tower up and running even if it passed. Also, the proposal to sell hasn't even been discussed by town officials. Am I right?"

Drew nodded, wishing his report had been far less detailed.

"What I'm thinking is, let's go ahead with the original plan to decommission and tear it down."

"But—"

Jim held up a hand. "My decision's made. I'm also expecting your performance review for McNaught by the end of the week, please." He turned his attention to the computer on his desk and Drew knew he was dismissed.

He stood in the hall a few minutes longer, his brain swirling with all kinds of unhappy thoughts and one in particular. *Grace.* Then he headed downstairs to Human Resources.

CHAPTER FOURTEEN

"GRACE?"

Ben looked up from the notes he was writing, surprise in his face. Grace scanned the small construction site office comprised of four desks, four chairs, a sink, microwave and what looked like a bar fridge along with a filing cabinet and cork bulletin board covering one whole wall. Of course, the company had a proper headquarters in Portland, but this was where her brother and other personnel hung out when they were "on the job" as her father would say. Since the town's first and only subdivision was still growing, Grace guessed the site might become a permanent fixture.

"Figured you'd still be here," she said. It was almost six and she'd come right after closing the store and feeding Felix, hoping she'd find Ben alone.

He pushed his chair away from the desk. "Have a seat and tell me what finally brings you to my home away from home."

"Hmm," she said, giving the room another once-over. "A bit cramped and definitely not as pretty as your actual home."

He snorted. "Yeah, but at least it's all mine. For now, anyway."

"You could always find your own place in town, you know. Move out."

"I could, but then I'd be making a statement."

"How so?"

"That I'm here to stay."

So, he's grappling with the same dilemma that I am. Leaving the Cove after a year or staying. "Yeah, I get it."

"Would you go back to Augusta?" he asked. "Especially now?"

"What do you mean by especially now?"

He shrugged. "You seemed pretty cozy with Drew Spencer last night."

"Cozy?"

"I got the impression you were a bit more than just friends but hey, I'm only your brother. What do I know?"

Grace knew her face was red. Her adult brother was a lot more insightful than his teen version had been. But she wasn't here to discuss her love life or even her imagined one.

"I have a favor to ask."

"Uh-huh?"

"You know my plan to restore the lighthouse as a memorial for Brandon?"

Ben's face darkened. "Not that again. I thought you were supposed to pass it by his family. And Dad."

"I talked to Dad today. He said if Aunt Jane and Suzanna agreed, he was okay with it."

"Dad said *that*?" Ben tossed the pen in his hand onto his desk. "I don't believe it. Is this Gracie interpreting events for her own purpose?"

"Cut it out, Ben. I'm not a kid anymore so stop treating me like one."

Another flash of surprise that was followed quickly by pursed lips. "Okay. Sorry. I deserve that." He rubbed a hand across his eyes and yawned. "It's been a long day but that's no excuse. I don't know why, but for some reason coming back home has catapulted me right back to those days when I was an actual teen."

"Yeah, I'm finding the same thing. I think it's hard for Mom and Dad, too. I bet they're having some difficulty looking at us as adults, especially since we've lived away from home for so many years."

Ben grinned. "When did you get so smart, little sister?"

Grace waved a hand. "Don't change the subject. If Dad and everyone else agrees, what's *your* objection?"

He took so long to reply she wondered if she'd touched on a sensitive subject. Though she had no idea why that would be. How could it matter to *him*?

Finally, he said in a low voice, "I suppose it's because those days after Brandon died were so hard and painful. And not just for our families. For other people, too."

Grace knew he was referring to Ella, who'd left the Cove a day after being questioned by police about the note Ben had passed on to them. She had never returned. It was a *very* sensitive topic for both of them and one she'd have to carefully tiptoe around. But she hadn't come here to discuss that night.

"That's why I think a proper memorial would give Brandon a presence in town. Something more than a bad memory. Did you know that some people consider the lighthouse haunted?"

"That doesn't surprise me. I guess it kind of is for his family. Though I don't understand why it should be for others." He stared blankly ahead, as if he were in another place and another time.

"Back to the lighthouse," Grace prompted.

The expression he shot at her was startled. Grace gave him a few seconds to get his mind back to the present. "If the rest of the family is on board—" she mentally crossed her fingers at that "—then all we have to do is get a structural inspection. Drew said that could take some time with the Coast Guard but—"

"That's the favor."

"Yes. I'm sure there's someone in the company who'd qualify to do that."

His nod was encouraging, and she quickly added, "As soon as possible?"

"Grace…"

"Stop rolling your eyes. Yes or no?"

"Okay, okay. There is someone, an engineer who also happens to be interested in lighthouses."

"Great!"

"When does this have to be done?"

"Like right away?"

Ben shook his head. "I don't know why, but suddenly I'm getting the feeling I really *am* back in the past. My little sister wrapping me around her finger again."

"You're not. This is the adult me, big

brother. Get used to it." She stood, grinning. "Let me know when," she said, giving him a small wave as she walked to the door.

SHE WASN'T EXPECTING Drew to call, but the sound of his voice reminded her of Ben's remark. *Yes, you're right, Ben. He is more than a friend.*

"Hi," she said, hoping she didn't sound as giddy as she felt. "How was your trip back?"

"Oh fine. How's Felix adjusting to being in his old home again?"

"Nonchalantly. He aimed right for the spot in the kitchen where Henry used to put his food dish."

"Nice to be a cat, oblivious to change."

"As long as food and water are provided."

"For sure. And speaking of Henry, have you heard from him since his doctor appointment?"

"No, but he'll be seeing me tomorrow when he comes to pick up Felix."

"Right. Well, say hi for me."

"For sure." This is almost as awkward as a high school phone call, Grace was thinking. "By the way, I spoke to my father and he's okay with the memorial project. Thought I'd call my aunt tonight and talk to her first before I approach Suzanna."

"Ah…uh…well that sounds like a good idea." After a long pause, he said, "Um, I've taken a couple of days—Friday and Monday—to make a longer weekend and thought I'd pay you a visit."

Pay me a visit? Was I one of his aunties? She stifled a sigh. "That's great. Will you stay with Henry again? I'm sure he wouldn't mind."

"I don't like to impose. I was thinking the hotel or maybe that motel up by the highway, closer to Portland."

"Sure, but—hey, why not stay at my place?" There was another long pause. Had she been too presumptuous? Misreading the cues?

"Oh well, that's a wonderful thought but—"

"I wouldn't be here. I mean, I can stay at my parents' for the weekend."

"That seems to be a lot of trouble for everyone."

"Are you kidding? They'd love to have me around." Well, Mom would anyway.

Another pause.

"It would be fine, Drew. Seriously."

"Okay, then. Thanks. I'm thinking of arriving midmorning on Friday."

"I'm having a guest author come to speak at the bookstore about ten. Why don't you come and hear him? I think you'd be interested. He's Henry's age and has lived in the Cove his whole life. Has lots to talk about."

"Great. All right, I'll see you then."

She thought he was about to hang up when he suddenly asked, "Anything else new there?"

"Um, not really. Same old." Her slight laugh sounded very nervous.

"Okay, see you soon. I…um… I've been thinking about you," he said just before he hung up.

The call had felt stilted. Grace knew the information she'd been trying to keep from him, but what was *his* excuse? Whatever it was, she phoned Aunt Jane immediately after.

When the small talk had finished, Grace broached the subject. "The other reason I'm calling is that I've been thinking of establishing a memorial for Brandon."

"Oh?"

Grace cleared her throat. This was something she couldn't hedge around. "At the old lighthouse."

"Go on."

"Someone from the Coast Guard has been

here as part of a survey of lighthouses along the coast."

"Oh. Does the Coast Guard look after them?"

"Yes, since the '30s or so I think he said. Anyway, it's in bad condition and he said it would probably be decommissioned."

"Which means what?"

"It would no longer be their responsibility so it would be sold or torn down, depending on its condition."

"I see."

Grace grit her teeth. The conversation was almost as frustrating as the one she'd had with Drew. But at least her aunt hadn't come out with a flat refusal. *Yet.*

"I'd like to try to get the town to buy it and set it up as a memorial for Brandon, with a plaque and everything." There was no response for so long Grace was certain her aunt had hung up. "My parents like the idea but want me to discuss it with you first—and Suzanna, of course."

"What would all this involve?"

"The lighthouse has to pass a structural test before it can be sold. Then I plan to write up a proposal and take it to the next town council meeting. I'm hoping the council will agree to kick in some money but may expect public fundraising, too. It would be a long process and getting your okay is just the beginning."

She heard her aunt sighing. "Maybe you'd prefer to think about this a bit?" Grace suggested.

"Yes, dear. I will definitely need to do that. You said you'd talk to Suzanna yourself?"

Grace hesitated. Not having to face Suzanna about it would be a bonus but also inconsiderate. She deserved to hear about it firsthand. "Yes, I will. It's best coming from me."

"Okay, then. Let me sleep on this and get back to you."

"Possibly by tomorrow?" Grace winced at her pushiness, but she was on a tight schedule.

"Hah! There's the Gracie I remember. Yes, dear, I'll call you tomorrow."

When she hung up, Grace was heartened by her aunt's light chuckle. *It's happening. My project is taking off.*

DREW KICKED HIMSELF for the ridiculous phone call. He knew he had to tell Grace his bad news in person, which had prompted him to take the days off. The problem was all the time he was talking to her he kept picturing how she'd look when he told her—the disappointment and hurt. Perhaps even an accusation that he'd misled her over the outcome of his report. He hadn't, though Jim had certainly misled *him*.

Perhaps he'd been foolish to take the days around the weekend. When would he tell her? Before, during or after they'd been having a good time? Or even worse, after a kiss? He doubted she'd want him to kiss her *after* she heard the news. A better plan would have been to go see her right away—tomorrow— and get it over with. At least he could use the days off to feel sorry for himself, alone in his own apartment.

The problem was he wanted to see her. To be with her. Badly. To be in her presence and see that impish grin, the tousle of her curly dark hair when she refused to listen to reason and yes, even the way she frustratingly leaped from a simple comment he might make to an assumption. Drew knew in his heart that when he announced Jim's verdict, she'd refuse to accept it. She'd forge on, amending her plan as needed if that's what it took. But she wouldn't give in.

He ran his fingers across his scalp, massaging the stress headache he felt coming on. There were a couple of days left in the week before he returned to the Cove. Maybe he'd take another shot at Jim, try to dissuade him from his decision. Surely there was a way out of this mess.

Drew smiled at the irony of the situation. It was the reversal of the one days ago, when Grace tried so hard to change his mind about tearing down the lighthouse. Now he was taking on her role, only with his boss. He hoped he could be as convincing as she'd been, though he knew her other attributes had factored into his decision. What miracle could he come up with to persuade Jim?

CHAPTER FIFTEEN

HENRY STROLLED INTO the store midmorning and waited patiently for Grace to finish up with a customer. As the woman left, he said, "I've come for Felix. And thank you for hosting him. I hope he wasn't too much trouble."

"Oh, he mewed pathetically all night," Grace complained, smiling at the same time. She came from around the counter and hugged him. "How are you? How did the doctor appointment go?"

He patted her on the back. "I'm good. The appointment went well and I'm on the waiting list for a hip replacement. I had a nice visit with my sister, though she may have to go into a retirement home." He sighed, shaking his head. "That's the tip of the slippery slope far as I'm concerned. Don't ever put me in one, Gracie."

"Are you kidding? You're going to be around pestering me for years."

Henry's face sobered. "Think you'll be here in the Cove for years?"

The unexpected question took her aback. "Well, um…"

He waved a hand. "No need to answer. I've never thought this situation here was permanent, though I'd hoped it might be."

He'd always been so good at reading her, even when she was a teen and couldn't comprehend her own self. "It's complicated," she murmured.

"Hah! Maybe not so much. My opinion is that people make things complicated as an excuse for not doing anything at all. Inaction. Waiting around for someone or something to compel them to act."

Grace grinned. "When did you get so philosophical, Henry? Come and sit down." She led him to an armchair in the reading nook. When they were settled, she told him the recent development in her lighthouse quest— her father's qualified approval.

"Charlie gave in, just like that?" Henry was shaking his head in disbelief.

The first time Grace heard Henry refer to her father as Charlie she'd been almost shocked. Everyone called him Charles, even her mother. But Henry had once told her he'd been in the same grade at school as her parents. Looking at his grizzled, potbellied self it was difficult to imagine him as a kid or a teenager. Imagining her parents and him hanging out together was even harder.

"He seems different since his heart surgery," she said. "I can't pinpoint exactly how different, but less inclined to engage in an argument. He more or less said the project was up to me." Then she gave a small laugh. "Everything is relative, isn't it? He still lets us know how he feels about things. Loudly."

"Hard to believe, though I suppose aging is an inevitable change, much as we like to fool ourselves otherwise. So, you got the green light, then? What about Brandon's family?"

"Aunt Jane called me this morning to say okay. She sounded a bit doubtful, but I think she likes the idea of having a permanent marker for Brandon. She told me that she and Suzanna have been visiting Brandon's gravesite in Portland regularly, at least several times a year." Grace paused, recalling her aunt's sad voice on the phone. "Especially on Labor Day weekend."

After a brief silence, Henry said, "Then it's a go."

"I still have to talk to Suzanna."

"Oh. That might not be as easy."

"Why?" she asked, though Grace guessed what he meant.

"I always got the feeling Suzanna thought she belonged somewhere else. Don't know why. But she used to come into the store and walk around as if it was too small and shabby for her. As if she'd rather be some place more exotic."

Grace knew what Henry meant. "She used to make me feel like I wasn't important."

Henry stared at her, then patted her on the arm. "That's the young Gracie talking, not the woman she's become. You were never kind enough to yourself, my dear. Too judging. Isn't that what they say now? Judging is bad, even though we all do it."

"You've always been so wonderful to me, Henry. When I was a kid, I sometimes wished you were my father instead—"

"Hah! Don't go there. Your parents love you more than you know." He struggled to his feet. "Okay, got to fetch Felix now and get home."

"Stay here. I'll go get Felix."

Much later, as Grace strode across the marble floor of her cousin's hotel, she tried to ease her anxiety by replaying Henry's words in her head. She wasn't responsible for Suzanna's temperament, but her sadness about Brandon was another matter. Grace forced her mind away from that thought. *You can't change what's done* had been her mantra since her therapy days, back in college when the full impact of that night hit her with a vengeance.

At the check-in counter Grace told the receptionist—a young man wearing a Rohan name badge—that she was there to see Ms. Winters.

"Is she expecting you?"

"No, but I'm her cousin. Grace Winters."

"I'll just ring her and see if she's busy." He pressed a button on the check-in counter phone and said, "Your cousin, Grace Winters, is here to see you." Then he nodded and hung up. "She said to go on through." He gestured to the office behind.

When Grace opened the door, she saw Suzanna close the laptop on her desk. Her cousin's face was pale and the dark circles under her eyes suggested stress. Grace remembered her mother's comment about Suzanna's marriage troubles. Probably this wasn't the best time to speak to her. If her emotions were high already who knew how she'd respond to Grace's request. *Well, I'm here now.*

"Grace? This is a surprise."

"Sorry for the interruption. If you're busy I can always come back."

"No, no, have a seat. Not busy. Just tired." She rubbed her face. "Is everything okay with Aunt Ev and Uncle Charles?"

"They're fine. Um, I'm here to ask a favor. Well, not exactly a favor as such. But to ask you to consider a project I'm working on."

"Oh?" She frowned. "Something to do with the hotel?"

Grace shook her head. "The lighthouse."

Suzanna leaned forward, resting her forearms on her desk. "What about the lighthouse?"

"It's going to be decommissioned by the Coast Guard. It hasn't been functioning for ages, even before you came back. Anyway, Drew—remember him from dinner last Sunday?"

Suzanna smiled. "I do. Very attractive and seemed like a nice guy. Are you two a couple, then?"

"Uh…well…we're friends. I don't know about the couple part." She could feel color rising into her face.

"Oh trust me, I picked up on that almost immediately."

Grace bristled, wanting to retort, "If you did, then why were you so chatty with him?" but she knew how childish that would sound. "Anyway, Drew works for the Coast Guard and he was in town recently completing a survey of lighthouses along part of the coast."

"Really? Funny he never mentioned that when we spoke about lighthouses, here in the hotel or at your parents' house."

"I'm sure he didn't think it was relevant. As for Sunday dinner, I asked him not to mention what he was doing."

"Why was that?"

Grace hesitated, already put off by her cousin's tone. *Too late. Just jump in and get it over with.* "Because I wanted to talk to you about my idea first. Drew said when the Coast Guard decommissions a lighthouse, it's either sold or torn down."

"Okay."

"And I've asked him if we can buy it and restore it."

"We?"

"Maybe the town."

"Why?"

"Because I want to erect a memorial to

Brandon there, on the site." She stopped then because her cousin was shaking her head back and forth, her pale face even paler now.

"No way. Absolutely not."

"Don't you want to hear my reasons?"

"I don't care about your reasons, Grace. It's bad enough that I have to look at that thing almost every day. Why would I want to go there to see some...whatever you have in mind...*memorial* for my brother? It should be torn down!"

"Then Brandon would really be forgotten. By everyone who knew him here and everyone who's heard the story."

"My mother and I will never forget him and that's all that matters."

Grace pushed on. "My family will never forget him either, Suzanna. I want to put up a plaque for everyone to see and to remember. I want him to be a permanent part of this town, where he was born and grew up."

"Until he was fourteen," she snapped.

Grace stopped, fighting back tears. Finally, she said, "The memorial isn't just a reminder of Brandon, Suzanna. It's a reminder to all of us who were on the beach that night. To everyone who picked on him at school. To everyone who gossiped afterward and said cruel things to…to some of the kids who were there that night. Even to anyone foolish enough to consider going out to the lighthouse when the tide's coming in." She took a deep breath. "Nothing is going to bring him back. I know that. I just want to see a tangible memory right here in town. For always."

Suzanna had dipped her head down partway through Grace's speech. Now she raised it, her eyes wet with tears. "I understand what you're saying, Grace. And I do remember some of the things people said after, especially about that friend of yours. The summer girl. *Ella?* If it weren't for her…"

"You don't know the whole story, Suzanna. Nobody does." *Except for me*, she thought. *And Cassie and Ella.*

"I heard enough. It's a good thing she and her family never came back here. I don't know what I'd do. I'll never forgive her."

Grace closed her eyes. She thought of her brother's comment. *This isn't a good idea, Gracie.*

The silence in the office was broken by Suzanna's hoarse whisper. "I can see this means a lot to you, Gracie. I'll call my mother and see what she thinks."

Grace looked up, as surprised by her cousin's use of her childhood name as she was by this unexpected concession. "I... I've already spoken to Aunt Jane, Suzanna. She agreed."

Her cousin's face tightened. "Very shrewd of you, Grace. Or calculated. I wouldn't have thought you'd have that in you."

Grace got to her feet. "I'm sorry you feel that way. I called Aunt Jane because she had the right to hear my idea first. My coming here was a courtesy, Zanna. Your mother's approval is all I need." She walked to the door. "And I'm sorry, for whatever personal issues you're going through right now. You don't deserve more bad luck." She was about to close the door behind her when Suzanna spoke up.

"Grace. Wait. I'm sorry if I seem unappreciative of your efforts. That you care. You've always been sweet that way. It's just that I need time to process this."

"I get that. Let me know." Grace left the office, unsure about her next move until Ben called to say his engineer was going out to the lighthouse to have a look at it.

She stood at the top of the steps leading down from the hotel to Main Street and looked across the harbor to the lighthouse, a solitary signal post in the distance. This was the view Zanna gazed upon every time she left the hotel—a constant reminder of her loss. The brother she never got to know as an adult. Unlike Grace, whose relationship with Ben was sometimes fraught with childhood baggage, Zanna had no siblings to share family issues with.

All because of her and Cassie. There was no way Grace could ever compensate for that moment of teenage ill-judgment—her failure to connect an act with a possible consequence. But she could atone.

DREW UNLOCKED THE door of his apartment and for the first time since he'd moved into it eight months ago, the utter loneliness of it hit him. There was no one to call out to, not even a cat to curl around his legs. He plopped his briefcase and laptop onto the nearest chair and clicked on the air-conditioning.

He smiled at the thought of Felix, Henry's elusive pet. The cat didn't need a lot of attention and seldom seemed to want it, but whenever Drew had settled into one of Henry's armchairs, Felix invariably ended up in his lap. Perhaps a pet might be something to consider, given that there was no end in sight to any change in his solitary and cramped living quarters.

Housing and rental units were pricey in Portland; hence the suburban sprawl to the northeast and Lighthouse Cove. The Winters family was sitting on a gold mine in development opportunities. He sighed. No matter how hard he tried, he couldn't clear his mind of a Winters. Especially the one who meant the most to him. Grace.

He loosened the collar of his uniform shirt and headed for the small bedroom to change. It had been a long day, complicated by his preoccupation with Jim's decision about the lighthouse along with his return to the Cove. One more day. No matter how many scenarios he constructed in his mind, he couldn't decide on the best possible time and place to talk to Grace. He planned to arrive early Friday morning because her guest author was due about ten and he didn't want to sabotage the event by blindsiding her with bad news. Dinner perhaps? Then ruin the weekend for both of them? There was no good time, he realized.

It was only later, after he'd exchanged his uniform for shorts and a T-shirt, and was sitting in his favorite chair, a cold beer in hand, that an irresistible idea occurred. He'd over-looked one sentence from Jim's announce-ment about the lighthouse—*you'll have to convince me otherwise.*

There was still a chance to change his boss's mind. He just had to come up with a very persuasive argument, one that wouldn't jeopardize his chance at getting the group commander promotion, to get Jim to under-stand the importance of the lighthouse as a symbol. Not merely to a grieving family but to a whole town.

In the few days he'd been in the Cove, Drew had heard and witnessed the effects of that past tragedy, not only on family mem-bers but on some of the town's residents. He didn't know all of the story—and doubted many people in town did, from what Henry had told him—but he did know how a tragic event can have an impact on people's lives.

CHAPTER SIXTEEN

THURSDAY WAS PROMISING to be a great day. Grace received an early morning phone call from Suzanna. "I had a long talk with Mom, who pointed out that although we didn't need the memorial for ourselves, maybe the town did. Besides, I don't have to go out there to see it if I don't want to."

Grace thought about that call most of the day. She wasn't certain that the town needed the memorial either, but *she* did. Zanna's comment about never going out to the site also suggested she couldn't be the mystery woman taking flowers. She must remember to tell Drew when he came the next day. Her excitement about getting the go-ahead from Suzanna rose even more when Ben called late afternoon.

"My engineer thinks the lighthouse is good for restoration. Bricks need replacing and repointing. A few floorboards need repairing and shoring up. The concrete base is okay, stable in spite of a few chips here and there. He didn't know anything about the light equipment but figures the Coast Guard will offer advice on that."

"We're good to go?"

Ben laughed. "It sounds like *you* definitely are, Gracie. Yeah, go for it. I'll email you a copy of his report."

She closed the store early, hoping Henry wouldn't come around on a surprise visit and scold her. Then she got to work, typing up an ad for *The Beacon* enlisting volunteers to fundraise, and composing a few signs for shop windows about the proposed project. She searched the town's website for information about the next scheduled budget meeting and if time would be allotted on the agenda for input from residents. When she discovered that the final meeting would be in early September, the surge of adrenaline from the morning slowed down. Her appeal for council funding and any town zoning permission would be bolstered by the public support she could garner in the meantime. Demonstrating that residents were contributing financially—and perhaps even volunteering time as well—would be the bestselling point of all.

Nothing to stop her now.

WHAT COULD BE more exhilarating than knocking on a door that would be opened by Grace Winters?

Drew had never considered himself a romantic. He'd always been too organized and precise in thought and manner, more concerned with the proper way of going about his life than a spontaneous one. But when the closed sign on the bookstore flipped over to reveal Grace's smiling face on the other side of the door's windowpane, Drew felt a rush of desire and longing. Desire to wrap his arms around her, hold her against him and to stay like that for as long as possible.

But neither option was possible because he was bringing bad news. Still, when she moved into his arms, his intention to give her the news right away vanished. Later, he told himself, when the best opportunity arose.

"Good trip?" she asked, stepping out from what Drew felt was an awkward hug.

"Yes." He couldn't take his eyes off her. She was full of life and enthusiasm. Everything about her glowing.

Then her expression altered. "Anything wrong? You seem a bit hesitant."

Drew pulled her close again. "I'm fine. It's all good."

"Come on upstairs with your things," she said. "Terry will be here soon and I still have to get the coffee urn going."

"Terry?"

"The guest author, remember?"

"Right." He followed her inside and through the interior door that led up to her apartment. She opened the door at the top of the stairs and stood aside to let him walk past.

"Take your things down the hall to the bedroom. I've got it ready for you."

Her bedroom was smaller than his in Portland, with basic furniture—double bed, bureau and a small desk. What got his attention though was the lack of personal touches—no photographs, pictures on the walls or even fancy pillows propped on the bed. She'd been staying in this room for at least five months, but there was little evidence of that. When he returned to the tiny living area, she handed him a set of keys.

"I've already moved my stuff into my parents' place, so I won't need to bother you later."

Drew wrapped his hand around hers. "You wouldn't be bothering me."

The glow reappeared in her face and he

was about to bring her closer when she murmured, "Terry's probably waiting."

He reluctantly let her go. "I'll be down in a sec."

"Take your time. I have coffee on downstairs."

Drew guessed he wouldn't see her for much of the day, nor even through the weekend. She had a business to operate and he gathered sales were slow. But he'd come prepared to entertain himself. He'd brought a thank-you gift of a bottle of Scotch for Henry, binoculars for a bird-watching hike and his laptop to prep for his job interview in two weeks. His stint as acting group commander was no guarantee he'd land the promotion.

By the time he got downstairs people were milling about the coffee urn or sitting in the chairs set up around the reading area. A man who looked to be in his sixties was chatting with a guest next to a lectern and Grace was putting the finishing touches to the display on the table nearest the cash counter. Drew picked up one of the books—*Stories of the High Seas*—to read the back-cover synopsis. The front featured a cloudy ominous seascape with a small boat struggling against an enormous wave. Drew's stomach lurched at the mere sight and he decided right then to pay Henry a visit rather than stay for the talk.

Fortunately, Grace was now occupied with a customer purchasing one of the books and as he made his way past her to the front door she glanced up, startled to see him leaving. He gave a small wave, held up the gift bag with the Scotch inside and motioned to the door.

The day was bright and sunny with a cooling sea breeze. Drew strolled down Porter Street to Main, then descended onto the boardwalk edging the marina. The town's sights were familiar now and he was beginning to feel less like a visitor. As he was passing The Daily Catch bistro, the chef-owner was sweeping the roped-off section of the boardwalk that served as an outdoor eating area.

"Hey," the man greeted. "How're things?"

"Great, thanks. Beautiful day."

"It is until it isn't." He laughed. "Maine weather, you know. I'm Tom Nakamura. You were here with Grace Winters a week or so ago." He extended his right hand.

"Yes, and we had an amazing meal," Drew said as he shook hands. "Thanks, too, for comping dessert."

The other man grinned. "Good customer service. Brings people back." Then he asked, "So do you live in town or visiting?"

"Visiting this weekend. And doing some work, too."

"Oh yeah? What kind of work?"

"I'm with the Coast Guard, stationed in Portland."

"No kidding! Like, search and rescue? That sort of thing?"

"Um, no. I'm with the lighthouse maintenance section. I've been surveying lighthouses in the greater Portland area and that's what brought me here to the Cove."

"No way!" Then he frowned. "Were you inspecting our own lighthouse?" He jerked his head toward the far rocky peninsula across the inner harbor.

"I did have a look, yes." Drew was beginning to wish he hadn't mentioned the lighthouse, thinking suddenly that Grace wouldn't want him to have this conversation. At the same time, he told himself she was far too obsessed with the tower.

"That thing hasn't worked for a few years," Tom was saying. "What's your verdict, then?"

"Huh?" Drew's mind shifted from Grace back to the man standing in front of him.

"I assume when you inspected it you had to make some decision about it, right? Get it working again or whatever?"

"Would you like that? For the lighthouse beacon to be shining?"

Tom shrugged. "Kinda. It would be pretty and maybe a tourist draw, which we badly need, though I suppose the light isn't necessary for safety anymore. The place has a sad history. Don't know if you've heard about it from Grace—she was right in the thick of it, she and her family."

"I've heard some of it."

"Yeah, well the whole thing cast quite a pall over the town. I was away at college for the aftermath, but my younger brother, who was in Gracie's year at school, remembers the story that went around. One of the summer girls had apparently been leading Brandon Winters on, knowing he had a crush on her, and sent him a note to meet her during the beach party. No one knows what happened after that or why Brandon was caught at the lighthouse in high tide. Anyway, it was all a long time ago. I'm sure most people have forgotten the story or never knew it in the first place."

Some hadn't forgotten. Drew pictured Grace's sweet but determined face.

"Are you still seeing Grace?"

Drew nodded.

"Good. She's a great person. Say hi to her for me." Nakamura began to sweep again.

Drew waved and continued on his way to Henry's, mulling over this different take on the lighthouse. Perhaps Grace was right about the need to preserve it. He'd have asked Tom his opinion about a memorial but there was no point, considering the tower was slated to be torn down. Unless he could come up with an alternate plan.

Drew spotted Henry sitting on his front porch when he turned the corner onto his street. He waved and as he got closer, held up the gift bag.

"Thanks for letting me stay," he said, climbing onto the porch. He handed the older man the bottle of Scotch, amused at the expression of delight in his face when he opened the bag.

"Sit, and you needn't have brought a gift. You looked after Felix for me. Going for a bird walk?" He gestured to the binoculars around Drew's neck.

"I am. Care to join me?"

"Thanks, but no. Taking it easy today."

"Grace told me you're on the list for a hip replacement. Any idea when that will happen?"

"Anytime in the next six months, they said."

"Hopefully sooner than later. Let me know when. I'll come visit you in the hospital."

"I'd like that. So, you here for the weekend?"

"Staying at Grace's. She's with her parents," he quickly added.

"'Course she is."

Drew caught the twinkle in his eyes and smiled. "Guess I should get on my way, then."

He stood. "Oh, thought I might also have another look at the tower. Can I get the key?"

Henry frowned. "Gracie still has it."

"She does?"

"Borrowed it the other day. I don't know why. She was all excited though. I'm sure there's a spare one around somewhere. Give me a minute." He struggled to his feet and went inside.

Drew wondered why Grace had needed a key. He knew she'd only been to the site a couple of times and doubted she'd visit it on her own. The place had too many bad memories.

A few minutes later Henry emerged, holding a small padlock key. "There you go." He passed it to Drew, who pocketed it. "Come back for a longer visit next time. We'll have a shot of Scotch together."

"I'd like that. Take care, Henry. I'll bring this back later."

"You can give it to Gracie. Then she'll have them both and you'll know where to find them when you make a decision about the lighthouse."

His keen eyes probed Drew's face, seeking a response that Drew wasn't able to make. *Yet.* He waved goodbye and headed for the shore. By the time he got there, he'd changed his mind about hiking into the dunes and aimed for the lighthouse instead.

He was only several feet away when he realized someone had been at the site recently. The flag and packet of firecrackers from the July Fourth weekend had been trampled and, as he reached the locked door, he noticed small sections of the white stucco exterior had been scraped, exposing the red brick beneath.

Drew unlocked the door and pushed it

open, covering his nose in anticipation of a billow of dusty air. But there were only a few motes whirling about and when he stepped inside, he noticed a chalk mark next to the gaping floorboard and another on the floor below the missing bricks on the far wall. Someone had definitely been inside and he didn't need to follow any dots to get to the answer. These were signs of an inspection.

Drew didn't bother going up to the gallery. He'd seen enough. Locking up behind him, he decided to forgo his bird walk and strode determinedly back to town.

TERRY WAS WRAPPING up his presentation, which had gone far too long in Grace's opinion, when Drew returned. She'd been a tad miffed that he'd left rather than stay for the talk but had gathered from his signals that he was going to see Henry. The event had drawn about twenty people, all of whom were buying books. They applauded when Terry finished and milled around him as well as the coffee table. Grace worked her way through to Drew, standing at the coffee urn. "Hi there. Did you go visit Henry?"

"I did." He smiled but his gaze didn't linger, drifting over her head to the group of people.

"Well, I'm glad you made it back. Terry's eager to meet you. I told him you were in the Coast Guard." She craned her neck to beckon to the author and when he drew near, she introduced them.

"Mighty pleased to meet someone from the Guard," he said, beaming as he shook Drew's hand. "Where are you stationed?"

"Portland. But I've only been there a few months."

"Search and rescue?"

"Um, no. Lighthouse maintenance."

"Ah!" Terry looked briefly at Grace. "Come to see our own tower, here in town?"

"I have."

Grace waited anxiously for Drew to mention his survey, but he didn't. In fact, she thought he seemed preoccupied. Usually he was friendlier, and she felt a slight disappointment at his apparent lack of interest in Terry.

But the author seemed oblivious. "Where were you before Portland? I know some people in the Guard."

"I was farther up the coast. Southwest Harbor."

"Were you there last year when that fishing boat disaster happened outside Bar Harbor?"

Grace was certain Drew stiffened.

"Terrible thing that was," Terry went on. "I heard there was some kind of inquiry after but never found out the result. Did you?"

Drew cleared his throat. "Uh, no." He turned to Grace and only then did she notice his white face and trembling hands as he set his coffee cup down on the display table.

He looks like he's going to be sick, was her first thought. Either that, or faint. She noticed that Terry was about to ask another question and she intervened. "Terry? I see some people are waiting to have their books autographed and I must get to the cash counter."

"Oh?" He turned around. "Goodness. Don't go away," he said, smiling at Drew. "I'm planning another book on marine disasters and would love to get your expertise. And take a book, won't you? On the house," he announced grandly.

"Is everything okay?" Grace asked Drew as soon as Terry had moved off.

He took a long deep breath, placing his fingertips on the table as if to steady himself. "I'll wait for you upstairs, Grace. There's something we need to discuss."

Grace watched him walk toward the door leading to her apartment, his shoulders pulled back almost in defiance, as if he were bracing himself against a sea wind. That gait and the iciness in his eyes a minute ago confirmed her sickening suspicion. He knew something.

CHAPTER SEVENTEEN

DREW PACED AROUND the apartment, waiting for Grace. He shouldn't make assumptions, but who other than Grace would have organized an inspection? Hadn't she mentioned mere days ago that the family company had engineers and couldn't one of them do the inspection? Despite his insistence that there was a protocol, a procedure to follow, she'd gone ahead anyway.

The irritation—no, the anger—that suffused him was a relief compared to the nausea and shakes he'd had when he first entered the apartment. Thank heavens he'd escaped any further questioning by that author. He'd felt so ill he was about to lie down on Grace's bed when he imagined her lying in it, too, and pushed back the temptation. Right then he didn't want to picture her in any other role than villain. Or manipulator.

No. Neither of those words were appropriate. They were unfair. He went to the kitchen sink to pour himself a glass of cold water and drank it in one go. But at the very least, he decided, she was either underhanded or lacking in judgment. Perhaps impulsive and obsessive could work, as well. By the time he heard her footsteps on the stairs almost an hour later, Drew had mentally scrolled through an entire thesaurus of adjectives that could apply to Grace Winters. And they all flew out of his head the instant he saw her pale, pinched face.

"What's happened?" she asked when she opened the door into the kitchen, where he stood waiting for her.

He ignored the pitch in her voice and forced himself to stay on target. "Perhaps you should be telling me."

She brushed past him into the living room area and sank onto the sofa, tucking up her legs. "I'm too exhausted, Drew, and I can only give myself an hour for lunch so please, just get to the point."

Drew hesitated. Unlike his father—and perhaps Grace's—he wasn't the kind of man who needed to take charge. There had been no upper hand in any of Drew's relationships with other women. There was only give-and-take. Respect and consideration. Speaking and listening. Taking in Grace's drawn face, he felt his anger dissipate. But not his hurt pride.

He sat down in a chair across from her. "I went out to the lighthouse," he began, and she straightened up immediately, about to say something when he held up his hand. "Let me finish. I noticed that someone has been there, making what looks very much like an inspection. Or part of an inspection, anyway. Was it someone from your father's company and if so, who arranged it?"

She set her feet onto the floor and leaned forward. "I asked Ben to do it. I know you said it needed to be done through the Coast Guard, but I couldn't wait, Drew. And even if a more detailed inspection is needed, at least we know now that the lighthouse is viable. It can be restored."

"Do *we* know that, Grace, or is that what *you* want to believe?"

"The engineer said it only needed some brickwork. Minor fixes. The structure is sound."

"All right, let's not get off track. The fact is that I told you my department handled the tests and that I'd organize it. Then you—"

"But you said it would take time."

He raised his shoulders, frustrated. "So

what? The tower's been sitting idle for at least two years. Your cousin has been dead how many years?"

"Seventeen." Her voice was a bare whisper.

She looked away but not before he saw tears welling up. He clenched his jaw, torn between rushing to pull her into his arms or to leave. Instead, he sat and grit his teeth, waiting for the wave of sympathy he was feeling for her to ebb. He wasn't ready yet to yield his point. He lowered his voice. "Then why now, Grace? And why didn't you talk to me first?"

"Because I got everyone's approval to go ahead and you weren't here. Because there's a town council budget meeting in early September and I wanted to get the project started and some fundraising done before I went to ask the council for support." She paused. "Because I was afraid you'd stop me."

Drew's head was spinning. "I see you've convinced yourself that what you did was reasonable—*from your point of view*—but I was only a phone call away. And we did speak on the phone, didn't we? Yet not a whisper of what you intended!"

"You would have tried to stop me."

"You don't know that." But he did, because she was right.

The talk came to a dead halt then. Drew leaned back in his chair, his mind racing through a series of possible options and ways to salvage Grace's project. Not a single one appealed. The problem was that although Jim had instructed him to revise his report to include the teardown recommendation, Drew had not yet done that. In a few days, Jim would expect Drew's final report on the Lighthouse Cove tower, its fate sealed. In a couple of weeks, Drew would interview for a job he'd dreamed about since he was a kid, holding his brand-new book about the Portland Head Light. There was no escape hatch for this emergency situation.

He wearily rubbed his face and sighed, exhausted not by any lack of sleep but by the high emotion in the room. "Is there anything else I need to know?"

"What do you mean?"

"You know what I mean, Grace." The woman could be frustrating.

"Well…"

"Tell me. We've got to clear this up now."

She stood and went into her bedroom, returning to hand him a sheaf of papers. He flipped through them, his heart rate accelerating with each turned page. They were flyers advertising the proposed lighthouse restoration/memorial project for the Cove and requesting volunteers as well as donations to the new Brandon Winters Memorial site.

Too dumbfounded to speak, he waved them at her.

"I told you that I'd need to show public support through funding to get town council approval. All of that would take time and—"

"That's not the problem, Grace. The lighthouse is going to be torn down."

She was struggling to speak and he waited, feeling that this was the moment he might look back on some day and realize how different his life could have been if…

"What?" A single word, but a whole book in her disbelief and hurt.

"I'm sorry. It's not how I wanted it."

"Then why?"

"Do you want the official summary of reasons?"

"No. I want to know why you changed your mind. You said—"

"That there was no guarantee."

"But it passed an inspection."

"By someone unauthorized by the Coast Guard." Her dismissive shrug rankled. She was the person at fault here. He'd given her plenty of warnings.

"You promised!"

Drew winced at this flash of the young Gracie. "Not really, Grace, and it's out of my hands now," he added, wanting to thrust the blame on anyone but himself.

After a minute, she said, "I've got to open up the store. Maybe we can finish this later, when I close up." Without a glance his way, she left the apartment.

Drew stared at the closed door, half inclined to dash after her and make everything disappear—the anger and hurt, the sense of being let down. And not just in him, he realized. Grace was clearly feeling the same. He remembered what she'd said about acts and consequences the time they went for a drink to discuss the fate of the lighthouse. He'd been totally confused by the cryptic remark, tossed at him as some kind of angry afterthought. But now he was beginning to understand her meaning. Consequences clearly did follow acts, but it was impossible to foresee what they would be.

He was the prime example of that truism. He'd acted last year, when his two-man crew pulled three fishermen into Drew's Coast

Guard response boat in the bay outside Bar Harbor. He'd acted when the winds picked up and the rough sea hampered their efforts to transfer the last man, the boat's captain. And when he'd shouted, "Abort!" against the blinding rain and thundering waves and struggled to turn his boat around, heading for shore. Those acts had had dire consequences—ones he lived with every day and would continue to live with in some form or another for the rest of his life. So, Drew knew all about consequences, which is why as hurt and angry as he was at Grace, he also felt a spark of empathy for her.

He needed to come up with a plan to fix the whole mess. It was only one o'clock and Grace would be working four more hours before she'd be free to spend time with him. He sighed, knowing that his plan to have a romantic dinner somewhere in town was seriously in jeopardy. The whole weekend was now in doubt. He resumed pacing, running his fingers through his hair as if to stimulate brain waves that at the moment were dormant.

Then it occurred to him that it was Friday. Jim would still be at work and Portland only a half hour away. Perhaps the drive there would give him a chance to think of some remedy he could apply to this gaping wound between him and Grace.

Half an hour later, Drew zipped into his parking space at headquarters and dashed inside, waving his security ID at the desk personnel, and raced up the stairs. He tapped on Jim's door and flung it open.

Jim looked up, startled. "Drew! I thought you were off this weekend."

"Yeah, I am but something's come up. Have you got a minute?"

"Sure. Take a seat."

"I've been thinking about your decision yesterday, to proceed with the teardown of that tower in Lighthouse Cove."

His boss frowned. "Oh?"

"Just that I've been thinking—"

Jim was rifling through his in-box. "I don't see your final report here. Did you email it?"

"No. I…uh… I haven't submitted it yet."

"Why is that?"

Drew knew the idea he'd had on the way here was far-fetched. He also knew he was taking a chance—one he could ill-afford considering his upcoming interview. But if his assessment of Jim's character was accurate, this might be his only chance at saving

Grace's project. *Saving the potential outcome of his whole life.*

"Are you busy tomorrow, sir? There's someplace I'd like to take you."

GRACE DRAGGED HERSELF up the stairs. She was wrung out, not by the unexpected rush of customers at the end of the day but by the horrible argument with Drew. Though to be fair, it hadn't been an argument as such, even though there were two opposing sides and no resolution. All afternoon she'd thought about his calm but icy cold expression. She could see that he was angry—maybe hurt, too—but he was so restrained she'd wanted to fly off the sofa and shake him.

Then he'd dropped his bombshell about the lighthouse and all her hopes fizzled away. The news had shocked her so much she was paralyzed by inaction, her mind blurred by useless questions like *Why? How could you?*

She waited at the top landing, her hand grasping the doorknob as she tried in vain to decide her next course of action. Making amends to Drew was on the list, but not at the top. Certainly below forgiveness, which she had grappled with all afternoon. He should have told her sooner, before she'd printed flyers and sent an ad in to *The Beacon*. The childishness of that thought brought a quick smile. Still, if she'd known... *What, Grace? Would you have changed your mind? Given up?* Not likely, she realized.

She took a deep breath and opened the door, stepping into a very quiet apartment. "Hello?" Nothing. She walked through the kitchen/living space toward the bedroom. Maybe the talk had drained him, too. The door was ajar and she couldn't see if he was lying on the bed so she tapped lightly.

"Drew?" She pushed the door to find an empty room. Very empty, she noticed immediately. No backpack, no laptop case. Only a piece of paper lying on the bed.

Hi, Grace, I would have texted but hesitated to interrupt you at work. Something's come up and I've gone back to Portland. I may or may not return tonight, but hopefully sometime tomorrow for sure. See you soon, Drew.

Something's come up? May or may not see you tonight? She balled up the note in disgust and threw it on the floor. As much as she'd dreaded the evening ahead, she hadn't given up hope that some of it could be saved; that perhaps the ambience of a nice dinner might have eased their disappointment in each other. Too late now, she thought, sitting on the edge of the bed and contemplating a lonely night ahead—until she thought of her old friend.

An hour later she was striding along Main Street to Henry's. By the time she'd called him, Grace had mentally transformed what had happened between her and Drew to a simple difference of opinion.

Henry's long silence when she'd phoned to ask if she could see him almost prompted her to add, "It's okay, this is very last-minute," but as he'd done so many times in her teens, Henry had come to her rescue.

"I've got one of those packaged frozen lasagnas for supper and it's far too big just for me. I'd be thrilled if you'd join me."

She had no appetite anyway. Her purpose in wanting Henry's company was only to sit in peace with someone who wasn't going to pepper her with questions or raise an eyebrow at the story she desperately needed to tell.

He was waiting for her in his favorite chair on the porch and stood to give her a bear hug. "I've a nice bottle of wine that Drew left behind when he was here. Would you like some?"

The sharp pang at his name startled Grace

and for the first time she considered what she'd put at risk by her impulsive actions. She was tempted to dig out her cell phone and call him right away, to stammer an apology that might bring him back. Instead, she said, "Thanks, Henry. I could use a glass of wine."

She sat in the chair next to his while he went inside. People were arriving home from their jobs in the small residential enclave where Henry's bungalow was located, and children were playing on the sidewalks or running to the beach for another swim before dusk. It was a scene she'd witnessed and taken part in throughout her own childhood until she left for Augusta and college. She could still remember those carefree summer evenings when the only instruction was to come home at dusk. All that changed for several years after Brandon's death.

The first Christmas Grace had come home from college—almost two years after that Labor Day weekend—her mother had told her how many parents held a tighter rein on their children, who were no longer allowed to run free until nightfall. And the unspoken, uncompromising rule was that no child or teen was permitted anywhere near the lighthouse without an adult.

She stood to get a better look at the lighthouse. Its white exterior was stained pink, reflecting the setting sun from behind the town. She tried to picture how it would look if it was operating—how it might look in the future—with its beacon cutting a shaft of brilliance onto the dark water. It would be beautiful. Then she wondered if her two friends from that summer would ever get to see it lit up again. *Cassie and Ella.* Or if *she'd* ever see *them* again. *Unlikely in my lifetime,* she figured. A sudden cool gust blew in from the sea and Grace shivered.

"Here you go, my dear," Henry broke into her thoughts, handing her a glass of chilled white wine from the tray he was carrying. He set it down on the table between them and passed her a plate of steaming lasagna.

"That was fast," Grace laughed.

"Miracle of the microwave. Tuck in. There's plenty more."

They ate in silence, watching the last stragglers trudge home from work or beach until the first stars appeared and Grace was ready to talk. She recapped most of it, going back to Drew's caution about the inspection process, touching briefly on her impatience and subsequent call to Ben and ending with Drew's reaction to her flyers. She couldn't bring herself to tell him the bombshell about the lighthouse. That awful news was tucked away in a far corner of her mind.

Henry sat quietly through the whole speech, his head bobbing thoughtfully a few times, and didn't utter a word until she reached the part where she'd discovered Drew had left. Then he reached across the table to clasp her hand and murmured sadly, "Oh, Gracie."

CHAPTER EIGHTEEN

GRACE SLEPT LATE and was opening up the bookstore when her mother phoned.

"Ben told us your good news, darling. That's so wonderful. Let me know what your father and I can do, other than contributing financially, of course. Would you like to come for dinner tomorrow night and talk about it with us?"

Later Grace would blame her grogginess for her failure to inform her mother of Drew's decision. She was still processing it herself. Her wakefulness all night hadn't produced a single idea to turn the situation around. She'd walked home from Henry's feeling better and when he'd mentioned that no doubt Drew would get over his tiff, as he'd called it, once the lighthouse restoration was underway, Grace almost told him the rest of the story. But she didn't have the emotional energy.

On her way back to her apartment, she'd

stopped at the end of Henry's street to gaze one more time at the lighthouse. The nearly full moon cast an eerie luminescence on it, spotlighting it against the pitch-black sea beyond. If a beacon shone into the dark, people would look at it and remember Brandon. Her father said people had moved on from what happened and that was a good thing, to move on from the pain and grief. But forgetting about the lighthouse meant they'd also forgotten about that fourteen-year-old boy. She certainly hadn't and never would.

These were the thoughts that had tormented her sleep and dogged her throughout the morning as she went through the motions of providing good customer service to the handful of people who wandered into the store. Grace was pleased the author event had garnered interest as well as sales. Something to consider for future plans, she thought, and was immediately struck by the fact that she'd just considered a future in Lighthouse Cove. Later, she would pinpoint that moment as the reason for her next move. She phoned Henry.

"How're you today, Gracie?"

"Not bad, considering my poor sleep. Thanks for everything last night, Henry. Especially your listening."

"Not the lasagna then?" he teased.

She laughed. "It wasn't that bad. Your company made it taste wonderful." She paused. "Anyway, I'm calling for a favor. Again!"

"Never use that word *again* when you ask me for a favor, sweetheart. What can I do for you?"

"Last night I mentioned the ad I'd placed in *The Beacon* about the lighthouse restoration and soliciting donations and volunteers."

"Uh-huh."

"I had a brain wave early this morning."

"Oh-oh. Not one of those Gracie brain waves?"

She had to laugh. He knew her so well. "Afraid so. In all the emotional drama with Drew, I neglected to tell him about the ad in *The Beacon*."

"Oh?"

His voice registered concern and she rushed to add, "It really doesn't matter. I doubt he'd see it anyway. The problem is that I might get responses and I thought I should make some kind of schedule or list of tasks that need to be done while we're waiting for the okay to buy the property." Grace closed her eyes, saying a silent prayer—*please let that happen.*

"And I know when we do," she went on,

"we'll need the involvement of the Historical Society. Some of the members know the lighthouse's history and can advise us what restoration materials will be appropriate to the time period and so on."

"When you say 'we' and 'us', Gracie, who are you referring to?"

"Well, to you, Henry. Are you still going to help me?"

There was a slight hesitation that worried her and she thought she heard a sigh before he answered. "Of course, Gracie. I'm always there for you."

"You're so wonderful, Henry," she said, her voice choking.

"Tell me what I can do."

"Could you ask some of the Society members to meet me at the lighthouse, say about noon? I thought I'd ask my friend Julie to look after the store for me."

"I'll see what I can do. It's Saturday and late notice."

"I know and we won't need a lot of people. Just a few to take a tour of it and give us some ideas of where to start."

"Sounds good. Bring the keys, then. I don't have a spare here."

"Keys? I only have the one you gave me."

"Drew didn't give you the other one?"

"No."

"Hmm, oh well. No matter. One will do. See you soon." And he ended the call.

Grace stared glumly at the phone in her hand. She hadn't been inside the lighthouse in many years, avoiding it only for what it symbolized—the place where Brandon drowned. *You can do this, Grace.* Then she called Julie before she could change her mind.

"Sure, I can do that, Grace," Julie said. "I'll come by earlier so you can show me the ropes."

"It won't be too hard, Julie. The cash operation is basic and I'll be a phone call away."

"Does this emergency meeting have anything to do with your lighthouse project?"

"Kind of." The front doorbell tinkled. "Oops, got to go, Julie. Customer. See you soon." A classic case of being saved by the bell, Grace thought, as she smiled at the woman and child heading her way. Now wasn't the time to tell her friend the whole sad story.

"Breakfast is on me, sir," Drew said as Jim climbed into the passenger side of his car.

"Appreciated, Drew, considering I'm giving up my Saturday morning golf round."

Drew flashed a smile. This trip was also going to be an opportunity to learn more about his boss. He just hoped what he already knew about the man—that he was flexible in his thinking and willing to take a chance on his personnel—was going to be enough for a successful outcome.

"I've never been to Lighthouse Cove," Jim said as Drew pulled out of the office parking lot.

"Not even when you were doing lighthouse inspections yourself?"

"Nope. Back then I was stationed in Rockland and took charge of the sites up the coast. It was always a Portland officer doing this area."

"Gary Hale?"

Jim sighed. "Most of the time. You took on a real challenge by stepping into his job. That hasn't gone unnoticed, by the way."

"Thank you, sir." Drew's nervousness about his plan to show Jim how important the tower was to the town eased slightly. *But you're not there yet*, he warned himself.

They made small talk on the half-hour drive to the Cove. When Drew had transferred to Portland, he'd connected instantly with his new boss. Something in the man's willingness to listen to another viewpoint appealed to Drew. He wasn't slack as a commander, but he also wasn't tied to any go-by-the-book rule.

Jim also knew about the disaster off Bar Harbor but had never pressed Drew for his own account. It was all in Drew's personnel file anyway—his testimony at the inquiry as well as that of the witnesses. Everyone at the Portland station knew most of the story, too, but they followed Jim's lead—acceptance without judgment. That had been the key to Drew's healing.

Yet he still had flashes of that day. The boat cruise with Grace reminded him that there were some memories he'd carry to the grave. For some reason, he felt intuitively that Grace would understand that, which was why this mission was so important.

There was too much at stake. When Grace had cried, "You promised," yesterday, Drew's response wasn't at all what he'd been feeling inside. He knew that he *had* made an implicit promise. He couldn't understand his overreaction to her admission that she'd arranged an inspection. The flyers, too, were basically of little importance. She hadn't even posted them! Had it been his wounded pride, that she'd gone ahead with something he hadn't approved? If so, then what kind of man was he, that his ego could be so easily threatened? He didn't want to be that man, whether he had Grace in his life ahead or not.

When they reached the road exiting the highway to the Cove, Drew said, "We'll get breakfast first, sir, then maybe a quick tour of the town."

"Sure, but I thought the point of this trip was to show me the lighthouse."

Drew looked sharply at his boss. He ought to have known Jim would figure that out. "Yes, it is. But the town factors in, sir."

"Uh-huh. As long as we get breakfast first. And don't keep using 'sir.' It's Saturday, your day off and mine, too."

Drew smiled, giving a thumbs-up to Jim. As he drove down the hill leading onto Main Street, he pointed out the harbor, the marina and the hotel. But not the lighthouse. That could wait. Luckily, he found a parking space in front of Mabel's Diner so he wouldn't have to look for one on Porter, where the bookstore was located. He was hoping the morning's ex-pedition could be accomplished without encountering Grace. Then if he was successful, if Jim were to reconsider his decision, Drew planned to return to the Cove later today or tomorrow to tell Grace the good news. But it all hinged on that one word—*if.*

Fortunately, the café wasn't full and they were able to get a table. Best of all, there was no one inside who would recognize Drew other than the waitress, who greeted him with a big smile. While they ordered, Drew nervously tapped his fingertips on the table.

"I'm getting the impression you've made more than one trip to this town," Jim commented after the waitress brought them coffee.

Nothing was lost on Jim, Drew thought. That could be a good thing or not. Of course, he could take him to the lighthouse right after breakfast, but then Jim wouldn't have a sense of the importance of history to its residents. And that history included what happened to Brandon.

"Yes, I have. Something about this town appealed to me. I grew up outside a small town a bit bigger than this one, so I understand what they're all about. The closeness that can sometimes feel too constricting. The converse of that is also what makes small towns unique. People stand together when they most need to."

Jim nodded. "I've heard that, though I grew up in a city too big to know more than a handful of neighbors on my street. That scenario had its benefits, too, especially for teenagers." He grinned.

Their orders came and both men devoted their full attention to pancakes and sausages. Later, as Drew was paying, he noticed a small pile of copies of *The Beacon* on the cash counter and picked up one for Jim. It would give him another aspect of the town. They headed for the car and as Drew was getting behind the wheel, he noticed a familiar woman going inside Mabel's front door. That friend of Grace's. The one he'd met at the July Fourth rib-fest. He couldn't recall her name. He hoped she hadn't noticed him. The last thing he needed was for Grace to find out he was in town.

"Where to now?" Jim was asking.

"Thought we'd take a spin around Town Square, see some of history and then—"

"On to the lighthouse?"

Drew sighed. There was a tinge of impatience in that question. "Yes, then on to the lighthouse."

The square was busy on a Saturday morning and the limited number of parking spots meant that Drew was only able to drive slowly around its perimeter, pointing out the imposing Town Hall and the statue of Hiram Winters in the center of the square.

"One of the founding fathers," he remarked.

"Uh-huh. Winters. That name's familiar."

Drew couldn't tell if Jim was teasing or not. "Over there," he said, changing the subject, "is the new library, under construction as you can see. The town is in transition from a fishing community to a satellite of Portland. It's growing. You saw the new housing development near the highway."

"How does all this affect the lighthouse?"

Drew stifled a sigh. Saving the tower wasn't going to be an easy sell, even to Jim Pitarokilis. "People here want to preserve as much of their history as possible. It's a changing world and icons from the past like the tower are important." He thought suddenly of Henry and his friends at the Historical Society. Too bad he hadn't thought to introduce the older man to Jim. Perhaps there'd be an opportunity after they visited the lighthouse.

He decided to drive back down to Main Street and take the waterside road for a view of the harbor and marina, rather than return to the highway and access the lighthouse from the road up top. Jim was only fifteen years or so older than he was and in good shape. Climbing up the dune to the lighthouse path wouldn't be challenging.

"Nice harbor," Jim said as they drove by it. "And I see the tower. Not very big, is it?"

"No. I included some of its history in my report. Started in 1917 and completed a year later."

"War anxieties, you mentioned?"

"That's what I heard. Not much has been written about it, but a man from the Historical Society said he's writing a book."

"There's a historical society?"

"Yes."

He found a parking space near the same ramshackle cottage he and Henry had sat by more than a week ago. *More than a week ago!* Drew marveled how so much can change in a person's life in such a short time span.

"Think you can manage?" he asked Jim as they stood, staring up at the dune and the lighthouse at the very tip of the rocky peninsula.

"'Course I can."

Smiling at the indignation in Jim's voice,

Drew led the way. It wasn't until they'd reached the top of the dune, pausing to catch a breath and enjoy the panorama of the town below, that Drew noticed they weren't the only people up there. About a dozen or more men and women were clustered at the base of the lighthouse.

"Watch your step along the path, sir," he cautioned as they walked toward the lighthouse.

"I'm fine, Drew, and…are we meeting people here?"

"I wasn't expecting to," Drew murmured, wondering if this was yet another of Grace's ideas, and despite his resolve not to judge, felt a rise of irritation.

As they drew closer, one man headed toward them. Henry.

"Drew!" he exclaimed. "I wasn't expecting to see you here."

"Likewise, Henry."

JULIE WAS RIGHT on time. As soon as she entered the store, Grace called out, "I'm just going to run upstairs and change. Have a seat."

Grace thought Julie was about to say something, but she was in a hurry. She knew Henry could be impatient and she didn't want to keep him waiting. She wondered if she ought to have told him about the possibility of a teardown but knew his response would probably be to cancel this meeting about a restoration that might not even happen. Thanks to Drew.

That's not fair, Grace. He'd said the decision was out of his hands, which implied it had been made by someone higher up. Maybe his boss. There was no point ruminating over what happened yesterday. She finished dressing, picked up the lighthouse key from her kitchen table and went downstairs, where she found Julie skimming through a copy of *The Beacon.* The sight of it brought a twitch of anxiety, until Grace reminded herself that the paper, a free weekly, usually disappeared completely in a day.

"I like your ad for the lighthouse project," Julie said, waving the paper. "I hope you get lots of positive feedback, as well as support. Put me down for whatever job you need."

"Of course, thanks, Julie."

Julie set the paper down and joined Grace at the counter. "I can't be sure, but I thought I saw your friend this morning."

"What friend?"

"The lighthouse guy."

"You mean Drew?"

"I guess. Forgot his name. The one you were so cozy with at the rib-fest."

Grace's mouth went dry. Finally, she managed to say, "Where was this?"

"I popped into Mabel's for some scones for my mother and caught a glimpse of two men in a car. One of them really looked like Drew." She frowned. "What is it, Grace? You look upset."

"I'm fine, Julie. But I don't think it could have been him. He went back to Portland yesterday and I have no idea when he'll be back." *Or if.*

"Look, I should go. Call me if there's a problem. If worse comes to worst, the store key is right there beside the computer. Feel free to just lock up if you have to." In her rush to leave, she thought she heard Julie protesting behind her but didn't stop.

Grace's mind whizzed through countless explanations for Julie's sighting. *She must be mistaken. Even if the man was Drew, who could the other man possibly be? It didn't make sense. Besides, surely he'd have phoned to let me know he was coming back, wouldn't he?*

Maybe not, she reasoned, *because you*

made such a fuss yesterday. By the time Grace reached the end of the beach road, she was almost sick with worry. Then she saw Drew's car parked in front of the old Fielding place. She stopped beside the car to calm herself before starting her climb.

When she reached the top of the dune, she had to pause again. She saw that the lighthouse door was open and, as she strode forward, heard the rumble of voices inside. She climbed up the two steps to the threshold and peered into the shadowy interior, waiting for her heart rate to slow down. A familiar face emerged from the group of people milling about inside.

Drew was walking toward her, his face tight and anxious with disbelief. "Grace? What are you doing here?"

CHAPTER NINETEEN

IN SPITE OF the urge to find out exactly what was going on and why, Drew was aware of someone exiting the lighthouse behind him and kept quiet. But his gut told him the woman standing before him, pale-faced and chin raised, was responsible.

Henry had been vague about why people from the Historical Society were at the lighthouse when he and Jim had arrived. "They've been meaning to come have a look around for ages," he'd explained. "Today seemed like a good time."

If Drew hadn't felt such respect for the old man, he'd have snorted. When he'd seen Grace standing hesitantly in the open doorway, he began to put it all together.

"I think *you* should be answering that question, Drew," Grace was saying in reply to his from a moment ago. "Why—" She stopped at the sudden appearance of the person on the lighthouse doorstep.

Drew turned and motioned to Jim. "Grace, this is my commander, Jim Pitarokilis. Jim, Grace Winters."

Grace took the man's hand, shooting Drew a look that might have made him cringe if she wasn't the one at fault.

"Winters? Are you the person who sent me the email about restoring the lighthouse?" Jim asked.

Grace nodded.

"And I guess a descendant of the man whose statue I saw in town."

"My great-grandfather."

"He was the man who got this tower built."

"That's right."

"I haven't been up in the lantern room yet, but from what I've seen so far, the place is in pretty bad shape."

Drew noticed that Grace was about to protest when he heard Henry's voice.

"That would be my fault, I'm sorry to say." The older man stepped forward to stand beside Drew. "As I was about to tell you a second ago, Jim, I had to abandon my duties as volunteer keeper because of hip problems the past couple of years. The keeper before my time—Leonard Maguire's father—managed just fine but after he passed away, no one took on the job until I agreed to. That was about six years ago."

"The tower has a history of some neglect then," Jim said.

"'Fraid so," Henry admitted. "Why don't you come back inside, meet some of my friends in the Society and have a look around?"

"I'd like that," Jim said, allowing Henry to guide him toward the door.

Drew's silent thank-you to Henry was interrupted as soon as the men went through the door.

"Why didn't you tell me you were coming back? Why is everything such a secret with you?"

Her flushed face and pitched voice might have spurred him to retort back but Drew clenched his jaw instead, knowing he did not want to have that argument then and there. He simply wanted an answer to one question.

"Did you organize this?" He gestured to the open door and the voices inside.

The flush deepened. She nodded, raising her chin higher.

"Why? What was the point after what I told you yesterday?"

"I won't give up, Drew. I *can't*."

Drew knew they'd reached an impasse. He felt a shiver of regret at that. Compromise seemed out of the question as far as Grace Winters was concerned. She wasn't going to settle for a mere plaque where the lighthouse once stood. And if his plan to persuade Jim to reconsider failed, there was nothing he could do. Defying his boss's orders wasn't going to happen. Not even for Grace.

"We might as well go inside, then, and join the group." He heard the flatness in his own voice, the lack of both energy and emotion.

She did, too. Because she shifted her gaze from his face to the ground at his feet. "I should get back to the store," she mumbled and walked away.

Drew would have gone after her but someone called his name and by the time he turned to signal Jim, standing in the doorway, Grace had disappeared.

"BACK SO SOON?" Julie called from the cash counter when Grace burst through the door. She met her partway. "What's happened? Are you okay?"

Grace wiped her eyes with the back of her hand. "No, not really." She leaned against the door leading up to her apartment.

"Tell me."

"Are we alone?" Grace asked.

"Yep. Last person left about ten minutes ago."

"The whole thing is a disaster, Julie. I think I messed up."

Julie clutched her arm. "Grace! Come and sit."

"No. I have to change and then go see my parents."

"Not without telling me something."

"I arranged with Henry to have people from the Historical Society check out the lighthouse and I planned to meet them there, to go over some ideas about the restoration."

"Okay."

"But you were right, Drew is in town. He was there with his boss from Portland."

"Okay, but so what?"

"Well, I didn't tell Drew about the other thing—the historical group meeting."

"So, he was surprised. What's the big deal?"

"He told me yesterday that his boss decided the lighthouse should be torn down."

"Uh-oh. And you—"

"Hadn't told Henry or the Society members."

"Ouch. Yeah, you kind of messed up."

"And then—"

Julie held up her hand. "You don't need to tell me the rest. I'm picturing it. What now?"

"I have to tell everyone—my parents, my aunt and cousin—the place is going to be torn down...right after I practically begged all of them to support me."

"But that's not your fault, Grace."

"I'm not so sure about that." She opened the door to go upstairs. "Can you stay a bit longer? Until I come back from my parents'?"

JIM FOLLOWED DREW down the sandy hill to the car below. After Grace left, Drew had accompanied Jim and Henry around the lighthouse and up to the lantern room, where Jim inspected the lens, bulb and reflector.

"All of this would need replacing," Jim had muttered. He'd cast a cynical eye at the missing brickwork and the gaping floorboards, but Drew was grateful that his boss hadn't uttered a single word about tearing the tower down.

On their way out, a couple of Society members thanked them for coming. "It's a crying shame," one man remarked, "to see this part of our history fall into disrepair. We're so happy it can be preserved."

Jim had shot Drew a baleful look but simply nodded. It wasn't until Drew turned onto the highway to Portland that Jim said, "I know you brought me here to show me the importance of the tower to the town, but whose idea was it to ask the Historical Society?"

"Um, that would have been Grace's, sir. Maybe Henry's, too. They kind of work together." For a split second he envied that partnership, wondering if he'd ever have the chance to forge one with Grace, as well. Maybe not now, he thought.

"I had the impression they didn't know about the teardown."

Drew cast a quick glance his way. "Umm, maybe not."

"But you told Grace?"

Drew kept his eyes on the road. "Uh-huh."

"I see." After a second of silence, Jim said, "She seems to be a fighter. Buying and restoring the tower is an ambitious project. Maybe too ambitious."

Drew wasn't about to have a conversation about Grace with his boss. He heard Jim leafing through the copy of *The Beacon* Drew had given him earlier and was grateful for the chance to think about the scene at the lighthouse and Grace. While he understood her desire to fight for her project—and Jim was right, she was a fighter—he couldn't accept her refusal to compromise. Life was full of situations demanding compromise. A person had to know when to give in to an inevitable outcome.

His thoughts zoomed automatically to Bar Harbor and that fateful day. He recalled vividly the agonizing seconds that felt like hours until he made the decision to yield, to give in to the inevitability of the high seas, the hurricane force winds and the boat, already crammed with crew and rescued fishermen. Grace's struggle was nothing compared to that dilemma, but considering the family tragedy connected to the lighthouse he could understand her tenacity.

"Drew?"

"Hmm?" He glanced across at Jim, who was holding up *The Beacon* and pointing to something on a page.

"There's an ad in this paper asking for community volunteers and donations to the Brandon Winters Memorial with a photograph of the lighthouse. Do you know anything about this?"

Bile rose into Drew's throat and he couldn't

speak. *I might have known. I should have
known there'd be one more thing she'd kept
from me. Even after I asked her just yesterday—is this everything?—and she'd handed
me the flyers.* But no word about the ad. He
looked at Jim and shook his head.

"Then can I assume it's the work of Grace
Winters?"

Drew swallowed. "I…uh… I guess so, sir."

"But you told her the tower was going to
be torn down."

Drew cleared his throat. "Yes, I did, sir."

"Then…" Jim was shaking his head. "I
don't understand why she'd place this ad." His
expression cast doubt on everything Drew
had just told him.

"I don't know why either, sir," Drew
croaked. Although he absolutely did know.
Because she was a fighter and refused to back
down.

Jim folded the paper and stowed it in the
console between their seats. After a moment, he said, "I know this is none of my
business…"

Drew closed his eyes, sensing what his
boss was about to say and wondering how
he'd respond.

"But is there a possible conflict of interest here? Between you and Grace?"

Drew inhaled and said, "I...um... I think there might be. Yes. There is, sir." He felt his boss's gaze on him but kept his own straight ahead.

"Okay," Jim finally said. "Well, that's definitely another complication."

The talk ended there until Drew pulled into the station parking lot, where Jim had left his car. As his boss opened the passenger door, he paused to say, "I guess I won't see you in the office until Tuesday. I believe you took off Monday, as well?"

Drew nodded.

"All right, then, I'll see you in my office first thing, with a revised report on the Cove tower." He climbed out and bent over to add, "If you come up with a solution to this problem before that, get in touch with me. And um, a word of advice, keep your eyes on the target. Don't be distracted by less important factors." He closed the car door.

Drew watched him get into his own car, going over what his boss had just said. What exactly had he meant by "the target"? What were these less important factors? As for the

problem? The answer to that was one word—
Grace.

He reversed onto the street, at a loss what
to do next. Shower and clean clothes for sure.
Then what? Long hours of mentally replaying the day or yesterday? No. However today's events ended up, he couldn't possibly
put off what he had to do right now. Go back
to Lighthouse Cove and Grace.

GRACE HAD CHANGED into the clothes she'd
worn earlier, after a quick shower, briskly
scrubbing off the dusty perspiration. If only
she could cleanse her mind of the rest of it—
the words and angry faces. Julie promised
another hour, so she didn't have a lot of time
to inform her parents. Just as well to have
a reason to escape the round of inevitable
questions.

"This is a surprise." Her mother looked up
from the magazine she was reading in the solarium. Grace's father sat opposite, a copy of
The Beacon in his hands. Grace sighed at all
the explaining she was facing. She hugged
both of them and sat on the love seat next to
her mother, hoping some of her mother's in-
nate empathy and acceptance would shelter
her from her father's interrogation.

"Who's in charge of the store?" Charles immediately asked.

"My friend Julie."

"Is something wrong, dear?"

Grace patter her mother's arm. "No, Mom, but there's something I have to tell you." There were some details she omitted in her recap, most of them connected with the other aspects of Drew, the ones only she'd seen: his unexpected kiss the night of the fireworks— a memory that still brought a smile; his curious reaction to Terry's questions about some sea disaster, which Grace hoped Drew would reveal. Most of all, the way he kept forgiving her.

Grace's fervent hope was that she hadn't misinterpreted the expression in his eyes at the lighthouse today, when he'd realized she'd gone behind his back yet again. Disappointment and hurt were more positive than anger, weren't they?

"Let me get this straight," her father said as soon as she finished. "There's not going to be a memorial after all because the lighthouse is going to be torn down."

"Yes. Well, no."

"Which is it?" He sounded bewildered rather than annoyed.

Grace studied his aging face, the new lines that had appeared gradually over the past year along with his heart problems. The fight was going out of him, she thought, and that was a worry.

"I'm not sure because I plan to appeal the decision. I'm going to rally the town and do whatever it takes to make Drew's boss change his mind."

"Hard to win against bureaucracy," Charles grumbled. "And there's a whole other level of government above Drew's boss."

"I know and I don't care. Somewhere in their official manual there must be an instruction…or a proviso…about coexisting with ordinary people and with the communities they serve. Semper Paratus? That's their motto, isn't it? Always at the ready to serve and protect. Shouldn't that apply as well to fostering a community's desire to preserve its history?"

Grace's parents stared at her as if they'd discovered their daughter was a changeling. She couldn't resist a smile.

"Did you say all that to Drew or to his boss? If not, you must. Word for word." Her mother wrapped an arm across Grace's shoulders and pulled her close.

"So what now?" was all her father said.

"I'm not sure. I need some time to think. Plus, I still have to phone Aunt Jane and Suzanna, to fill them in." She stood, feeling so much lighter now. "I should go. I told Julie I wouldn't be long."

"Come for dinner tomorrow, dear," her mother said. "We can talk some more. Maybe plan our next steps."

Grace loved her mother for that faith in her, that her daughter would accomplish exactly what she intended.

"And bring Drew, if he's still in town. He needs to be part of the discussion."

He did, Grace thought, wishing she'd realized that much earlier. Before yesterday and especially today. "I'll let you know about dinner, Mom. I can't promise." She didn't mention Drew. Right at that moment, she wasn't sure when—or if—she'd ever see him again.

Julie was waiting for her near the door, clearly ready to leave and eager to hear her news. "I hope you weren't too busy and sorry I took a bit longer," Grace said.

"Things were slow. A couple of customers—a man looking for a book on lighthouses, which struck me as either a weird coincidence or a direct result of the ad in *The Beacon*—and a young girl looking for a new young adult book that I couldn't find, so you must not have it."

"What's the title?"

"I wrote it down. It's by the computer. So how did it go with your folks? Was your dad upset?"

Julie's friendship in senior year of high school meant she'd had plenty of encounters with Charles. "He was surprisingly matter-of-fact although he did want to know who was in charge here at the store."

"Probably picturing my seventeen-year-old self and wondering why me."

Grace grinned. "No doubt. Listen, thanks so much, Julie." She hugged her and waited by the door while she left. Then she checked the time. More than two hours until five and closing.

As she'd gloomily predicted, the rest of the afternoon dragged and the knowledge that Grace had no plans for the night lowered her mood further. She rearranged some books, checked the calendar for upcoming important events—*none*—and decided she might as well close the store on Mondays now, as well as Sundays. Couldn't she use a two-day break like everyone else?

She glanced at the note Julie had left beside the computer—the book a girl had inquired about.

Always Be Mine. No author's name. She'd check it out later.

About an hour before closing, the doorbell tinkled. Grace looked up sharply from the laptop. A teenage girl with a backpack was walking toward her and Grace sighed. Not Drew.

"Can I help you?"

The girl's eyes darted everywhere but on Grace. Her face was bright red, with an anxious expression that Grace wanted to alleviate right away.

"Is everything okay?"

The girl nodded. "I was here before, when there was another lady working."

"Oh. Are you the girl asking about this book?" Grace held up the note.

Another nod.

"I'm sorry I don't have it but I'll be happy to order it for you. Do you know the author?"

She shook her head. "My friends told me about it. They said it's brand-new and supposed to be good. But don't order it just for me 'cause…"

"Because?"

"I won't be able to buy it anyway." Then

she pulled off her backpack and opened it, pulling out a paperback, which she set on the counter.

Grace recognized it. One of her new purchases on the display table in the children's book section. She frowned.

Before she could speak, the girl blurted, "I'm awful sorry but I took that book on my way out of the store. Before. When that other lady was here."

This was a first and Grace had no idea how to handle shoplifting.

"I knew it was wrong, but I wanted a book so badly. And we only have one car and a new baby so my mom can't drive me to the library in Portland. And my allowance is too small." She gulped a breath. "Books cost a lot."

They did, Grace thought. She gazed at the girl, who was fighting back tears, and remembered all the times she herself had come in for new books. She'd been lucky back then, because occasionally when her allowance ran out, Henry would let her read a book in the store. "No dog-ears," he'd whisper, winking.

"What's your name?"

"Becky," the girl mumbled, staring at the floor. "Becky Oliphant."

"I'm Grace, Becky, and this is my bookstore."

The girl looked up.

"How old are you, Becky?" Grace impulsively asked.

"I'll be fifteen next week."

"Well, would you like to earn a bit of money this summer?"

Becky's eyes widened.

"A part-time job?" Grace went on. "Maybe a couple of hours a day for the summer? If your parents allow, of course."

A big nod, followed by, "Yes, please."

Grace was still smiling at the girl's beaming expression when she flipped over the open sign and locked up for the day. She knew she was taking a chance, but she reasoned Becky didn't have to come back with the book. And she'd come on her own, not dragged in by an embarrassed parent. There were plenty of small tasks she could have her do. As for books...well, perhaps Grace could follow Henry's lead there.

She closed the laptop and turned out the lights. Maybe she'd have dinner in town. Getting out and away from regretful thoughts would be good for her. Then tomorrow, after calling Aunt Jane and Suzanna, she'd begin planning her appeal to the Coast Guard.

She was heading up to her apartment when a hard tapping on the window of the front door stopped her. She closed her eyes, debating whether to ignore this late customer or open up again. It had been a tiring day and her brain urged for the first option. But a sale is a sale, she reminded herself. And this better be one. She unlocked the door and flung it open, thinking if the customer wasn't intending to buy, the show of force might deter her. *Or him.*

Drew's smile was a bit wobbly and his face strained. At his feet sat a medium-sized cooler and he had a blanket tossed over one shoulder, which almost made Grace laugh. Except if she did, she might also cry.

"Are you free to join me for a picnic supper on the beach?"

She was nodding long before she could manage to say, "Yes. Yes, I am."

CHAPTER TWENTY

DREW WAITED DOWNSTAIRS while Grace changed, pacing around and occasionally picking up a book to flip through. He had no idea how this impulse was going to play out, if it was headed for disaster or not. Judging by Grace's smile and the way her eyes lit up when she saw him standing at the door, he figured he had a good shot at fixing things.

He noticed there were still several copies of that author's book, *Stories of the High Seas*, on display and he thumbed through one to the index, curious to see if his own story was there. No, thankfully. Though hadn't the guy mentioned he was thinking of writing another book to include it and perhaps Drew could give him some information? *Not a chance.* But Drew realized it was time to tell Grace. He hoped she wouldn't be pitying.

When she breezed out of her apartment entrance, tote bag in hand, he asked, "Got your bathing suit?"

"Wearing it," she said. "You?"

"Yes, though to be honest, the Maine sea isn't my favorite place to swim."

"Too cold?"

"You bet. Plus, the desire to immerse oneself in water isn't a natural trait in an Iowan farm boy."

Her laugh echoed in the store. "But you joined the Coast Guard!"

"What can I say? Piloting a boat isn't the same as swimming." Though it doesn't always keep you dry, he almost added.

"Do you know that you've barely spoken about your job? Here I've been thinking you've always been connected to lighthouses."

"I guess we still have more to talk about than...well...the current situation. And excuse the bad pun," he added with a nervous laugh.

"Yes, we do."

Drew saw the determination in her face. He'd made the right decision to come back today, rather than wait till tomorrow. As she was locking up, it occurred to him that they could drive. His car was parked in front.

When he suggested it, she said, "That's a good idea, but parking spaces will be at a premium. Summer holidays, you know. Lots of tourists." She thought for a minute and said, "We could park it at Henry's and walk from there. He wouldn't mind."

She texted Henry as he stowed their things in the back of his SUV and when he climbed behind the wheel, she was smiling. "He sent a thumbs-up emoji."

The short drive was quiet, as if neither one wanted to get into a serious conversation. Best done after a swim and a full stomach, Drew figured, but he felt his anxiety build. He needed to focus on reconciling and not reverting to the futile cycle of blame they'd established.

Grace was right about the parking. Despite the supper hour, people were still heading for the beach and Drew wondered if he'd made a mistake in planning a picnic supper there. He'd thought they'd have some privacy and more important, that the neutrality of the place was a better option than the bookstore or her apartment. Now he was doubting that, especially since the end of the beach near Henry's place was closer to the lighthouse. Too late now, he thought as he parked in front of the bungalow.

If Grace had similar concerns, she wasn't revealing them as she helped him unload.

There was no sign of Henry. Drew had thought the old man might come out to greet them and he was thankful he hadn't. This picnic wasn't intended purely for pleasure and Drew feared any distraction would set him off course.

By the time they found a reasonably private place—being at the farthest point of the beach helped—they were both ready for a swim. Like Grace, Drew had worn his bathing suit under his clothes and as they undressed, his gaze kept shifting from Grace to the lighthouse and back to her. Especially to the bikini—*and Grace in it*—which was a serious distraction though one Drew didn't mind.

She was in the water before him, dashing through the foamy waves and dunking almost immediately, a feat Drew admired without any urge to imitate. He was in up to his knees when she emerged and waded back to him, grinning as she extended her arms in what he knew was going to be a bear hug.

"No, no," he said, backing away, but the awkward move coupled with another wave pushed him down. He came up spluttering, reaching for Grace's hand. She was laughing and soon he was, too, until he wrapped his arms around her and held her close, so close she pressed her palms against his chest.

He loosened his grip but kept his hands on her arms and gazed down into her dark eyes, still shining with laughter. "You're beautiful," he said and lowered his mouth to hers.

Her lips were salty-sweet and he might have stood there longer, waves lapping against his legs, but the shouts of nearby children reminded him they weren't alone. "Guess we'd better get dry. Warm up."

"I'm not sure we need warming up." She giggled, taking his hand as they waded to shore.

They toweled off and after she spread out the blanket, Drew opened up the cooler.

"I'm impressed," Grace said as he set food items on the blanket. "You seem to be a pro at this."

"Nope. First time at organizing a picnic, though I have attended a few."

"I think I'm jealous," she murmured.

He looked up from unwrapping a piece of cheese. She was lounging on the blanket, her elbows propping her up, and smiling. The early evening sun behind them gilded the upper part of her body in hues of pink and gold. Drew thought of taking a photo but didn't want the moment to slip past him while he fumbled at his cell phone.

"Jealous of my organizing a picnic?"

"No. Jealous of you having picnics with someone else." She ducked her head to pick up a slice of red pepper from a plastic container of cut vegetables, but he'd seen her face turn pink.

For a minute Drew worried the outing might veer into a direction he'd love for it to go. *Forget the talk. Forget the soul-baring. Just lie on the blanket next to her, bask in the glow she emanates without effort and fill your senses with her presence.* But he knew as much as he wanted to delay having that talk, he couldn't put it off much longer.

"I'm starving." She was looking expectantly at him and the cooler.

Perfect timing, Drew thought. He passed her cheese, a packet of prosciutto and two containers of salad. Then he reached into the grocery bag for the baguette, cutlery and paper plates.

Drew couldn't remember when he'd eaten with such enjoyment. Not even the dinner at The Daily Catch days ago, at the very beginning of the roller-coaster ride that brought them to this moment. He ate half reclining on one elbow so he could watch her, the sea and, off to their left, the lighthouse. She ate with pleasure, licking her fingers and once in a while making sweet humming noises that enchanted Drew. Seagulls careened overhead, occasionally diving for fish or food scraps left behind by other picnickers. Dusk was creeping up on them by the time they could eat no more. People had begun to leave, heading for parked cars or their cottages and homes.

Grace reached for her T-shirt and shorts, pulling them on over her bikini.

"All dry?"

"Yes. And you?"

"Yes." He sat up, reluctant to end this part of the day for the next scene. The one he was now dreading.

By the time he dressed, she'd packed up leftovers and the rest of the picnic items. "My place?" she asked.

"Uh, well, I'd thought we could sit here longer. Watch the sunset." Then an idea occurred. "Let's go up there, to the tower."

When she didn't answer, he turned around. She was staring unhappily at the lighthouse, her face clouded with some emotion he couldn't define. "I've got a key," he added, hoping that might reassure whatever doubts she had.

Still she didn't move.

"Grace," he murmured, "it's okay. Come on. It'll be special to see the last of the sunset from inside, up in the lantern room." He reached for her hand and led her along the road to the path leading up the dune. He was expecting her to balk and hold back but when she didn't, he let go of her hand and proceeded ahead. Once he looked back to see her standing in front of the shuttered cottage where he and Henry had sat, his first day in the Cove. She was staring at it with what looked like a forlorn expression. Then she noticed him waiting for her and began to climb.

She caught up to him a few seconds after he'd reached the spot in the path where remnants of flowers were scattered. The wind had blown away the flag from days ago and the tide had disintegrated the firecracker packet.

"It isn't Suzanna," Grace said.

Drew swung around from unlocking the door. "Huh?"

"The person who brought this stuff isn't Suzanna. When I was talking to her the other day, she said she hasn't been out here."

It was a mystery that no doubt would be

answered at some point in time, he figured. He reached the two concrete steps leading up to the lighthouse door and unlocked it. When he tugged the door open, he turned to see her peering down at the ruined shrine.

"Grace?"

She looked at him, her eyes both sad and fearful.

"What is it?" He moved toward her.

"I haven't actually been inside for years. Long before Brandon. I... I'm not sure I can do this."

Drew reached for her hand. "You can, Grace. It's just a place. There are no ghosts here."

The look in her face cast doubt on that but he refused to let her retreat. Whatever fears she had, he sensed this was the time to face them. With him.

"Come," he whispered. "I'm with you." And he slowly led her inside.

HE WAS A kind man, Grace thought. The way he guided her into the lighthouse, one arm draped casually over her shoulders as if they were taking an evening stroll. He seemed to know intuitively that her legs were numb, frozen to the grassy path, and her heart rate so sluggish she could hardly breathe. He spoke the whole time, pointing out things in the small room they stepped into.

"This is where the keeper would store things. Tools, extra bulbs, cleaning materials and so on. The keeper for a tower like this would have had a place of his own nearby. Maybe one of those old cottages at the foot of the dune, like the one you were just looking at."

Cassie's place. She watched him move around, touching the walls and the dusty shelves.

"It looks like someone has stayed here at some point in time though. These candles have been lit, maybe with that cigarette lighter." He suddenly looked her way. "Are you okay?"

She nodded but inside she was crying, *No, I'm not. Had Brandon been the one who was here, lighting the candles? Waiting impatiently for the tide to recede?* She remembered hearing from other kids that the door wasn't always locked back in those days.

It was getting darker outside and in. Drew flicked the cigarette lighter, but its fuel had long evaporated. "Guess I won't be lighting the candles, so this will have to do." He held up his cell phone. "Come on. Let's go up top and watch the rest of the sunset."

She hesitated at the base of the spiral staircase, watching him climb nimbly up the steep, narrow stairs. Then she slowly followed, pausing on each step to take a calming breath. The space at the top was smaller than she'd expected.

"Come and see this." Drew was staring into a large fixture. "There's the lens and the lamp—basically a big light bulb. You can see it's burned out—has been for a while. That tarnished bit of metal behind it is the reflector. Or was. And see the windows, how filthy they are?" He stopped to wipe at some grime on one of the panes. "I'm afraid we're not going to see much of the sunset after all. Most of the dirt is on the outside but come here anyway."

Grace reached for his hand, letting him lead her to the west side of the room.

He peered through the glass on the land side of the lighthouse. "Darn. Can't see much. Guess this wasn't such a great idea after all." He smiled at Grace. "Let's go back down. We can talk there, if you like."

If you like. He was giving her an out. Yet she knew postponing the talk until they returned to her place might bring other complications. She thought of his kiss when they were in the water and the way he held her so tightly she had to push against him, afraid she'd smother. At the same time, she'd wanted him to shield her from the chilly water as well as the misery of the past couple of days.

"Okay," she finally said.

THERE WAS NO view down below, but the semi-darkness lent a coziness to the room. Drew sat on the floor, leaning against the brick wall, and patted the space next to him. Grace had been so silent he wasn't sure if she'd talk at all. But that was okay. He would. He needed to. When she sat beside him, he put his arm across her shoulders and drew her closer.

"You said earlier that you knew very little about my role in the Coast Guard. I've been giving the impression that I've been in the lighthouse division for some time, but actually it's only been a few months."

She pulled back to look up at him. "Seriously? You seem like such an expert."

Drew laughed. "Researching lighthouses as a hobby growing up made me an amateur know-it-all. I'm sure some of the people in the Historical Society could tell you a lot more about them. No, I transferred to Portland eight months ago to a desk job but shortly afterward, I took over the lighthouse maintenance team section when its former head retired. Before Portland, I was stationed in Southwest Harbor."

"I remember you telling Terry something about that, at his book talk. I didn't hear it all 'cause I was dealing with customers. Something about a disaster?"

We got to that pretty quickly, Drew thought. Just as well. No chance of backing out now.

"I was the pilot—or captain—of a search and rescue boat. It was a small one—what's called a response boat. There was just me and my mate, Jake. We got an SOS from a fishing trawler in trouble up the coast off Bar Harbor. A long way out. The tail end of a hurricane had swept through the area the day before and winds were still high. I've no idea why those fishermen decided to go out, but they did. We had a couple of bigger boats at Southwest Harbor station, but they were out on the water and not close enough to take the call. My Defender—or Response boat—was the only one available.

"By the time we reached the trawler, it was capsizing, turned on its port side. The winds had picked up, too. The men were hanging off the upended starboard side. I heard later they'd been in that position twenty minutes or so. Jake and I set about lifting them off and onto our boat. It was an experience I never want to go through again." He closed his eyes, the memory of his panic and fear sweeping over him. Grace's hand pressed gently on his forearm.

"We had everyone on board with just the trawler's owner still clinging on when we spotted a super wave rolling our way. I had seconds to decide whether to attempt to get him and risk my own boat with the men we'd rescued getting caught in the wave, too, or leave him." Drew stopped, seeing again the terrified faces of the fishermen, staring at him with both hope and sorrow. They'd known he really only had one choice.

"You had to leave," Grace whispered, taking his hand in hers.

Drew couldn't speak. They sat silently for a long time, listening to their own breathing and the whoosh of night breezes outside the tower. Then Drew straightened up, letting go of her hand and straining to hear a new sound. One he didn't want to hear. Water washing against rocks.

"We've lost track of time, Grace," he said. "I think the tide is coming in. We have to go."

When Drew pushed open the door, he saw in the shaft of moonlight that the six to eight feet between the tower's concrete base and the grassy path was now covered with seawater. The problem was that in the dark, they could be jostled by the tide's current onto the rocks around the base.

He kept his tone casual. "Yeah, so we're going to have to be careful to avoid those," he said, pointing to the rocks. "It's dark and they're wet and slippery. I'm going to close the door behind us but won't lock it until later, after the tide's gone down."

"Why don't we just stay inside until then?"

He turned to see her staring intently at the black water. "That'll be hours, Grace. The water's still rising. It won't be deep yet. Trust me."

She looked from him to the open doorway again, her face waxen in the faint light.

"This is what we're going to do." He was saying this as much for himself as for her. "I'm going to step onto the first step here and when both my feet are steady on it, I'll go onto the second. When I'm steady, I'll take your hand and you'll go down onto the first step. When you're beside me on the second, I'm going to close the tower door. Okay?"

She gave a solemn nod.

"Then I'm going to move slowly off the last step." He didn't want to contemplate this next point but had to warn her. "Once our feet touch the sandy bottom, depending on the depth, we will wade or even breaststroke but," he swiftly added at the alarm in her eyes, "I doubt the water will be deep enough for that. I promise you I won't let go of you until we're both on dry ground." He managed a smile. "Okay, shall we do it?"

Her "okay" was barely a whisper.

Drew stepped off the threshold, the shock of the cold water catching his breath. It was already knee-deep, and he felt a surge of doubt over his decision to vacate the tower. When he set his other foot down, waiting for a second to make sure he was stable, he reached for Grace's hand. She stood frozen on the doorstep. "You can do this."

After what seemed a long moment, she placed one foot into the water and gasped. Because of their height difference, the water reached her thigh. She swayed against him and Drew held his breath.

"Now the other one," he said, urging her on

in his mind, the water's temperature already numbing his legs.

When she was next to him on the second step, Drew felt behind him for the tower door and closed it. Then he placed a foot onto the sandy bottom and it was then he felt the strength of the tide current. They didn't have time to waste. He set his other foot onto the bottom and waited until he was stable enough to help her down. Her body was trembling as she leaned against him, thrown off-balance by the depth—almost at her waist now—and the tide surge.

"Okay. Almost there." But staring at the six feet of dark water ahead, Drew wasn't feeling so optimistic.

They inched forward, pausing whenever the current pulled at their legs. He could barely feel his hand enfolding hers and he prayed the water's depth would keep steady until they reached dry land. If only his mind held steady, too, but snips of memory attacked his concentration, spinning him back to that day a year ago.

Suddenly a wave surged, knocking Grace over. Her hand slipped out of his and she disappeared beneath the water. Drew's shout was drowned out by the wind and waves. For a paralyzing second, he was back at the helm of the response boat, unable to move.

CHAPTER TWENTY-ONE

IT WAS A darkness so dense her mind could feel it. But not her body, as it instinctively tried to push her up. Except where exactly was up or down? For a terrifying instant Grace couldn't tell and her arms flailed at the water, as if it were a beast she was trying to tame. Until something grabbed her arm and she panicked, thinking she'd been snagged by an underwater creature. She kicked hard to break free. Then she broke the surface, choking and gasping for air. Drew's arms were around her and he was dragging her through the water, the waves rolling against them, pushing and pulling in every direction. Grace stumbled when her feet hit dry ground and Drew's grasp loosened. They both fell and lay panting on the hard, sandy surface.

Another wave hit Grace—one of nausea. *This is what Brandon went through.* The panic and the relentless power of the tide. And he didn't have someone like Drew to help him. When the pounding in her chest eased, Grace whispered, "Thank you."

Drew rolled over onto his side and smoothed away the strands of hair plastered on her cheeks and forehead. "I don't know how high the water will rise and we need to get dry," he said.

His voice was strained and raspy. Grace watched him get up on his knees and then wait, his chest heaving with exhaustion. There was enough light to see that his face was ashen. She thought at once of his steady tone as they went into the water and his story about the sea rescue. Whatever memories probably swept over him as he was dragging her to safety, he'd been able to push them aside.

When he was on his feet, he reached down for both of her hands and gently pulled her to her feet. They staggered down the dune to where they'd left their things. Grace watched, numb with cold, while Drew tossed items aside until he found the blanket. He rubbed her arms and legs with it until they tingled and wrapped it around her.

When her trembling eased, she said, "I'm okay. You get dry now." In spite of the balmy night, they were both shivering. Grace still couldn't move. "I kept thinking about Brandon the whole time I was underwater. That maybe this was my punishment." She saw him frown.

"Let's get to the car, Grace," was all he said. He picked up the cooler and her tote bag, then clasped her hand in his free one.

There were no lights in Henry's place when they reached the car. "I wonder what time it is," Grace said as Drew helped her into the passenger side. She sensed she wasn't thinking clearly. Everything around her—Henry's bungalow, the halo around the streetlight and the cool leather of the car seat—melded in a blurry collage of touch and sound. There were no edges to hold on to.

Suddenly Drew was revving the engine and the car was moving slowly down the street, around the corner and onto the waterfront road. Grace dug her fingers into the armrest.

"Where are we going?" Her voice sounded peculiar—thin and taut, like a wire. She saw him look sharply at her, as if he'd only discovered she was there. The notion made her giggle.

"Grace," he said in a tone that immediately got her attention. "We're going to your place."

Later she tried to recall the interval be-

tween leaving Henry's and sitting on the sofa
in her apartment, holding a mug of something hot—maybe tea—but the time span
was blank until Drew sank down beside her.
He was drinking from a mug, too, and she
watched him set it down on the coffee table
in front of them before reaching for hers and
placing it next to his.

"Where's your cell phone?" he asked and
she wanted to laugh again, the question was
so unexpected. But a tiny part of her brain
suggested she shouldn't. Slowly objects
around her began to form into recognizable
shapes with stark outlines.

"Um, I think I left it here somewhere."

"Okay. Just that mine's toast now. Where
do you usually leave it?"

She noticed him glance around the room,
as if waiting for the phone to raise its hand.
Here. Another suppressed giggle. Grace took
a deep breath and released it in a long exhale.
"Maybe on the nightstand beside my bed?"

She watched him get up and head for her
bedroom, returning seconds later with a
phone in his hand. "Why?" she asked as he
sat next to her again.

"In case I need to call someone to come
and stay with you."

"You're here. *You* can stay."

His eyes were serious and he kept them fixed on hers. "I will, Grace. And right now you're going into your room to change and get into bed."

She nodded. "This sofa isn't big enough for you."

His smile was the first she'd seen in hours. Or so it seemed. "If you've got an extra pillow and blanket, I'll be fine on the floor."

A faint disappointment breezed through her. It would be nice to feel his warmth and his strength close beside her all night long, to chase away the nightmares she anticipated once the lights were out and she was alone in the dark.

By the time she was under the covers, the familiarity of everything around her had returned. Drew tapped on her door and opened it slightly when she said, "Come in."

He moved to the bedside and silently watched her for a long moment. Then he bent down and kissed her on the forehead. "You look better now," he murmured. "I can see some color in your cheeks."

"Are you still going to stay?"

He smiled. "I am. I found a pillow and blanket where you said, in the hall closet."

Had she? She couldn't remember telling him that but knowing he would be in the next room eased her mind. "Drew?"

He turned around on his way out of the room. "Yes?"

"You saved my life."

He shook his head. "You'd have been fine, Grace. You just slipped. The water wasn't over our heads."

"But it was strong. I couldn't fight against it."

"We managed, Grace. Together." He looked down at her for a long moment. "Sleep well. We'll talk in the morning." He switched off the lamp on her nightstand.

After he closed the door, Grace lay for what seemed hours, forcing her mind away from the rush of water and suffocating blackness. None of her nightmares over Brandon equaled the intensity of those seconds underwater and for the first time she'd caught a glimpse of the panic and fear that he must have been feeling that night. She knew there was no way she could ever make up for what happened. No memorial would bring her cousin back. But she could do something. She could tell the truth to those who deserved to know. Her family—all of them. This revelation kept her awake most of the night. What finally lulled her to sleep was Drew's calm face, his worried eyes and strong hands. The kind of hands Grace would like to have nearby, always.

The aroma of coffee roused her next morning. She'd slept well after all and felt energized, relieved to have her old self back. She slipped into sweatpants and a T-shirt, wanting something cozy for the talk she knew she had to have with him. *Wanted* to have. If anyone could listen without interruption or judgment to what she'd done all those years ago, it would be Drew. Still, Grace hesitated at her bedroom door. She wasn't certain about the judgment part. What if a teeny seed of doubt about her—worry about the kind of person she was now—were to spring up in him and ruin everything? What if he didn't like her anymore, afterward?

She took a deep breath and opened the door.

HE KNEW HE needed to give her plenty of time. They'd finished the coffee and scones he'd brought back to her apartment from Mable's and had a brief debate about immersing his cell phone in a bowl of dried rice.

"What've you got to lose?" she'd teased,

grinning, and he felt such relief that the Grace he knew and loved—*yes, he told himself, it is love*—was back. When she suggested they leave the kitchen for the sitting area, he guessed by her sober expression that she was ready to talk.

"This is a long story," she began, "going back to the summer I turned fifteen. Seventeen years ago. I had just finished my freshman year and was pretty insecure in those days. I was a bit of a nerd, with few friends. Reading was my pleasure and main pastime. But a girl in tenth grade took pity on me toward the end of the school year. She started talking to me and soon we were friends. She lived near the beach with her mother. You must have seen her place. It's all boarded up now. I heard her mother is in a nursing home in Portland."

Drew nodded, trying to keep his focus through this meandering start. "Uh-huh," was all he said, reluctant to distract her further with any question or comment. Maybe she needed to begin this way.

"Her name was—*is*—Cassie Fielding and I worshipped her. She was daring and unafraid to speak her mind to anyone, like boys and sometimes even teachers. She was popular, too, in her own way although looking back now, I think some kids might have been intimidated by her. But I would have done anything to keep her friendship. I have to emphasize that fact, so maybe you can understand what happened later."

That got Drew's attention. "Okay," he said.

"There was another girl, too. Ella Jacobs. She was a summer kid. In those days, there were two groups—the full-time residents, like me and Cassie, and the summer kids who came for July and August every year. They were regular vacationers and we all got to know and accept them. But at the same time, they weren't from the Cove. The difference between us was always there. Do you know what I mean?"

"I think so. We had something similar back in Iowa. The farm kids and the townies."

"Yes! We were the townies, here all year round in good weather and bad, with families and neighbors going through hard times, like divorces or unemployment and sicknesses. We knew all about each other whereas what we knew about the summer kids was only what we saw or heard during vacation. They told us things about their lives in the cities they came from, but they were things we could only see in our imaginations."

Drew suppressed his impatience. Her story, however convoluted it seemed, needed to be told—and heard.

After a pause—perhaps to gather her thoughts?—Grace continued.

"I was actually friends with Ella long before Cassie. Every summer for years her parents rented a cottage that my father owned. He's sold most of them now, but back then he had a few near the beach that he rented out. I think we started being friends when I was about twelve and she was thirteen." Grace suddenly smiled. "We met here. Well, downstairs in Henry's bookstore. She loved to read, too, and she was buying a book that I had just finished. I recommended the book and we left the store together, talking about our favorite authors. And that was it. We just clicked. We were together almost every day and at the end of the summer, we traded the books we hadn't read, so we'd have something new to read when we had to say goodbye after Labor Day." Grace stopped then. "Is there more coffee? I feel like a boost."

"I can make some for you."

"I'll do it. I need a break." She got up from beside him on the sofa and stretched.

Drew watched her lithe body move and had an abrupt image of the Grace from last night—smaller and forlorn—lost in her fog of shock. He wanted to take her into his arms and kiss her but knew she had to finish her story. He followed her into the kitchen while she brewed another pot of coffee and was content to simply observe her every move—the quick opening and closing of cupboards, squinting at the water level in the glass coffeepot before pouring the water into the machine, flicking the on switch and spinning around unexpectedly to face him and quip, "Too bad the scones are gone."

He smiled. "I could get some more."

She pursed her lips. "No. I need to finish this." Then she glanced away. "Otherwise all of what I felt last night will be for nothing."

Drew tensed, remembering her cryptic remark about being punished. The story that minutes ago was ordinary now seemed ominous. The coffee maker beeped then and the chance to ask her about that was gone.

"Do you need to go somewhere today? I mean, is it okay if I finish?" she asked, pouring their coffee. She raised her head to look at him.

He saw the uncertainty in her face and wondered whether she was hoping for a reprieve. Or maybe she was worried about how he was processing what he'd heard so far? He chose his words carefully. "If you feel you want or *need* to tell me what happened that summer, Grace, then you should."

"Thanks. Yes, I do need to."

He saw the determination in her face and wanted so much to take her into his arms and tell her everything was going to be all right. At least, that was his hope.

When they took their coffees back to the living room, she sat in the armchair opposite the sofa where he was sitting. Drew wondered if she wanted that small distance between them as a kind of buffer.

She started where she'd left off—the summer that Cassie became the third person in the Grace and Ella friendship. Drew imagined what was about to unfold—a teenage threesome of friends could be complicated.

"Cassie wasn't into books the way Ella and I were, but she was fun and so was Ella. They had that in common. The three of us were always together, especially at my house." She paused. "Ella and Cassie were my friends and I had been the link, the one who connected the three of us until suddenly… I wasn't."

Although Drew was guessing where this familiar tale was heading, he couldn't figure out how it led to the lighthouse and Grace's cousin Brandon.

"It's funny to think about now but at the time it definitely wasn't. See, I wasn't the one attracting their interest, it was Ben. What made things worse was that I didn't know about Cassie's feelings for him either, until after. She kept dropping hints about Ella, but I didn't want to believe her. When I realized Cassie was right, I was angry at Ella and at the same time, jealous of my brother who was getting her attention."

Grace gave a sad smile. "So I was all too willing to go along with Cassie's plan." She brought her hands to her face, massaging her forehead and temples.

He could see the toll the memories were taking on her and wondered if she wanted to take a break. He was about to suggest that when she said, "That's why I agreed to take notes to Ella and Brandon. It was supposed to be a practical joke, but it ended up a tragedy. For all of us."

Her voice caught. Drew thought about getting her a glass of water but decided not to. Instead he sat still, hearing the rest of it and forcing his mind away from the pain in her eyes. When she reached the part where Brandon and Ella realized they'd been tricked, Drew leaned forward on the sofa.

"We ran back to the bonfire and a few minutes later, Ella showed up. She didn't say a word to us, just tossed her note into the flames and left. I never saw her again." Grace's eyes brimmed with tears. "Cassie and I weren't friends any longer either."

Drew watched her struggle to compose herself.

"I thought Brandon had gone home, but he didn't. No one knows for sure what happened but the police inquiry and coroner's inquest determined that he might have gone to the lighthouse—it wasn't always locked in those days and teens often hung out there. Then the tide came up and he tried to swim to shore but got caught in the currents." She stopped to catch her breath. "Just like we did last night. Except Brandon had no one to save him."

Drew closed his eyes. *This is what her insistence on the memorial is all about and why it means so much to her. Atoning in some way for her part in a thoughtless, childish prank.* He heard her softly cry. Tears were rolling down her cheeks and Drew saw the weight of that seventeen-year-old burden in the slump of her shoulders and the resignation in her eyes. He knew that, like his own role in the botched sea rescue, there was no way back for either of them.

"Grace," he murmured. "You were fifteen. You were a kid. It's all right." He got up from the sofa to pull her up into his arms, shushing her weeping until it finally stopped.

CHAPTER TWENTY-TWO

CONFESSION WAS SUPPOSED to be good for the soul and Grace did feel lighter inside. At least she was no longer the only person to know how much she regretted her actions seventeen years ago. Now there was Drew. If only confession could also erase memory.

Somewhere in the apartment a cell phone was ringing. Grace wiped her eyes with the back of her hand and looked up at Drew. "Yours or mine?"

"Well, mine is sitting in a bowl of rice so…"

"And wherever mine is now, it can—"

"Go to voice mail."

Laughter was good, too, she decided. She moved out of his embrace and arched her back, yawning.

"Tired?" Drew asked, grinning. He tugged her back to him, kneading the tension at the nape of her neck.

Leaning against him, Grace murmured, "Relieved."

He gently turned her around. "Thank you," he whispered.

"Why are you thanking *me*?"

"For trusting me enough to tell me your story."

For *loving* you enough, Grace wanted to add. "I do trust you, even *more* now that you know my story. Only two other people do and neither of them is likely to return to the Cove."

"So where do you go from here?" he asked.

"What do you mean?" But she knew what he meant.

"What's your next step?"

"My parents," she whispered. "And Ben. Then Aunt Jane and Suzanna."

"Want me to go with you? Whenever you decide to speak to them, I mean."

"No. But thank you. I appreciate your thoughtfulness. I need to do this on my own."

"I figured you might want to but if you change your mind…"

She leaned toward him, kissing him on the cheek. "I won't. I can't. In fact, I'll call them right now." She stepped away from his arms and started to walk away. "Where is my phone, by the way? I think you had it last night."

"On the kitchen table. You were a bit out of it last night. I wanted to keep it handy in case I had to call emergency or something."

His smile wasn't reassuring. "Um, I hope I didn't embarrass myself."

"Not at all. The aftereffects of…you know…what happened. I was worried."

"The whole night was like a movie, wasn't it?"

"A bad one," he said quietly. "Until this morning."

"Yes." She was afraid to ask the question that had been troubling her since her talk. *Do you feel differently toward me now? No*, she decided. *Sometime soon I'll ask him that but not yet.* "I should listen to my voice mail," she said, heading to the kitchen for her phone.

There were three messages. Two from her mother. "I didn't hear back from you about dinner today. I hope everything's all right. Maybe you'll come for lunch instead? To talk about your plans for the lighthouse?" And the last one from Ben, who said, "Mom's worried because you haven't replied to her messages. Can you call her, please? And I emailed you that report."

Drew came into the kitchen while she was listening and when she finished, she said, "Mom's asked me to lunch today—to talk about the lighthouse. Ben was calling to say she was worried when I didn't reply. I guess it's back to real life now."

His face was thoughtful, but he didn't respond to her mention of the lighthouse. What had happened yesterday—the unexpected meeting with the Historical Society and Drew's boss—had yet to be discussed. Grace waited a few more minutes for him to comment about their unfinished business.

"I better call Mom now and tell her I can make it for lunch." She kept her eyes on Drew, but he simply nodded.

As she turned to go to her bedroom, he suddenly asked, "Do you want me to wait for you here?"

"I don't know how long I'll be, but we still need to talk later. You know…"

"Yes," he said, keeping his eyes on hers. He didn't speak again for a frustrating few seconds. Then, "I think I'll head back to Portland. I have some business to finish up but I'll be back, I promise. Later today or maybe tomorrow."

Grace hid her disappointment. There

wasn't time to continue their talk about the lighthouse, but a sign from him about his intentions would have bolstered her spirits, especially now that she was about to face the biggest challenge of her life—admitting to her family what she'd done seventeen years ago.

"Okay," was all she said. On her way to the bedroom, she heard him gathering his things and by the time she'd changed, he was gone.

An hour later she was sitting at her parents' kitchen table and biting her fingernails.

"I haven't seen you do that since you were a teenager," her mother remarked as she popped a quiche into the oven. "And in spite of what Ben might have told you, I wasn't worried because you didn't answer my calls last night. I wanted to know before I went to the trouble of making this." She gestured to the oven and the quiche inside it.

But Grace knew otherwise. She'd heard the relief in her mother's voice an hour ago when she returned her phone call. "How long till the quiche will be ready?" she asked.

"About forty-five minutes. Why, are you hungry?"

"I can wait, but when is Ben coming?"

"I told him noon and it's almost that now.

I always give him some leeway, you know, because he's so seldom punctual."

"True enough," Grace said. "And Dad?"

"He's upstairs. He'll come down when everyone's here. What's this all about, dear?"

"I have something to tell everybody but not until Dad and Ben are here."

"Does it have to do with tearing down the lighthouse? Because Ben has some thoughts about that."

"It kind of does, but not the tearing down part."

Her mother's frown prompted Grace to add, "You'll understand."

"If you say so though right now, I'm very puzzled and these ambiguous remarks don't help at all."

Grace sighed, wishing she hadn't said anything. There was still the quiche to be eaten, unless she told them beforehand. No. Then no one would have an appetite once they heard the truth and her mother had gone to some trouble to bake the quiche. She sighed again. She didn't even like quiche that much.

Lunch was eventually consumed and in record time even for the Winterses, Grace thought as she watched Ben take their empty plates to the sink. Meals had often been anxiety-inducing when she was a teen—rushed, sometimes fraught with tension or outright arguments. Most of them centered on Ben, whose impatience and occasional temper matched his father's.

But except for small talk, this meal had been mostly silent. No one wanted to raise the lighthouse situation, which was okay with Grace because she didn't want to be sidetracked from her real purpose in coming for lunch. When her mother asked if anyone wanted tea and they all shook their heads, Grace knew it was time.

"I need to tell you something," she began when her mother and Ben were sitting down again. "And it's not about the lighthouse." She knew they were anticipating a different story. She took a moment to calm her nerves, picturing Drew's face and his steady, encouraging eyes.

"It's about Brandon." She hesitated, noting her father's frown, took another deep breath and said, "It wasn't Ella Jacobs who sent him the note about meeting her that night near the lighthouse. It was me."

Much later, Grace realized that for the first time in ages no one in the family had interrupted her and, ironically, she'd been wishing someone had. Their silence had been unnerving, though facial expressions and eyes had revealed much—shock, horror, disappointment. Not blame and for that, she was grateful. But when she finished, they did have questions.

Her mother pulled her into a hug, stroking her hair and cheek. "Why didn't you tell us right away?"

"I was afraid to. I thought you'd be angry or even worse. When Ben told me he found the note I'd left for Brandon and gave it to the police, I knew I should have said something but I was afraid. Then I heard that Ella was questioned and I thought if they knew Cassie and I were responsible, we'd be arrested. I don't know why Ella didn't tell the police about us. Maybe she tried to but because she'd thrown her note into the fire, she couldn't prove anything."

Her mother shook her head. "Oh, Gracie, how frightened you must have been. I wish you'd told us, so we could have helped you."

"What were you afraid of?" her father wanted to know. "There was no actual crime here. Just a very unfortunate decision to play a mean trick on your cousin."

"I was fifteen. I didn't know anything about

criminal acts. I just knew that something I did led to Brandon's death and I thought you would never forgive me," Grace said, watching her brother pacing about the kitchen.

"It wasn't even your idea," her mother went on. "That girl, Cassie. She had some kind of control over you as I recall."

"Cassie didn't make me do it, Mom." It was difficult for them to accept what she'd told them without editing her story, lessening her role in it.

Suddenly Ben spun around to face her. "Ella had nothing at all to do with this whole thing? She was basically a victim, too, of that—I won't call it a joke because there was nothing funny about it—that thoughtless plan you and Cassie cooked up."

Grace flinched. She hadn't expected this reaction from Ben, who'd always been her staunchest supporter in almost everything. But of course, she ought to have factored in Ella.

"Ella was—" he said no more, leaving the room and seconds later, slamming the front door.

Evelyn turned to Grace. "He'll be okay. He's going through a rough time right now with his divorce and—" she shifted her gaze briefly toward her husband "—at work. Don't worry about him."

Grace figured he wouldn't be the only person in the family, or even the town, to be angry at her.

"You'll have to tell Jane and Suzanna," Charles said.

"I plan to. I phoned Suzanna before I came here and asked her to have Aunt Jane come to the Cove for an important meeting. Something we couldn't discuss on the phone. She thinks it's about the memorial."

Evelyn looked at Grace, sitting on the edge of the chair across from her. "Do you want to stay here for a while? Have a rest in your old bedroom, perhaps?"

Grace struggled to smile. "Thanks, Mom, but I should go back to my place."

"And what about the lighthouse being torn down? Is it really going to happen? Can Drew do anything about it?"

Grace shook her head. "I don't know, but maybe not. I got the impression his boss told him it had to be torn down."

"That doesn't sound good. He can't go against his boss."

"I guess not. Anyway, I don't think Drew

would ever consider that." *Maybe not even for me*, she thought.

"He's nice. I like him and I hope we see more of him."

Me, too. Though her earlier optimism about any kind of future with Drew Spencer was slowly fading. There was still the lighthouse problem to be solved.

Her father suddenly cleared his throat and stood. He'd never been the kind of father to reveal his emotions—unless they were connected to impatience or anger. "Think I'll go have a nap," he mumbled, but on his way out, he paused beside Grace and placed a hand on her shoulder. "You did well, Gracie. That took courage. Come and see us tomorrow. We can talk some more."

He left the room before Grace had a chance to speak. It was the first time in years that he'd used her childhood name. She looked at her mother and burst into tears.

DREW BOOTED UP his laptop as soon as he was back in his apartment. The drive to Portland had been a good opportunity to gather his thoughts. Well, he amended, *some* of them— the ones that hadn't been devoted to Grace. Those had bombarded his weary mind basically the whole way. He was still processing her story, especially the part she played in it. The entire narrative was a compelling portrait of the teenage Grace. *Gracie.*

He wished now he'd thought of something more to say than "you were only a kid," but his focus had been on the regret in her eyes that he knew no words of comfort could erase. Experience had taught him that. Even now, a year after Southwest Harbor, he sometimes caught that same expression reflected back from his bathroom mirror. Perhaps there were no words anyway, only shoulders to lean on. Or cry on.

Yesterday, Jim had asked for a revised report. Drew couldn't recall his boss's exact words. Something about keeping his eyes on the target, whatever that meant. They'd been talking about the conflict of interest with Grace, and Jim had leaped to the right conclusion, Drew thought.

He stared glumly at the computer screen. What he was about to do could likely jeopardize his chance at the promotion. But it was no coin toss. There was only one solution to the problem Jim had mentioned. He began to type.

Later that night Drew called Grace, after his phone had finally begun working.

"You were right," he said.

"About what?"

"The rice. I'm obviously using my phone right now. I wanted to find out how things went today with your parents."

Her hesitation worried him until she said, "Better than I imagined. Tomorrow I'll call on my aunt and cousin while I still have the nerve."

"It's not nerve, Grace. It's courage." She was quiet then and he thought he heard a sniffle. "Are you sure you're okay?"

"I am…just that my father said almost the same thing and it was so unlike him that I spent most of the rest of the day thinking about him and all these random things from my childhood."

"We have lots of things to talk about ourselves, Grace."

Another silence. Then, "We do."

After he assured her he'd return to the Cove the next day, Drew ended the call. He took a few minutes to read over his revised report one more time before emailing it to Jim and going to bed.

Early the next morning he was standing

in front of Jim's desk, squeezing his hands into fists and releasing them over and over behind his back while his boss read the print copy of the report.

"I don't check my email on the weekend unless I'm expecting something important. And you were supposed to be here tomorrow morning, not today," Jim had announced at Drew's question on entering the office moments ago.

The terse reply hadn't been a good sign and now that Jim seemed to be unreasonably slow going over the report, Drew's anxiety level soared. His heart rate picked up and he guessed circles of perspiration were already visible in his uniform shirt.

Finally, Jim set the report down and raised his head. But he took his time, clearly thinking before he spoke. Drew wasn't sure whether that was promising or not. At least he hadn't flung the paper back at him and ordered him from the room. That wasn't Jim's style.

"It was obvious to me yesterday that you have feelings for Grace Winters. Now, I don't know if they're reciprocated and that's none of my business, but I was worried that your judgment might be clouded by your emotions. Hence my decision to have you take another look at your report. I wanted to know how much it would change from your original one."

Drew cleared his throat. "I—"

"I'm not finished, Drew. I can see that you have very wisely heeded my advice when I suggested yesterday that you keep your eyes on the target. This report tells me that you have done so."

"I'm not sure I understand, sir."

"The target was always the lighthouse, correct? Whether it ought to be torn down or sold."

Drew nodded.

"I worried your personal target was to please Grace—her memorial plan. I know that's important—for her at any rate—but I was looking for something more about the community in that town. *Lighthouse Cove*. What you've written here shows me how much you've come to like and care for it. I saw some of those feelings the other day when you were with the people from the Historical Society and that friend you've made— Henry. You've presented a solid case for the tower's preservation, given the aftermath of that tragedy and its importance to the town."

Drew unclenched his fists. Every muscle in his body slowly relaxed as he listened to Jim, though his mind was racing far ahead, out of the office and halfway to the Cove before Jim finished reading.

But then his boss looked up, frowning. "I see that a structural assessment has already been done, but not by one of our engineers. Did you authorize that?"

Drew sensed he wasn't off the hook yet. "Um, no, I didn't, sir. It was arranged by a civilian."

"Ah. I'm thinking that civilian might have been someone you know?"

If Drew hadn't seen the glimmer of amusement in Jim's eyes his anxiety might have reappeared. He nodded.

"Okay, well perhaps you can get a copy of that report and send it to me." Jim continued staring at the paper in his hand for what seemed an interminable moment to Drew. Then he raised his head and smiled. "All right then, I will endorse your report and add my personal recommendation, as well." He studied Drew a minute longer. "But I ought to warn you, I can't guarantee the success of your job application. Though I intend to support it."

"Thank you, sir. I appreciate that very much."

"Relax, Drew. You've done well. The town can apply to purchase the lighthouse and I'm sure you'll be able to assist Grace with that."

Drew thought his boss had winked but decided later he must have been mistaken.

GRACE BELIEVED WITH all her heart that Drew would come back. He'd promised and although she still had so much more to learn about him, she knew he kept his promises. Even if they weren't always in her favor. That was one of his traits she admired most. He was flexible when it came to plans or decisions, but not with principles or ethics.

It had been a mixed-up morning, complicated further by information that left her already busy mind spinning. She'd noticed the slip of paper Becky had handed her yesterday, with the title of the book that had garnered rave reviews, and decided to order a few copies. This new interest in the bookstore surprised her and she wondered if it had something to do with Drew. Or the beginning of a future she'd never dared dream about.

When she typed *Always Be Mine* into the Google search bar, a flurry of sites appeared and with them, the name E. M. Jacobs.

Grace clicked on the author's website and gasped. *Ella Mae Jacobs*. And there she was in some photographs—older, but even more beautiful—smiling confidently into the camera. Grace logged on to her book supplier's website and ordered a dozen copies of the novel. She suddenly thought of Ben's face when he realized Ella hadn't been involved in the prank and his voice when he'd uttered her name. Perhaps there was something she could do about that—another way to make up for that day.

But right now, she had a meeting to attend with her aunt and cousin. The stomach rumbling she had prior to talking to her parents was nothing compared to the stress headache, the clammy hands and rapid heartbeat she was experiencing as she set out for the hotel where they were waiting. Yesterday when she'd confessed to her parents, she'd feared their disappointment and questions she couldn't answer—like *how could you or why?* But they were her parents. Forgiveness would come. With Brandon's mother and sister, Grace had no such assurance.

When the hotel receptionist told her to go on into Suzanna's office, Grace had stood, her cold hand grasping the door handle, a full thirty seconds before opening it.

Suzanna, sitting behind her desk, and Aunt Jane in a chair opposite, stopped whatever they'd been discussing to stare at Grace as she closed the door behind her.

"Have a seat, Grace," Suzanna said. "And some tea?" She gestured to the tea tray on the desk.

Grace shook her head. She didn't dare lose her momentum. "Thanks for coming, Aunt Jane. I know this is last-minute but it's important and really couldn't wait."

"Something about the memorial, dear?"

"Not really, but kind of." She took a deep breath, trying to focus on the main story rather than digress as she so often tended to do. "It's about Brandon, but specifically what really happened the night he drowned." She saw her aunt's face pale. "I'm sorry that this is going to be painful for both of you—" she turned toward her cousin, whose face was bright red "—but I've kept this inside for seventeen years and I need to get it out. Not just for my own sake, but for all of us."

"Grace—"

"Zanna, please, if I stop now I'm afraid I'll lose my courage."

Jane reached out to pat her on the arm. "Go on, Gracie. We won't interrupt."

"You know that Brandon went to the lighthouse that night because he had a note signed by Ella asking him to meet her on the path. He had a crush on her that summer. You probably didn't know about that part and why would you? He was a teenager. But he confided in me early on. He didn't realize that Ella had a crush on Ben. That scenario was the reason why my friend Cassie Fielding—maybe you remember her?" She looked at Suzanna, who was frowning. "Maybe not. She was younger than Ben and you were just finishing your freshman year at college. I think you stayed in Augusta that summer to work."

Suzanna nodded but other than a quick glance at her mother, said nothing.

"One day Cassie was complaining how Ella never showed any interest in us anymore when Ben was around. I foolishly told her that it was too bad Ella didn't have a crush on Brandon, because he had one on her." Grace looked down at her hands clenched together in her lap, embarrassed suddenly by her story. Such a teen cliché. She took another breath. "At the time, I didn't realize Cassie also had a crush on Ben and was jealous, because he so obviously was more interested in Ella. Unfortunately, I didn't figure that part out until afterward, when it was too late." She risked a glance at her aunt and cousin, both staring intently at her.

"Cassie thought it would be fun to play a joke on Ella. She wrote a note, supposedly from Ben but just signed with a *B*, asking Ella to meet on the lighthouse path during the beach party. I was allowed to go for the first time." Grace sighed. "I wish now I hadn't. Anyway, Cassie wrote the same note but signed it Ella and got me to deliver it to Brandon."

She peered down again but heard someone gasp. When she continued, she couldn't look up. "We thought it would be funny to see their faces when they realized what was happening. Cassie said no one would get hurt because it was only a joke and I was stupid enough to believe her." Her eyes welled up and she had to stop. She thought someone was about to speak and swiftly raised a hand. "I need to finish. So when we saw first Brandon and then Ella leave the bonfire, we sneaked away, too, and ran toward the lighthouse path. We hid behind some shrubs and of course, it played out exactly as we'd guessed. Both of them were stunned, then angry. But they were angry at each other for some reason. I guess because they didn't figure out right away who was responsible until Cassie giggled and Ella heard her. Brandon ran off then and so did we. We got back to the party seconds before Ella and we could tell right away she knew what we'd done. I remember she threw the note we'd given her into the fire." Grace paused again. "Maybe if she'd kept it, she wouldn't have been blamed for what happened. I know you heard most of this at the time from the police that Ben went looking for Ella and came upon Brandon. There was some kind of argument. Ben never really said what it was about but Brandon dropped the note he had onto the ground and ran off toward the lighthouse. I just want you to know that I had a part to play that night, too. A big part."

An intake of breath from Jane stopped Grace. "Oh no. I can't bear to think about this again." She lowered her forehead onto her hand and began to cry.

Suzanna gave a choking sound. "Mom..." and got up to walk around the desk, skirting Grace, to kneel at her mother's side. She wrapped her arms around her mother's shoulders and laid her cheek against her head. For a long moment the only sound in the room was weeping.

Grace dabbed at her eyes with a tissue and waited until she could speak again. "I'm so sorry. If I could live my life over…if I had refused to go along with it…if only I had…"

Suzanna raised her head. "What, Grace? *If* doesn't mean anything. I'm only sorry I spent so many days—*months*—hating Ella Jacobs when…"

I should have been hating you! Grace finished the thought for her. The pain it brought steadied her, reminding her that she was not the victim. That she deserved this and more. She stood up to leave, wanting them to process all she'd admitted in private.

But just as she got to the door, she heard her aunt say, "Gracie. Don't go. The three of us need to finish this talk. Over some tea."

When she turned around, Grace saw her aunt holding out a hand to her. There was still a long journey ahead, but Grace knew she was forgiven.

WHEN DREW PHONED at the end of the afternoon to say he was on his way back, Grace immediately called Henry to ask him to fill in at the store for her.

"Go," he'd said when she explained what she planned to do. No questions or concerns. And he'd send Drew to her.

Grace arrived at the lighthouse. The morning tide was still receding so she could only walk as far as where the flowers had been a week or so ago. This was the first time she'd come to the site by herself and it was something she knew she had to do. She walked around, looking for the best place to locate the memorial plaque and jotting notes in the sketchbook she'd brought with her. She was still feeling shaky from her morning meeting with her aunt and cousin but was heartened by their parting insistence that she do whatever needed to be done to make the memorial happen.

Grace felt a twinge of guilt, knowing that by proceeding ahead she was risking more than Drew's irritation. In the hours after her confession to her family, she'd decided not to give up. She couldn't blame Drew for acquiescing to his boss. He had a job to consider and she'd seen his obvious respect for the man.

But she could fault a bureaucracy for being

blind to what was important to a community that had suffered long enough. The whispers, the pointed fingers and blame from all those years ago had had a dire effect on the town—on all of them. Suzanna, her parents, Ben and Ella—even Cassie, who'd finished off her high school days without friends and had left the Cove forever.

There was no going back. That's what Drew had told her and he was right. But she could go ahead if Drew...

She heard him before he came up beside her.

"Henry told me you were here." He wrapped his arms around her and ducked his head to kiss the hollow of her neck. When she pulled back a long minute later, he was smiling.

"Where were you thinking?"

"What do you mean?"

"The memorial plaque. Where do you think you'll place it?"

Was he reading her mind now? "I...uh... I'm not sure what you mean."

His burst of laughter sent a nearby gull screeching skyward. "Don't deny it, Grace. I know you well enough now to figure out your presence here is all about some new idea and I can guess what that might be."

She tried to avoid his eyes, but his finger on the tip of her chin held her firmly in place. "Then tell me," she said.

He ran the finger along her jawline to her lips. "I'm not playing this game," he murmured, outlining her mouth with his fingertip.

"What game?"

"Where?" he repeated.

"Over there, near the flowers," she whispered.

"That's a good place." He lowered his head, about to kiss her when she stopped him.

"Is that all you're going to say?"

"Hmm. No, come to think of it, it isn't all I have to say. I also want to add that you can continue making your plans, Grace Winters, because the lighthouse isn't going to be torn down."

She gasped but before she could speak, he said, "There's a condition however."

Wasn't there always? "What is it?"

"I have to be included and involved, every step of the way."

"You already are," Grace said and moved slowly into his arms.

She tilted her head back as his lips found hers and when the kiss that seemed to go on forever ended, Grace broke away to gaze up at him. "I can't believe we've come this far and I still haven't told you."

She saw the instant worry in his eyes and laughed. "It's okay. I'm not about to drop another idea on you. At least, not just yet." She couldn't resist the tease. Then she ran her fingers down the side of his face. "I love you, Drew Spencer."

His arms tightened around her. "And I love you, Grace Winters…along with all your pet projects, whatever they may be."

Grace laid her head against his chest, listening to the steady rhythm of his heart. She pictured herself standing on the threshold of an opened door and for the first time in seventeen years she felt free.

* * * * *

Be sure to look for the next
Harlequin Heartwarming book
by Janice Carter,
coming in 2021!

THE WESTERN HEARTS COLLECTION!

#343 MONTANA WISHES
The Blackwell Sisters • by Amy Vastine

A life-changing family secret, two impulsive proposals and best friends navigating feelings they're both afraid to share. Will Amanda Harrison and Blake Collins's new relationship survive when truths are revealed on the Blackwell Ranch?

#344 RESCUING THE RANCHER
Heroes of Shelter Creek • by Claire McEwen

Firefighter Jade Carson had no problem handling the Northern California wildfire evacuations until Aidan Bell. The stubborn rancher refuses to leave his sheep and appears to care little for his own survival. Will they survive the night—and each other?

#345 HILL COUNTRY SECRET
by Kit Hawthorne

Lauren Longwood lived a carefree existence, but pregnancy from a failed marriage leads her to a friend in Texas. There she instantly connects with Alex Reyes, a man who can't afford the distraction from saving his family's ranch.

#346 ALL THEY WANT FOR CHRISTMAS
The Montgomerys of Spirit Lake
by M. K. Stelmack

After her aunt passes away, Bridget Montgomery is surprised when her ex-fiancé, Jack Holdstrom, returns with two adopted daughters in tow. But she's downright shocked to discover Jack's been willed the other half of Bridget's home and business!
